BELOW
SUSPICION

BELOW
SUSPICION

A Detective Novel by

John Dickson Carr

PUBLISHERS

HARPER & BROTHERS
NEW YORK

For

Violet Loxley

and

Wallace Geoffrey

BELOW
SUSPICION

1

HOLLOWAY PRISON, which houses female prisoners and those women awaiting trial, is in Islington. You will find it no very cheerful neighbourhood even in summer. This evening, with a cold March wind rushing and whining at the few street lamps, might have been the evening before an execution.

The Rolls-Royce limousine—its owner, forbidden by law to run a small car, could have both limousine and chauffeur as 'expenses'—drew up before the prison gates. In its tonneau sat Mr. Charles Denham, the solicitor, and Mr. Patrick Butler, K.C., the barrister.

Yet, when Butler opened the door of the car and Denham made a move to follow, the barrister waved his companion back.

"No," Butler said in his warm and friendly voice.

Denham's eyebrows, dark against the thin sincere face, drew together in anxiety.

"But don't you think I ought to be there when you talk to her?"

"Not at a first interview, Charlie. No. I want to"—Butler waved his hand with an easy gesture, and smiled—"take her emotional temperature, as it were."

That smile, the complete ease of manner for so comparatively young a man, seemed to inspire in Denham a kind of professional agony.

"The charge against her," Denham cried, "is murder."

"Of course it is," Butler assented cheerfully. "Or I shouldn't be here, should I?"

"Well," muttered the other, as though half conceding a point. "Well!" He peered out of the limousine towards the ugly, dim-lighted bulk of Holloway. "I hate women's prisons!" Denham added.

The handsome Mr. Patrick Butler, known to some as 'The Great Defender' and to others as 'that damned Irishman,' stood with one foot on the running board of the car, facing in; and he laughed. In another ten years he might be too heavy, and with a far more florid tinge in his face. At the moment he was forty years old, and looked about thirty. His arrogant nose was offset by a wide humorous mouth, his intellectual contempt for others offset by a twinkling blue eye. If he had not been genuinely kind-hearted, and free with money to a point of idiocy, there might have been those who hated him.

"I tell you," repeated Denham, "I hate women's prisons!"

"You exalt the sex," Butler told him dryly. "Now I love 'em, mind you! I love their ways and their eyes and their lips." He mentioned other charms as well. "But I keep 'em in their place, Charlie. Have you ever talked to Ferguson?"

"Who's Ferguson?"

"The Governor of the prison."

Denham, whose tight-drawn thin face appeared older than Butler's though actually he was younger, shook his head impatiently as though to clear it.

"Ferguson," he said. "Of course! Stupid of me. But—"

"Do you know how to keep 'em happy in prison?" Butler pursued amiably. "Give each one a mirror in her cell, and a decent comb. Don't appear to notice what fantastic makeshifts they use for powder and lipstick. Besides, in this year '47, are their lives more dreary than the life we lead outside?"

Denham swallowed hard.

"Look here," he said. "We didn't come to this place to talk about female convicts. We're here to help Miss Ellis, an innocent girl." His voice sharpened. "You do think she's innocent?"

All amusement died out of Butler's manner. His expression became almost portentously solemn.

"My dear fellow, of course she is! Give me half an hour with her; that's all I ask."

And, with his confident swing like the walk of an emperor, he strode away.

Fifteen minutes later, hat in hand, Patrick Butler was standing in a little whitewashed room with two barred windows that showed a muddy red sky westward. A single electric bulb, in a wire cage, hung from the ceiling. Its light stippled the room with cold cage-shadows, weaving the net round a plain deal table and two chairs.

Patrick Butler had been here many times. And yet, despite his light tone to Denham, he had never liked it. It was too much like being locked up in a room at the heart of the Great Pyramid, with a suffocating sense that invisible hands were beating at the bars all around you. Big and comfortable in his fine overcoat, obtained after much wangling with black-market coupons, he sat down at one side of the table. And a matron brought in Miss Joyce Ellis.

"Lord!" was Butler's thought. "A good-looker! Handsome's the word, rather. That is, if she had any animation. Not my type. But attractive."

Joyce Ellis, a middle-sized, dark-haired girl with large grey eyes, looked startled as he rose to his feet. She had to clear her throat before she could speak.

"Mr. Denham?" she said inquiringly, and looked round the room for Charlie without finding him. She was frightened.

"I'm afraid Mr. Denham couldn't make it," said Butler, with his best big-brotherly manner. He smiled deprecatingly. "But you won't mind me, I hope? I'm your counsel. My name is Butler. Patrick Butler."

"Patrick Butler?" echoed the girl.

He saw that the name had registered.

The matron—female attendants are never called 'guards' or 'wardresses'—did not remain in the room with them. But the blue-clad matron would be just outside the door, watching through a glass peephole; she would be into that room if Butler so much as tried to shake hands with his client.

For a moment, after the door had closed, Joyce Ellis stood staring.

"But I . . . I haven't any money!" she cried. "I can't . . . I mean. . . ."

Butler laughed outright. He was a product of Westminster and Christ Church, Oxford. But often, very deliberately, he would inflect his speech with a trace of Dublin accent which the English called a brogue; they loved it and fell for it.

"Faith, now, and what does that matter?"

"But it does matter!"

"Not the least bit in the world," he told her truthfully. He was so genuinely contemptuous of business matters that fortune, in turn, showered money on him. "If it makes you feel better, my dear, I'll take my fee out of the next rich blacketeer who really is guilty."

Unexpectedly, and though she hated it, tears came into the girl's eyes.

"Then you believe I didn't do it!" she said.

Butler's smile implied assent. His mind, a cool weighing-scale, was appraising thus:

"She's got a beautiful figure; those dowdy clothes hide it. Probably she's as sensually passionate as the devil; I'm glad there's no man mixed up in this. And she'll do well in the witness-box. Those near-tears look almost real."

"I ought to have known," Joyce said with fierce sincerity, "you wouldn't believe I was guilty. I've—I've read about you."

"Oh, they overrate my poor services."

"They don't!" said Joyce, and clasped her hands together and lowered her eyes. She was sitting opposite him at the table, with a cage of shadow-bars across her face.

"Anyway," she went on, "let's leave my thanks for another time. I don't want to make a fool of myself and cry. Do you want me to tell you . . . what happened?"

Butler considered for a moment.

"No," he said. "Let me tell you what happened; and I can ask questions as I go along. For instance, how old are you?"

"Twenty-eight," Joyce answered. She looked at him in surprise.

"And your background, my dear?" His rich inflection made it 'me dear.' "Your family, now?"

"My father was a clergyman in the north of England." She swallowed hard. "I know that sounds like a stupid joke in a book; but he really was. My father and my mother were killed during an air raid on Hull in '41."

"Tell me something about yourself."

"I'm afraid there isn't anything to tell. I worked fairly hard at home; but I wasn't brought up to do anything very useful. During the war I was in the Waafs. I—I didn't like it much, though I suppose I oughtn't to say that."

"Go on."

It was very casual, even inconsequential. Yet Butler's presence, radiating confidence like a furnace, was drawing the tensity from her body, the black misery from her mind.

"Well!" she said. "After the war, of course, there wasn't much for me. I was fortunate to get this position as a sort of companion-nurse-secretary to Mrs. Taylor."

"You are accused," Butler said quietly, "of poisoning Mrs. Taylor, with antimony or tartar emetic, on the night of February 22nd."

And then, for one terrifying instant, both of them were conscious of the matron's eye at the glass peephole. It was as though that eye swallowed up the room.

Joyce, with her eyes fixed on the table, merely nodded. Her fore-finger traced a vertical line on the table-top, then a horizontal line across it at the lower end. Her black hair, cut in a short old-fashioned bob, gleamed under the harsh bulb-light. The sense of the prison, where she awaited trial two weeks from now, again became suffocating.

"How long were you with Mrs. Taylor?"

"Nearly two years."

"What was your opinion of her?"

"I *liked* her," said Joyce, and stopped drawing designs.

"According to my notes," pursued Butler, "Mrs. Mildred Taylor was about seventy. She was very rich, very fat, and an imaginary invalid."

The grey eyes flashed up.

"Wait!" said Joyce. " 'Imaginary invalid' doesn't exactly . . . Oh, I don't know how to describe it!"

"Come, my dear! Try to describe it."

"Well, she had a passion for taking medicines. Any kind and every kind. If she thought she had heart trouble, for instance, and she acci-dentally came across somebody's box of indigestion-pills, she'd swallow the indigestion-pills just to see what happened. And she always kept dosing herself with Epsom salts and Nemo's salts."

Butler nodded.

"Ever since her husband died, I understand," he continued, "she's been living in Balham, on the edge of the Common. In a big old-fash-ioned place with a coach-house at the back."

"Yes!"

"But Mrs. Taylor and yourself were the only persons who actually slept in the house?"

"Yes! The servants all slept in rooms over the coach-house. That's what makes it so awful for me!"

"Aisy, me dear!" The Dublin accent soothed her again. Butler's ruddy face was a study in sympathy. How well, he thought in admira-tion, Joyce Ellis acted the part of trembling innocence!

"You see," the girl persisted, "Mrs. Taylor didn't often go out. And she hated motorcars. When she did go out, the coachman always drove her in a carriage called a landau. There's a stable attached to the coach-house; she's kept a horse there for years. And that's where. . . ."

"That's where *somebody* got the poison?"

"Yes. I'm afraid so."

"In a wooden cabinet attached to the wall of the stable," said Butler, "there was an old Nemo's salts tin that hadn't contained any salts for some time. It was a quarter full of a deadly poison called antimony. The coachman . . . what was his name?"

"Griffiths," said Joyce. "Bill Griffiths."

"The coachman," Butler went on, "used it in solution for keeping the horse's coat glossy." He fixed his eyes on her. "Antimony is a white crystalline powder, easily soluble in water; it looks exactly like Nemo's salts."

"*I didn't kill her, I tell you!*"

"Of course you didn't. Now take up the story: tell me exactly what happened on the afternoon and evening before her—death."

"Nothing much happened. It never did."

Butler's face, despite himself, must have betrayed impatience. Fear, and a pouring contrition, shone in her grey eyes.

("By George," he thought, "she's falling for me!" His female clients often did, and it was damned awkward.)

"It was a cold day, with a high wind," said Joyce. She wrenched her gaze away from him, and looked at the past. "Mrs. Taylor stayed in bed all day, with a big coal fire burning. I did her hair in the morning—Mrs. Taylor liked her hair to be as blonde as a copper kettle, for all her age—and she wasn't as jovial as she usually was. In the afternoon she had visitors."

"I see. What visitors?"

"Dr. Bierce, that's her regular doctor, dropped in about half-past two. Young Mrs. Renshaw (Mr. and Mrs. Renshaw are Mrs. Taylor's only relatives), young Mrs. Renshaw got there about three o'clock. That surprised me."

"Oh? Why did it surprise you?"

Joyce made a hesitant gesture.

"Well! The Renshaws live a long way off: at Hampstead. They seldom get as far into the wilds of South London as Balham and Tooting Common. Anyway, Lucia Renshaw was there. She's a natural blonde, and awfully pretty."

Joyce's tone implied, "Whereas I'm a frump." She started to add something else, but checked herself and bit her underlip.

"Go on!" said Butler.

"Mrs. Taylor and Mrs. Renshaw and Dr. Bierce were in Mrs. Taylor's bedroom—it's a sitting-room, really, with a big old-fashioned wooden bed in it—at the front of the house. I was in my bedroom at the very back of the house, reading, when the electric bell rang in my room."

"You see," Joyce explained, "Mrs. Taylor wanted a lot of attention. But she didn't want anybody near her, 'fussing,' when she wanted to be alone herself. So she had this electric bell installed in my room. It's —it's going to hang me.

"No, please don't interrupt!" cried Joyce, as her companion made a gesture. "Let me tell it!

"When I heard the bell ringing like mad, I almost ran to Mrs. Taylor's room. Dr. Bierce and Mrs. Renshaw had gone. Mrs. Taylor was sitting up in bed, with her hand still on the bell-push. It's the sort of bell-push they have in hospitals, with a long white cord fastened on the wall behind the high old headboard of the bed. Sometimes it gets swung round to the back of the bed, and then you have to stand on the bed to fish it up again.

"Mrs. Taylor was furious. I'd never seen her like that before. I know it sounds silly and ludicrous, but the reason was: she'd gone into the bathroom adjoining, and the tin of Nemo's salts was empty. Now she was craving salts as—as a drunkard craves whisky. She looked even fatter in a pink silk nightgown.

"Of course I immediately offered to run down to the 'village' and get another tin. It isn't a village really; only a suburban shopping-centre at the foot of Bedford Hill Road, near the Underground station. But, when I got halfway down the road, I suddenly remembered it was Thursday. Early-closing day. There wouldn't be a chemist's open unless I took the Underground all the way in to the West End.

"I looked back up the road, with the spiky trees all blowing and the houses as though they were frozen; and I didn't know what to do. Mrs. Taylor had said to come back directly. So I went back. When I got there. . . ."

Here Butler interrupted her.

"Just a moment," he said. "Was there anybody else in Mrs. Taylor's room when you returned?"

"Oh. Yes! Alice was there. Alice Griffiths is the coachman's wife; she's a kind of general housemaid and parlourmaid. Alice is middle-aged and a bit crotchety; but she's always been very nice."

"Go on!"

"When I told Mrs. Taylor about early-closing day, and said I'd go in to the West End straightaway, she was so angry that she wouldn't hear of it. She said she wouldn't have any Nemo's, now, if her life depended on it. She said everything was against her. She also looked at me and shouted, 'I know a young lady who'll get no bequest *now*, just as soon as I ring my solicitor.' And Alice heard her.

"You see, Mrs. Taylor had left me five hundred pounds in her will. I knew it; everybody knew it. I hadn't done anything to deserve it. But she had. Mr. Butler, please believe I wouldn't kill anybody for five hundred pounds—I mean, or for money of any kind. The trouble is, you can't explain afterwards. And nothing else happened, until the dreadful thing happened."

Joyce pressed the palms of her hands over her face, fingers hard against the eyes. Then, gritting her teeth for the worst part of what she had to say, she stumbled into it.

"At half-past seven," she said, "I took Mrs. Taylor her dinner on a tray. She'd—well, thawed out a good deal, though once or twice she talked about Nemo's salts and how good they were for the digestion. I simply don't know what to say to remarks like that; so I didn't say anything.

"Did I tell you there were three servants, if you don't include me as a servant? Anyway, the servants were Alice Griffiths, and Bill Griffiths, and Emma the cook. All of them, by Mrs. Taylor's order, had to be out of the house by nine o'clock. And they were.

"Then, as usual, I remade Mrs. Taylor's bed. I propped her up, and put some books and a packet of cigarettes on the night table. My last job of the day was to go round and lock up the house like a fortress: doors, windows, everything. The last thing I did was turn the key in the back door.

"My bedroom is near the back door. I read for a while, and then went to sleep in spite of the high wind. And all night, Mr. Butler, *that bell in my bedroom didn't ring.*"

Joyce bent forward, hands locked together.

"They say I'm lying, Mr. Butler. They say the bell was in perfect working order; and it was. They say Mrs. Taylor *must* have rung the bell when she felt that horrible pain coming on. But she didn't. I swear she didn't. I'm a light sleeper, and I should have heard it.

"Oh, God, I almost wish I *had* lied! I wish I'd said I took a couple of sleeping pills, or something. There were plenty of them in Mrs. Taylor's medicine cabinet. But if you're innocent, I thought, the law won't hurt you. It can't. That's what we're brought up to believe. I never had a life. And now I'm locked up here, waiting to be hanged."

("Never had a life?" thought Butler. "With that face and especially that figure? Come, now!")

But no hint of his sardonic amusement appeared in his big, ruddy, long-nosed face.

"You're getting ahead of the story," he reminded her sharply, as a slap for hysteria.

"I'm sorry!" said Joyce, pulling herself together. Again contrition shamed her. "I'm terribly sorry. I've got a whole army on my side when you believe I'm innocent."

"Yes. Well." Suddenly he flushed. "Next morning?"

"Every morning," said Joyce, "I woke up at eight o'clock to unlock the back door and let Alice in. Alice would light the fire in the kitchen range downstairs, and any other fires that had to be lighted. A little later Emma, that's the cook, would come in and prepare Mrs. Taylor's morning tea; Alice took it to her at half-past eight.

"*That* morning I woke up—automatically, you know how it is—at a few minutes before eight. When Alice tapped at the back door, I went out in a dressing gown and unlocked the door. But it was very cold, so I went back to bed again and dozed for a while. Mrs. Taylor usually didn't call me before ten o'clock at the earliest.

"Then, when it was barely quarter to nine, the bell started ringing frantically.

"Frantically! In long bursts with little spaces between. I thought it was Mrs. Taylor, angry all over again. So I rushed out without troubling to get dressed. But it wasn't Mrs. Taylor. When I got to that front room. . . ."

Joyce paused, with a little trembling jerk of her head and body.

"Alice Griffiths met me in the front passage," she said, "and took me in. Alice stood at one side of the bed, with a tea tray. On the other side of the bed, Emma the cook had just dropped the bell-push. The bell-push was hanging just beside Mrs. Taylor's cheek.

"And Mrs. Taylor—well, she was lying on her side, drawn up together, in a tangle of bedclothes. I knew she was dead. Her face had that awful caved-in look of dead people. Alice and Emma just turned round and looked at me, glassy-eyed, as though they'd been drugged.

"On the bedside table was a tumbler, with a teaspoon in it and whitish sediment at the bottom. Beside the tumbler was an open tin of Nemo's salts. Mrs. Taylor's fingerprints were on that tin." Joyce added with no change of tone. "So were mine."

2

OUTSIDE the two barred windows, the muddy red sky had changed to blue-black. The electric light was bleaker, harsher, more merciless.

Patrick Butler's grey hat and gloves lay on the table. His dark-blue overcoat hung open as he teetered back in the chair, making the chair squeak. With his eye fixed on a corner of the ceiling, the big man smiled a far-off enigmatic smile. Then the chair bumped back on the floor again, and he looked at Joyce.

"This tin of Nemo's, I believe," he said briskly, "was the tin usually kept in the stable. It contained only antimony?"

"Yes."

"Nemo's salts," Butler pursued, "are not effervescent. If somebody had given her that tin—"

"Given it to her!" said Joyce, and closed her eyes. Her words were edged with horrible irony.

"Mrs. Taylor," said the barrister, "would have poured two or three teaspoonfuls of pure antimony into a glass of water. She'd have stirred it round and swallowed the lot without noticing anything wrong. Antimony is odourless and tasteless, like arsenic."

"But I'm the only person who could have given it to her! Don't you see that?"

"We-el . . ." He pursed his lips.

"I was alone with her. The house was locked up inside. Nobody could have got in. They don't believe me when I say the bell didn't ring. I did inherit money from her; and I—was upset and angry about that afternoon." Then out came the question she had been trying to strangle back from the first moment. "Mr. Butler, have I got any chance?"

"Look here," he said gravely. "I want you to trust me just a minute or two more, until I've finished examining this story. Can you do that?"

"All right. Of course. If you say so."

"Then think back to the time you first saw Mrs. Taylor dead in that bed. Can you see the picture clearly?"

"Horribly clearly!" She did not tell him that she felt almost physically sick because he had not answered her question.

"When you first saw the tin of Nemo's on the bedside table, did you connect it in your mind with the one in the stable? The tin of antimony?"

Joyce stared at him.

"Good heavens, no! Nobody thought of it, until the police began asking questions. I—I just thought it was a real tin she'd found or dug up somewhere."

"Tell me what you did after you saw the body."

"I went to Mrs. Taylor, and touched her. She was cold. Alice and Emma were so frightened they couldn't talk straight; I could hardly understand them. I picked up the Nemo's tin from the bedside table, and looked at it and put it down again. I kept wondering where on earth she'd got it."

"And that was why the police found your fingerprints on the tin?"

"Yes. It was."

"Was this the only time you touched the tin?"

"The only time."

"You know, of course, that both Alice Griffiths and Emma Perkins say they didn't see you pick up the tin?"

Joyce's sick feeling had increased.

"Yes, I know," she answered. "And it isn't true. Please understand me! I don't say they're not honest. They are honest. But they were too horribly upset; they just don't remember. People often don't remember things like that, even when you remind them."

Butler gave her a quick, curious look, with the same enigmatic quality as the smile he had directed at a corner of the ceiling.

" 'Even when you remind them,' " he repeated. "I wonder!" Then: "Had Mrs. Taylor vomited during the night? Don't look so bewildered at the question, my dear. Had she?"

"No. That—that was the first thing that Dr. Bierce asked. But we looked all over the place; and she hadn't."

"When someone swallows a large dose of antimony, you know, the person is usually violently sick inside fifteen or twenty minutes."

"But she was poisoned with antimony!" cried Joyce. "When they

had me up before the magistrate for committal, and they presented
the evidence they're going to give against me in court, the pathologist
said it was antimony!"

"Ah, yes," murmured Butler with satisfaction. He raised his eyebrows. "That's one of the best features of our legal system. They've got
to present their whole case before the magistrate. Whereas we don't
have to; we merely reserve your defence. By God! They don't know a
single card in my hand!"

His bass voice, though low-pitched, rang with exultation.

"I can't stand this!" Joyce said uncontrollably. "Please, please, please!
Is there any chance for me at all?"

"I'll tell you," he answered quietly. "If you trust me, and follow my
advice, the prosecution haven't a leg to stand on."

Again Joyce stared at him, her soft mouth opening. He was regarding
her with a beaming and humorous quirk which, to anyone less under
his spell than Joyce Ellis, might have seemed almost horrible.

"The *prosecution* haven't got a leg to stand on?" she cried.

"Exactly."

"Don't make fun of me! Please don't make fun of me!"

Butler was genuinely hurt. "Do you think I'd make fun of you, my
dear? I mean exactly what I say."

"But the evidence before the magistrate . . ." She searched her mind.
"You weren't before the magistrate!"

"No. But my junior was."

"And as for—for preparing a case to defend me. . . ."

"Acushla!" he chided her, with Dublin again tinging his voice. "I've
already prepared your defence. I've been out at Mrs. Taylor's house,
and questioned the witnesses. That's why I want you to stop worrying."

"But suppose you're wrong!"

"I am never wrong," said Butler.

He did not say this in the least arrogantly, though intellectual arrogance was at the root of it. He stated a fact as simply as he might have
said he always spent his holidays in the south of France.

Joyce's mind was befuddled, whirling with only a few coherent
thoughts. She was quite innocent; she really hadn't killed Mrs. Taylor.
But this, to the impassive faces and pointing fingers which hemmed
her into a corner, hadn't seemed to matter. She had raged and screamed
—inwardly; never letting it show—against the filthy injustice of it. And
now. . . .

It was not quite true, as Patrick Butler believed, that she had fallen in love with him. But it was as nearly true as makes no difference, and a few more meetings would make it desperately true. To her he seemed godlike, almost like . . . and again she traced designs on the table. She would do anything for him, anything to preserve his good opinion! Her heart beat so suffocatingly that she could hardly see him.

Butler laughed.

"Mind you," he pointed out, "it's not that I can't be wrong about other things. I can be wrong about backing a horse. I can be wrong, God knows, about making an investment. I can even be wrong, though seldom, about a woman."

Joyce, despite her position, with the hangman almost touching her shoulder, felt a stab of jealousy.

"But I'm never wrong, believe me, about the outcome of a trial or in sizing up witnesses. Now!"

Here Butler's tone sharpened, and he leaned forward.

"There are just two points, vital to your defence, that I want to have clear before I go."

"Go?" repeated Joyce. She looked round the room. "Oh! Yes! Of course you've got to go." And she shivered.

"The first point," Butler went on, "is about the bell-push hanging over Mrs. Taylor's bed."

"Yes?"

"I've seen it, you know. As you say, it's a white button-bulb, on a long white wire. It hangs above and at one side behind a brown walnut bed, from the 'sixties or 'seventies, with a high scrolled headboard and peaked top. When you saw Mrs. Taylor dead in the morning, you say the bell-push was hanging almost against her cheek?"

"Yes; that's true!"

"Good!" Butler agreed with relish. "But, when you put her to bed the night before"—he leaned farther forward across the table—"where was the bell-push then? Was it hanging near her, or had it got swung round behind the bed?"

Fiercely Joyce searched her memory. "Mr. Butler, I honestly don't remember."

"Think, now! Surely you'd have noticed its position automatically? In case she called you during the night?"

"No. Because she never did call me during the night. Mrs. Taylor honestly thought she never got a wink of sleep—Alice will tell you that, because Alice was in the house before Mrs. Taylor employed me—but actually she slept like a log."

"Think!" insisted Butler, with his hypnotic blue eyes on her. "Picture the room! The yellow-striped wallpaper, and the old sitting-room furniture, and the bed! Where was that bell-push?"

Joyce did her best.

"I've got a vague sort of impression," she answered honestly, "that it was swung round behind the bed. Mrs. Taylor gestured a lot when she talked. But I. . . ."

"Excellent!" breathed her counsel, with a keen compliment in his glance. "My second and last question—"

"But that's only an impression!" protested Joyce. "Anyway, what difference does it make? I can't think. . . ."

"Stop!" said Butler. "Don't try to think. Let me do the thinking. Now my second and last question, I repeat, is about the back door and the key to the back door."

"I remember all about that, anyway!"

"Ah? That's splendid, my dear! You told me, I think, that the last thing you did before going to your room that night was to lock the back door?"

"Yes!"

"There's no bolt on the back door, as we both know. Only the key. Now tell me: is this the key to the back door?"

Fumbling inside his overcoat, he reached into his side pocket and produced a key. It was an old key, middle-sized, with a touch of rust-stain, common to the back doors of mid-Victorian houses.

"Is this the key?" he repeated.

"Where on earth did you get—?" Joyce checked herself, swallowing. "That's the key," she replied. "I mean: it looks like the key."

"Better and better" beamed her counsel, returning the key to his pocket. "You further stated"—something of the Old Bailey manner touched his voice—"that you unlocked the back door for Alice Griffiths next morning?"

"Yes! At eight o'clock."

"Exactly. Now I feel sure," said Butler urbanely, "you've forgotten something that will be of great help to you."

"Forgotten something?"

"Just as you said yourself: when people are very upset, they forget things and have to be reminded." Then he looked her straight in the eyes. "I feel sure that, when you went out to unlock the door, the key wasn't in the lock at all."

"Wasn't in the lock?" Joyce echoed stupidly.

"No. I feel sure," his glance was meaning, "that you found the key lying on the floor of the passage just inside the door. And you had to pick it up, and fit it into the lock, before you could admit Alice."

For perhaps ten seconds there was an intense silence. Butler could hear his wrist-watch ticking in this tomb. So as not to embarrass her, he let his gaze wander incuriously over the white-washed walls, himself a figure of blandness and innocence, whistling between his teeth.

"*But that isn't true!*" Joyce blurted.

Patrick Butler, K.C., could not have been more startled if the roof had been shattered as the quiet was shattered.

"Not true?"

"No! The key *was* in the lock."

Again silence; and she flinched as Butler studied her. His astonishment was mingled with a rising wrath, which tinged his cheeks. What the devil, now, did this girl think she was playing at? She was intelligent; she must see the value to her defence if she said that key was not in the lock. Well, then, what the flaming hell? Unless. . . .

Stop! He'd got it. And, as he thought he understood the reason, all Butler's wrath dissolved in a kind of intellectual admiration. It would be a little more awkward if Joyce Ellis still persisted in play-acting; but he understood. He even saluted her for it. She was a woman after his own heart.

"Mr. Butler! I—"

Butler rose to his feet, picking up hat and gloves.

"You understand, of course," he told her cheerfully, "that this is only a preliminary talk. I shall see you again in a day or two. By that time, I feel sure, you'll have remembered."

Panic was in her voice. "Mr. Butler, listen!"

"After all, you know you've been very lucky."

"Lucky! Oh. You mean in having you to defend me? Believe me, I know that! But—"

"Tut, now!" said Butler. If the matron had not been watching, he would have chucked her under the chin. "I told you before: you overrate me. No. I mean lucky in the course of events. Poor Mrs. Taylor died on the night of February 22nd. You were arrested . . . when?"

"Just a week later. Why?"

"Well! Your case, as it happens, has been crowded into the present term at the Central Criminal Court; that'll be in a little over a fortnight. You'll have been suspected, arrested, tried—and *acquitted*—in just less than a month. Not bad, eh?" His personality enveloped and smothered her words like a feather-bed. "Good-bye, my dear! Keep your courage up!"

"Mr. Butler, please listen! It isn't that I mind telling lies. It's only that. . . ."

But Joyce saw, with a feeling of being trapped afresh, that the matron was already in the room. A blue-clad male warder, his footsteps echoing in the passage, appeared to escort the visitor out.

Five minutes later, when Joyce was weeping hysterically in her cell, Patrick Butler emerged from Holloway Prison a good deal pleased with himself. The sleek dark limousine stood a little way off. Johnson, Butler's chauffeur, climbed out to open the door for him. And in the back seat, on a wire of nerves, was Old Charlie Denham.

"Well?" demanded the solicitor.

"All well, me bhoy. And I want a drink. Johnson, drive to the Garrick Club!"

"Wait!" said Denham. He made so imperious a gesture that the chauffeur's hand dropped from the starter. Then Denham switched on the interior light, so that he could see his companion's face.

'Old Charlie' Denham was about thirty-two. He was a lean, strong-built young man whose sombre bowler hat, sombre overcoat, hard collar and colourless tie were as professionally correct as the man himself. But he had never been so sombre as he appeared tonight.

Under a moonlight glow from the roof of the limousine, which shut them into grey-cushioned luxury with the dark and cold outside, there were shadow-hollows under Denham's cheek-bones. He wore a thin dark line of moustache, under idealistic eyes and dark eyebrows.

"Well?" he demanded again. "What did you think of her?"

Butler considered this.

"Not my type," he answered amiably. "But very attractive, I admit. Exudes an aura of sex."

Muscles worked down Charles Denham's jaws. He looked at Butler as though his question had been answered by a bawdy joke.

"Pat," Denham said slowly. "I think you seriously believe that three-quarters of the women in this world are preoccupied with nothing but sex."

"Oh, I shouldn't say exactly that." The barrister's grin implied that he meant nine-tenths of them.

"I suppose it's because that's the only sort of woman who ever gravitates towards you."

"Well," said Butler, "she gravitated towards me. Very definitely."

"That's a lie! I don't believe it!"

"A-a-isy, me son!" exclaimed Butler, genuinely surprised. He studied the other man. "Smitten yourself, are you?"

"No. Not exactly. That is. . . ."

"Now the divil burn ye for an old rake!" suggested Butler amiably. His tone changed. "I knew you were old Mrs. Taylor's solicitor, Charlie. But I was wondering why you were so much concerned with the Ellis girl."

"Because she's innocent, that's why! You believe she's innocent, don't you?"

Butler hesitated before replying. These two had been friends for several years; but you could never tell about Old Charlie and his British ideals and his infernal conscience.

"Do you want an honest answer to that," he asked, "or do you want the usual fine pretence between solicitor and barrister?"

"I want an honest answer, of course!"

"She's as guilty as hell," smiled Butler. "But don't worry, Charlie. I prefer to have my clients guilty."

For a moment Denham did not comment. He lowered his head and looked at the tips of his well-polished shoes. A thin wind whistled round the car, making the chauffeur beyond the glass panel pull up the collar of his coat.

"What makes you think J—Miss Ellis is guilty?" Denham asked.

"Partly evidence, but mainly atmospheres. I can always tell by atmospheres."

"Can you? What if you happen to be wrong?"

"I am never wrong."

Denham had heard this remark before. Sometimes it maddened him almost to committing what his precise mind called assault and battery. He was losing his sense of judgment and had already lost his sense of humour; nevertheless he was goaded into giving battle.

"So!" Denham said, and raised his head. "You prefer to have your clients guilty?"

"Naturally!" said Butler, raising his eyebrows. He chuckled. "Where's the credit—or the fun—in defending somebody who's innocent?"

"Then you regard the whole thing as a game to beat the other fellow? Is that your conception of the law?"

"Well, what's your conception of the law?"

"Justice, for one thing! Honour. Ethics—"

Patrick Butler laughed outright.

"Listen, Charlie," he urged gently. "Do you know what you sound like? You sound like a nineteen-year-old who gets up at the Oxford Union and solemnly asks, 'Would you defend a man whom you knew to be guilty?' Answer: of course you would. In fact, it's your duty to do so. Every person, under the law, is entitled to a defence."

"To an honest defence, yes! Not to a faked one."

"Has it ever been suggested that *I* faked a defence?"

"No, thank God! Because even rumours might ruin you." Denham's voice was almost pleading. "You can't get away with that sort of thing in England, Pat. One of these days you're going to come a hell of a cropper."

"Let's wait until I do, shall we?"

"And there's more to it than ethics," pleaded Denham. "Suppose you win the acquittal of a cold-blooded murderer who's killed for greed or hate or no reason at all, and might do it again?"

"Were you referring to our client?" Butler asked politely.

Silence. Denham passed a hand across his forehead. His face looked white and dazed in the moonlight glow.

"Let me ask you just one question, Pat," he urged. "Do you think Joyce Ellis is a complete nitwit?"

"On the contrary. She's a very clever woman."

"Very well! Then if she *had* poisoned Mrs. Taylor, do you think she'd have been such a fool as to leave all that damning evidence against herself?"

"In a detective story, no. She wouldn't have."

"Meaning what?"

"It's a good card," Butler conceded, "and of course I'll play it. But jurymen," he shook his head, "jurymen keep their detective-story minds and their courtroom minds locked in separate compartments. Now murderers, bless 'em—"

"Stop joking!"

"I'm not joking. Murderers, I repeat, are in a foolish state of mind and they do incredibly idiotic things. Every newspaper reader knows that. And any counsel who relies on that nobody-would-have-done game is a goner before they've even sworn the jury. Not for me, Charlie!"

Denham's throat seemed dry. Before he spoke next, he reached out and switched off the roof-light.

"What about Joyce?" he asked out of the darkness. "Are you going to fake her defence?"

"My dear Charlie!" The other sounded shocked. "Have I ever faked a defence?"

"Oh, stop it!"

"Two of my chief witnesses," Butler said dryly, "will be witnesses for the prosecution. One of them, Dr. Bierce, will be telling the truth. The other, Mrs. Alice Griffiths, will be telling what she now believes to be the truth."

"I hope I can trust you. You sail so close to the wind that— My God, Pat, suppose something goes wrong?"

"Nothing will go wrong."

"No?"

"I will bet you the price of this car against the price of a dinner," Butler told him coolly, "that the jury bring in a verdict of 'not guilty' within twenty minutes." Then he leaned forward to tap the glass panel behind the driver. "Garrick Club, Johnson!"

3

THE jury had been out for thirty-five minutes.

Courtroom Number One at the Central Criminal Court, otherwise the Old Bailey, wore an air of somnolence and looked more deserted than it actually was. The clock—up under the ledge of the small public gallery—indicated five minutes to four on the afternoon of Tuesday, March 20th.

One way or the other, it was all over now.

A running sting of sleet rapped across the flat glass roof over the white-painted dome of the courtroom. Below its whiteness the walls were panelled to some height in light-brown oak. Concealed lighting, under the edges of this panelling, threw a somewhat theatrical glow up over this sleepy, deadly room.

Sleet lashed again. Somebody coughed. Distantly there was the whish of a revolving door. Even sounds, in this room, seemed to come in slow motion. In the public gallery the spectators sat motionless, like dingy dummies; none would leave lest he lose his place. A verdict of Guilty, of course, would provide them the greatest lip-licking thrill as they watched the prisoner. A verdict of Not Guilty held less drama.

Below the public gallery, in the long tier of benches reserved for counsel, Patrick Butler also sat motionless towards the left-hand side of the front bench.

He was alone there. His grey-white wig, with its couple of precise curls at the sides, framed an expressionless face. His shoulders did not move under the black silk gown. He looked steadily at the wrist-watch on the desk-ledge in front of him.

Why didn't that jury come back? Why didn't that jury come back?

He wasn't going to lose the case, of course. That would be unthinkable. Besides, he had wiped the floor with poor old Tuffy Lowdnes—that is, Mr. Theodore Lowdnes, K.C., who had been instructed by the

Department of Public Prosecutions and led for the Crown. All the same. . . .

Why was he so concerned about the infernal case, anyway?

Patrick Butler glanced towards his left: towards the enormous dock, now empty, whose waist-high ledge was enclosed with glass walls on every side except that facing the judge. Two matrons, who guarded Joyce Ellis there, had taken her below to the cells while awaiting the verdict.

Well, it was certain now she was in love with him. For some reason this infuriated him. He could not understand her strange attitude, her strange replies to his questions, during the past two weeks.

And Butler's mind moved back to yesterday morning at ten o'clock—the opening of the trial which had now concluded. Again he heard the whispers, the rustlings, as benches of barristers' wigs nodded towards each other like grotesque flowers. Again he saw the 'red' judge on the bench, in the tall chair just to the left under the gold-gleaming Sword of State.

And again the chant of an usher:

"If anyone can inform my Lords the King's Justices, or the King's Attorney-General, ere this inquest be taken between Our Sovereign Lord the King and the prisoner at the bar, of any treasons, murders, felonies, or misdemeanours done or committed by the prisoner at the bar, let them come forth and they shall be heard; for the prisoner now stands at the bar upon her deliverance. And all persons who are bound by recognizance to prosecute or give evidence against the prisoner at the bar, let them come forth, prosecute, and give evidence, or they shall forfeit their recognizance. God save the King!"

The Clerk of the Court rose to his cadaverous height below the judge's bench. He faced the dock across the long, crowded solicitors' table in the well of the court.

"Joyce Leslie Ellis, you are charged with the murder of Mildred Hoffman Taylor on the night of February 22nd last. Joyce Leslie Ellis, are you guilty or not guilty?"

Joyce, standing up in the dock between the two matrons, was a surprisingly vivid figure in her 'best' clothes of a brown tailored suit and yellow knitted sweater. But she did not lift her eyes.

"I—I plead not guilty," she answered.

"You may sit down," said the judge, indicating the chair behind her.

Mr. Justice Stoneman, whose wig might have been real hair for his wrinkled old face, seemed a small and remote figure under the scarlet robe. The jury, eleven men and one woman, were quickly sworn without a challenge from either side. Mr. Theodore Lowdnes, a short and stout man with a pontifical cough, arose to open the case for the Crown.

"May it please your lordship; members of the jury."

Mr. Lowdnes's opening speech was studiously fair, studiously moderate, as all such speeches must be. But he was known as a bustler, a pusher. For all his quiet-voiced "We shall attempt to show—" and "I suggest—" he drew the picture of a woman, furiously angry and fearful of losing a bequest of five hundred pounds, who had poisoned her benefactor and then had listened without emotion to peals of help from a ringing bell.

Had Mrs. Mildred Taylor screamed out and demanded these salts? Very well! She should have that which she believed to be Nemo's salts —easily obtainable, the prosecution would demonstrate, from an unlocked cabinet in an unlocked stable.

"You will hear," continued Mr. Lowdnes, "that this poison does not act immediately. You may ask yourselves whether Mrs. Taylor, or anybody else in that position, would not have called for help. Yet the prisoner denies that she did. You may ask yourselves why the only fingerprints on the tin were those of the prisoner and of the deceased. You may ask yourselves, indeed, who else could have administered the antimony in a house described by the prisoner herself, in her statement to Divisional Detective-Inspector Wales, as being 'locked up like a fortress.'"

A faint whisper and creak, as though thoughts themselves spoke, trembled in the courtroom.

"This is nasty," muttered one of Butler's fellow-silks in the bench behind. "How's the Irishman going to meet it?"

"Dunno," muttered another. "But there ought to be fireworks before long."

There were. The fireworks began to explode during Mr. Lowdnes's examination of his fourth witness, Mrs. Alice Griffiths. After the usual preliminary questions:

"Will you tell us, Mrs. Griffiths, where you were about a quarter to four on the afternoon of February 22nd?"

"Yes, sir. You mean when I went into Mrs. Taylor's room to see if the fire was all right?"

Mr. Lowdnes's fat face, twinkling with a pair of pince-nez, was tilted with chin up high.

"I don't want to lead you, Mrs. Griffiths. Just tell your story."

"Well, I did."

"Did what?"

"Went into the room!" said the witness.

The slight tremor of a laugh, especially from the privileged spectators in the seats of the City Lands Corporation behind counsel, hovered near. Mr. Justice Stoneman looked up, very briefly, and even the ghost-tremor died.

Mrs. Griffiths was a determined, thick-bodied little woman in the middle forties. Though necessarily as shabbily dressed as any woman in the court, she wore a new hat with bright pink flowers. Lines of discontent drew down the corners of her mouth. She was flustered, over-awed, and therefore angry.

Mr. Lowdnes regarded her imperturbably.

"Was the deceased alone at this time?"

"Yes, sir."

"What did she say to you?"

"She said Mrs. Renshaw and Dr. Bierce had been there, but they wouldn't stay to tea. She said Dr. Bierce had gone first, and then Mrs. Renshaw. She said she'd 'ad words with Mrs. Renshaw. About religion."

"About . . . Ah, I see. The deceased was a very religious woman, then?"

"Well, she always said she was. But she never went to church."

"What I am getting at is this. Did Mrs. Taylor say anything about the prisoner?"

"Well . . . yes, sir."

"Your reluctance does you credit, Mrs. Griffiths. But please speak up so that we can hear you."

"The madam called Miss Ellis a—a bad name. She said. . . ."

"What was the bad name?" interposed Mr. Justice Stoneman.

Alice Griffiths went as pink in the face as the flowers on her hat.

"She said . . . what means a streetwalker, sir."

" 'What means a streetwalker,' " repeated Mr. Lowdnes in a ruminating tone. "Anything else?"

There was an audible throat-clearing. Patrick Butler, his black gown sweeping round him like the cloak of a Regency duellist, rose to his full height.

"My lord," he said in his rich voice, "I must apologize for interrupting my learned friend. But may I ask whether my learned friend will introduce evidence to show that the prisoner was, in fact, a street-walker?"

"My lord, I imply no such thing!" exclaimed Mr. Lowdnes. "I merely wish to show that the deceased was in a state of anger!"

"Then may I suggest, my lord, that my learned friend confine himself to literal facts? It might be confusing if I, in a state of anger, should refer to my learned friend as a ba—"

("Wow!" whispered counsel in the bench behind.)

"Your illustration is not necessary, Mr. Butler," interrupted the judge in a steely voice. "At the same time, Mr. Lowdnes, you might make your meaning clear."

"Beg-ludship's-pardon," counsel said grimly. "I shall try to do so."

Then out poured the ugly story of Mrs. Taylor's rage, of the will, of the five-hundred-pound bequest, and of Mrs. Taylor's scream: "I know a young lady who'll get no bequest now, just as soon as I ring my solicitor." Mr. Lowdnes was well satisfied.

"Now, Mrs. Griffiths, we come to the morning of Friday the 23rd. You have stated, I think, that you and your husband—as well as Emma Perkins the cook—occupied rooms over the coach-house?"

"Yes, sir."

"Will you just look at the surveyor's plan, there? Perhaps the jury will wish to consult their plans too. Thank you."

There was a long rustling as plans were unrolled.

"Was it your custom, every morning at eight o'clock, to go from the coach-house to the back door? And there be admitted by the prisoner, who unlocked the door for you?—I think you nodded?"

"Yes, sir."

"And the prisoner unlocked the door for you on the morning of February 23rd? Just as usual?"

"Yes, sir." Then the witness stiffened, and her faded blue eyes opened wide. "Oh! I almost forgot. There was something else—"

"Something else, Mrs. Griffiths?"

"Yes, sir." The pink flowers on the hat bobbed determinedly. "The key wasn't in the lock that morning."

Silence. Mr. Lowdnes blinked at her.

"Will you explain that statement, please?"

"It wasn't in the lock." She told him, simply but insistently. "The key was a-laying on the floor in the passage, inside the door. And Miss Ellis had to pick it up and put it in the lock before she could open the door."

There was a mild sensation. The judge, who had been taking down his notes in longhand and in a notebook as big as a ledger, glanced round at her.

("If Butler," muttered a voice among the whispers, "can prove some-body got into that house with another key. . . .")

"One moment," Mr. Lowdnes said sharply. He was now in the horned position of having to cross-examine his own witness. "This evidence was not mentioned to the police, I believe? Or in the magistrate's court?"

"No, sir, because nobody asked me about it!" returned the witness, quite obviously believing every word she said. "I thought about it since."

"Come, Mrs. Griffiths! Was the door closed and locked?"

"Yes, sir."

"Then how can you say the prisoner picked up the key from the floor inside? Could you see her?"

"No, sir. Maybe I shouldn't 'a' said that. But I 'eard her put the key in the lock—rattling like, and moving forward till it caught hold."

"Yet you saw nothing whatever, I take it. Had you looked through the keyhole?"

For some reason Mrs. Griffiths was outraged. "No, sir, I never did in me life!"

"I put it to you," said Mr. Lowdnes, extending his finger impressively, "that what you heard, or thought you heard, was the ordinary rattle as someone turns a key in a lock?"

"Sir, it was not! Besides," added the witness, "that door was open at some time in the middle of the night. Because Bill—I mean, Mr. Griffiths—and me 'eard it banging till the latch caught and it stayed shut."

This time there was a real sensation.

And the witness's words came as a complete surprise to Patrick Butler himself.

Hitherto he had been pretending to study his brief, with a deaf and detached air. Now he was so startled that he almost betrayed it. That tale of the key being out of the door, so far as he knew, was untrue. With long and patient questioning, with insidious suggestion, he had

conjured it into Mrs. Griffith's mind—or thought he had—until she
believed it herself.

But now Alice Griffiths, an honest woman, blurted out a story of the
back door banging in the middle of the night. Somebody could have got
in. Suppose his fake defence was a real defence? Suppose Joyce was not
guilty after all?

He glanced at her in the dock. For the first time Joyce had raised her
head, deathly pale, and was staring at Mrs. Griffiths. Then the grey eyes
swung round towards Butler, and away again hastily. He was for a
moment so off-balance that he did not hear question and answer until
his junior, George Wilmot, plucked hastily at his sleeve.

"You tell us, Mrs. Griffiths, that this banging door woke you up in
the middle of the night. What time was it?"

"Sir, I don't know! We didn't turn on the light and look at the
clock."

"We?"

"My husband and me."

"Can you state an approximate time, Mrs. Griffiths?"

"Well, it might 'a' been about midnight. More or less."

"What made you think that this noise you heard was that of the back
door banging?"

"Becos," retorted the witness, "I went to the window and looked out.
It was blowing a gale, but there was a dancy kind of moon. I could see
the door, sir. It banged again, and then stopped like as if the latch had
caught. It's true! You ask Mr. Griffiths!"

The judge's voice, though soft, had the chop of a butcher's cleaver.

"You will confine yourself," he told her, "to answering counsel's
questions and refraining from comment until it is asked for."

Mrs. Griffiths, terrified of this awesome little mummy-face with the
red robe, attempted a curtsy in the witness-box.

"Yes, me lord. Sorry, me lord."

"At the same time," the judge continued gently. "I want to be quite
clear about this. Did you mention this banging door to the police?"

"No sir, me lord."

"Why not?"

"Me lord," blurted the witness, "becos I didn't think it was important. Is it important?"

The very naïveté of that question compelled belief. Patrick Butler's
soul exulted. For a moment the judge looked steadily at Mrs. Griffiths,

shoulders hunched as though he were about to crawl along the top of
the bench. Then he made a slight gesture.

"You may proceed, Mr. Lowdnes."

"Thank you, my lord. Putting aside for the moment this new testimony," said counsel, with a meaning glance at the jury, "you tell us it
was the prisoner who unlocked the door and admitted you at eight
o'clock? —Very well! Was it the prisoner who told you the tale about
the key 'lying inside on the floor?' "

"No, sir!"

"It was not?" Mr. Lowdnes's voice poured with amused skepticism.

"She didn't say nothing. Just went back to her room."

"What did you do?"

"I went downstairs to the kitchen, and lit the fire, and made meself
a cup of tea."

"And then?"

"Emma—Mrs. Perkins got there. And she 'ad a cup of tea. And then
I got the madam's tea ready, on the silver service, and took it up to her
room."

"Describe what happened then."

Framed in the oaken witness-box, with its tall supports holding up a
wooden roof, Mrs. Griffiths's sturdy figure appeared to shrink.

"Well, sir, I drew back the curtains. And I was going to put the tray
on the table, when I saw Mrs. T. I come over so queer that it's a mercy
I didn't drop the tray. She was dead."

After a moment of silence, so that the brief words conjured up their
image, Mr. Lowdnes nodded.

"Will you take the bundle of photographs, Mrs. Griffiths, and just
look at the first picture in the book?"

One of the yellow-bound booklets, in which official photographs are
enclosed, was handed up to the witness. Several members of the jury
had also opened theirs.

"Is that how the deceased was lying when you first saw her?"

"That's it, sir. All twisted up in the bedclothes, like as if she was in
pain. The dark spot is the rouge on 'er cheek."

"What did you do next?"

"I ran into the back-stairs passage, and called over the banisters to
Emma."

"That is Mrs. Perkins, the cook?"

"Yes, sir. I said, 'Emma!' And she said, 'What?' And I said, 'For
God's sake come up here; something awful's happened.' "

"Mrs. Perkins did come up from the basement?"

"Yes, sir. We stood on each side of the bed. I was still 'olding the tray. We thought she'd 'ad a stroke."

"You mean, that Mrs. Taylor had suffered a stroke?"

"That's it. And Emma said, 'I'll ring the bell for Miss Ellis; she ought to know.'"

"Now look at photograph number two. You will see the white cord of the bell-push, hanging down beside the deceased, and within easy reach of her hand. Was it in that position when you first saw the deceased?"

"No, sir," the witness answered promptly. "It was hanging down behind the headboard of the bed."

It would not be true to say that Mr. Theodore Lowdnes made a noise like a man hit in the stomach. He was much too dignified. But he was holding his brief in his hands; he dropped the brief on the desk in front of him, and a pink sheet of blotting-paper flew wide.

"And I didn't tell that to the police," Mrs. Griffiths blurted, "because they never asked me. They saw it there, and I expect they thought it was always there!"

A sharp rebuke from the bench cut her short. Mr. Lowdnes glanced at the long solicitors' table in the well of the court, where the exhibits lay neatly ticketed. One of the men sitting there—now rigid, with the sudden consciousness of an obvious duty neglected—was Divisional Detective-Inspector Gilbert Wales.

Mr. Lowdnes had to make a split-second decision, and he made it.

"If the police did not question you," he remarked lightly, "no doubt they had good reason to think it unimportant. Was it easy to reach the bell-push, even in that position?"

"Oh, yes, sir!"

"Even though the deceased had swallowed antimony, she could quite easily have reached the bell?"

"Oh, yes, sir! Easy!"

"How?"

"Well—like Emma did when Emma rang it."

"And how was that?"

"She stood on the bed, and reached for the bell-cord, and pulled it up over the back of the bed. Then she rang it and kept on ringing."

"Did the prisoner immediately reply to the summons?"

Mrs. Griffiths hesitated, as though some emotion swelled inside her.

"No, sir. We knew the bell was working, 'cos you could hear it all the way down in her room. I went out into the passage, to go down to 'er room and fetch 'er. But I met her coming toward me."

"You met her in the passage?"

The pink flowers on the hat were agitated by a violent nod.

"What did the prisoner say to you?"

"Miss—the prisoner said, 'What's the matter? Is she dead?' "

"I see. The prisoner used the words '*Is she dead?*' before you had referred in any way to the deceased?"

"Yes, sir."

"And, in fact, before you had spoken at all?"

"Yes, sir."

Joyce Ellis, in the dock, hardly seemed to breathe. Over the courtroom flowed one of those waves of feeling which are as silent as thoughts yet as palpable as the hangman's rope. All eyes were on her.

"How should you describe her expression as the prisoner said this? Calm, or agitated, or what?"

"She was all upset, sir."

"What did the prisoner do?"

"She went into the madam's room, and looked at the madam and touched her. Emma and me was crying. Miss Ellis sat down in a chair. She put her hands over her face—like this, sir—and said, 'No, no, no!' like as if she was grief-struck. Emma and me were crying again."

"Now, Mrs. Griffiths. Did you notice anything on the bedside table at the right hand of the deceased?"

The witness replied that she had. Up to her for identification was handed a tin bearing the painted label, NEMO'S INVIGORATING SALTS, surrounded by blue flowers in love-knots. Next Mrs. Griffiths identified a tumbler with sediment in it, and a teaspoon. She told the grisly story of the antimony in the stable.

"When the prisoner was in the deceased's room, did she make any reference to this tin?"

"I—I don't remember as she did, sir."

"What did the prisoner say?"

"Well, sir, all of a sudden she got as calm as she usually was, and said, 'You'd better 'phone for Dr. Bierce.' "

"And did someone telephone?"

"Yes, sir. Emma did."

Mr. Theodore Lowdnes's manner grew very impressive. Putting his hands flat on the desk in front of him, he rested his weight there and leaned forward.

"You were in that room, I believe, from the moment you discovered the body until the police arrived?"

"I never left the room for a minute; that's gospel truth."

"Look at the Nemo's tin, Mrs. Griffiths. Did the prisoner touch or handle that tin at any time while you were there?"

"No, sir, she didn't."

"Then, if the prisoner's fingerprints were on the tin, she must have handled it before you discovered the deceased's body?"

"I—"

"On your oath, Mrs. Griffiths: did the prisoner touch that tin at any time?"

"No, sir, she didn't!"

Mr. Lowdnes, with his pince-nez and his ultra-refined voice, allowed a second to elapse while his eyes strayed towards the jury. Then, wrapping his black gown round him, he sat down.

And Patrick Butler rose to cross-examine for the defence.

4

JOYCE ELLIS, sitting there quietly and facing across towards the judge, felt herself already condemned to death.

It was easy, while you were in prison awaiting trial—and they allowed you your own clothes, and newspapers, and books, and even visitors—to shut away the memory of what they might say against you. Especially after what Patrick Butler had told her.

But the inexorable day came. And, when she found herself actually walking up that little iron staircase, through the trap and into the dock, Joyce's knees shook and she was afraid she couldn't speak when they spoke to her.

At first her sight was blurred. This court, she thought vaguely, was like a schoolroom, the more so because nobody ever hurried or raised his voice. She felt she could have stood it better if people had shouted and stamped about as they did in the films. Ahead, and towards her left, was the jury-box. Ahead, and towards her right, were several rows of barristers—with, as she afterwards learned, certain privileged spectators sitting behind them in the seats of the City Lands Corporation.

The first person her unsteady eyesight noticed, among the spectators, was an incredibly stout man in a cape, with a bandit's moustache and eyeglasses on a black ribbon. He was a stranger to Joyce. But the next person she saw was Lucia Renshaw.

Lucia Renshaw, Mrs. Taylor's niece. Lucia Renshaw, who had paid that harmless, laughing visit on the afternoon of the . . . death.

"What on earth," Joyce thought almost with panic, "is *she* doing here?"

Joyce, at the moment, didn't feel either like or dislike for Lucia. She never had. But Lucia's presence, her face and figure and clothes, all were as vivid as those of an actress on a lighted stage.

Lucia, her golden-yellow hair gleaming and with little curls at the back of her head, was wrapped up in a mink coat. Lucia was plump, but not too plump. Her beauty, of fair complexion and blue eyes, was so skilfully heightened by make-up that it seemed merely an effect of nature.

And Lucia really enjoyed life, even in these drab times of cigarette-queues and frustration. She raised her thin eyebrows at Joyce, smiled, and made a pout of encouragement.

"Don't fret, my dear!" that look said. "This charge against you is simply preposterous!" Then Lucia, with frank curiosity, began to study the court like a child at a pantomime.

"Little innocent!" furiously thought Joyce, the clergyman's daughter.

Joyce was roused with a start by the Clerk of the Court's voice.

"Joyce Leslie Ellis, you are charged with the murder of Mildred Hoffman Taylor. . . ."

Then up rose the horrible little man with the pince-nez, and began twisting facts so that Joyce grew frantic. Alice Griffiths, who followed him, held out help and cheer with one hand; after which (poor old Alice!) this same woman turned the case as black as nauseous medicine against her.

And she wasn't guilty! She wasn't guilty!

When Patrick Butler got up to cross-examine, Joyce's heart seemed to stop beating. Not once had he looked in her direction; at least, when she had been watching.

Butler looked amiably upon Mrs. Griffiths, who gave him something like a nervous smile. He looked amiably upon the jury. His voice, seeming so full of commonsense, made the tones of Mr. Lowdnes sound rather la-di-da.

"Well, Mrs. Griffiths," he began, "we've discovered some things. Haven't we?"

"Sir?"

"The house wasn't really 'locked up like a fortress'—to quote my learned friend?"

"No, sir, not a bit of it!"

Taking as his thesis the banging door in the middle of the night, the absence of a key in that door, Butler used vivid and picturesque questions to show that anyone—anyone with a key to fit the door—could have entered that house.

"I don't want to detain you, Mrs. Griffiths," he continued like an

old friend. "But I do want to suggest that perhaps the prisoner's words
'What's wrong; is she dead?' were not *exactly* what you heard?"

"It was, sir. That's gospel truth!"

"My dear madam, I'm not in the least doubting your good faith."
Butler sounded shocked, then warmly confidential. "But let me put it
like this. You say Miss Ellis appeared 'upset' when you saw her then?"

"Yes, sir."

"But you had seen her nearly three quarters of an hour before, hadn't
you? When she admitted you at the back door? —Exactly! Did she appear upset at that time?"

"Well—no, sir."

"No. And yet, if she had really poisoned Mrs. Taylor, she must have
been just as upset at your first meeting. But she was not?"

"Come to think of it, no!"

"Exactly! Now you further tell us that Emma—Mrs. Perkins—rang
the bell to summon Miss Ellis. Would it be true to say that she rang
loudly and continuously?"

"Oh, ah! For a minute or so."

"Was it usual for Mrs. Taylor, in life, to ring so early in the morning
for her secretary-companion?"

"Never, sir! Not until ten o'clock."

"Exactly. Not until an hour and a quarter after that time. So I ask
you to put yourself in Miss Ellis's place. Eh?"

Butler, despite his grave and earnest bearing, was enjoying himself
hugely, without a single thought for the shivering girl in the dock.

"Let's suppose, then," he went on, "that you are lying in bed, dozing
—as Miss Ellis was. All of a sudden, more than an hour before you expect it, the bell rings violently and continuously. Wouldn't you be, to
put it mildly, a bit startled?"

"Oh, ah! I would that!"

"And upset, Mrs. Griffiths? In the sense of being annoyed?"

"Couldn't help but be, sir."

Butler leaned slightly forward.

"I put it to you, Mrs. Griffiths, that you heard the prisoner use these
words: *What on earth is the matter? Is she dead or something?* And
expressing only a very natural annoyance?"

A whole shiver of convulsions and creaks affected the otherwise silent
court. Mrs. Griffiths, her mouth open and her eyes glazed, appeared to
be staring at the past.

"Yes!" she answered at length.

"On reflection, then, can you say that this was the prisoner's attitude and that those were the words she used?"

"I can say it," cried the witness, "and I do say it!"

"Finally, Mrs. Griffiths, about this unfortunate matter of the antimony tin on the bedside table." Here Mr. Butler, with a slight but majestic turn of the head, directed a brief glance of pity at Mr. Theodore Lowdnes.

"You say," Butler pursued, "that when you first went into the deceased's bedroom you believed she had died of a stroke?"

"Yes, sir. I couldn't think of nothing else."

"You did not suspect that Mrs. Taylor had died of poison?"

"No, no, no!"

"Were you in any way suspicious of the tin on the table?"

"No, sir. How could I be? I 'ardly noticed it, as you might say."

"Precisely!" beamed counsel. "You hardly noticed it." He grew very grave, very earnest again. "Therefore it would not be true to say that you watched the tin, would it?"

The witness's eyes grew more glazed. "Well! I—"

"Let me put it in another way. To say you weren't very conscious of it, and yet at the same time you watched it, would contradict your own story?"

Mrs. Griffiths was growing flustered.

"Forgive me if I express myself badly," Butler soothed her. "Did you watch the tin?"

"No, sir. Not like you're saying!"

"At what time did Miss Ellis come into the deceased's room?"

"It was about a quarter to nine, I think it was."

"Very well. And at what time did the police arrive?"

"Oh, that was much later. Maybe an hour. That Inspector didn't come until Dr. Bierce had been to see us."

"And, all this time, you did not watch the tin. Can you swear, Mrs. Griffiths, that the prisoner never once—never once!—touched the tin of antimony?"

A stricken expression crossed Alice Griffiths's face. She looked round, as though for help, and saw only stony faces, except the kindly tenderness of Patrick Butler.

"Can you swear that, Mrs. Griffiths?"

"No, sir. I ain't even sure of it."

"Thank you, Mrs. Griffiths. That will be all."

And he sat down.

Mr. Lowdnes, who had now lost his temper and was as red in the face as a peony, bounced up for a re-examination which only hardened Alice Griffiths's obstinacy. She was followed in the witness-box by William Griffiths, coachman, gardener, and odd-jobs man, who corroborated his wife about the banging door and gave further evidence about the antimony in the stable. Emma Perkins, cook—after a longer and even more adroit cross-examination by Patrick Butler—wavered and admitted that Joyce might have picked up the poison-tin.

But there were no more fireworks until, just before the midday recess, the prosecution called Dr. Arthur Evans Bierce.

"My name is Arthur Evans Bierce," runs his testimony in the printed record, as you may read it today. "I live at 134 Duke's Avenue, Balham. I am a doctor of medicine in general practice, and serve as part-time police-surgeon to K Division of the Metropolitan Police."

Medical men, like police-officers, are as a rule the canniest and most discreet of witnesses. But Dr. Bierce, though no doubt canny, was clearly prepared to speak his mind on any subject.

A lean, bony man in his late thirties, Dr. Bierce had receding brown hair which gave him a narrow, freckled dome of skull. It dominated his long nose, his sandy eyebrows and straight mouth, even the steady brown eyes. As he stood with hands folded on the ledge of the witness-box, set at an angle between the jury-box on one side and the judge's bench on the other, Dr. Bierce radiated capability.

"At approximately 8:55 on the morning of Friday, February 23rd, I was summoned to Mrs. Taylor's house, called 'The Priory,' by a telephone call saying that she was dead."

Mr. Theodore Lowdnes waved a mesmeric hand, the sleeve of his black gown flapping.

"Did the news surprise you, Dr. Bierce?"

"Very much so."

"You had been for some years, I believe, her personal physician?"

"To be exact, for five years."

"For five years. Was there anything organically wrong with her?"

"There was not. In my opinion, she could have walked to China and carried her own suitcase. But her state of mind was not healthy."

Mr. Lowdnes frowned. "Not healthy? Will you explain that?"

"Mrs. Taylor, at the age of seventy, was in the habit of dyeing her hair, painting her face, and asking me whether I knew of any rejuvenating drug which would still make her attractive to men."

"A harmless peccadillo, surely?"

Dr. Bierce raised his eyebrows, sending many wrinkles up the domed freckled skull. "That depends on the point of view."

"If someone had handed her what appeared to be a tin of Nemo's salts, do you think she would have swallowed a dose?"

"If someone she trusted had offered it to her, I should have expected her to swallow anything."

" 'Someone she trusted.' I see. Can you tell us whether her relations with the prisoner were, or were not, cordial?"

"In my opinion, much too cordial. The whole house was unhealthy. I did not consider it a good atmosphere for one"—here Dr. Bierce glanced briefly towards Joyce—"with so little knowledge of the world."

"You refer to the prisoner?"

"I do."

Mr. Lowdnes spoke dryly. "As a medical man, Doctor, have you heard of the vilest crimes committed by those with little knowledge of the world?"

"In books, yes."

"I referred to real life. Have you never heard of Marie Lafarge? Or Constance Kent? Or Marie Morel?"

"Those ladies, I fear, lived before my time."

"I tell you this, sir, as a historical fact!"

"Then I accept it . . . as a historical fact."

"When you arrived at 'The Priory' in response to the 'phone call, what did you do and what were your conclusions?"

"I examined the deceased." Dr. Bierce locked his fingers together even more closely. "I concluded that death was due to a large dose of some irritant poison, probably antimony."

"At what hour had the death occurred?"

"Again in my opinion, at some time on the previous evening between ten o'clock and midnight. I can go no further than that."

"What did you do next?"

"I telephoned the police, saying that I was unable to issue a death certificate. Later I received instructions from the coroner to perform a post-mortem examination. I removed certain organs from the body, and put them in charge of the Home Office analyst."

"Did you examine the Nemo's tin and the glass on the bedside table?"

Dr. Bierce had done so, and stated it emphatically. The tin contained pure antimony, the dregs of the glass a solution of water and about one-tenth of a grain of antimony. Whereupon Mr. Lowdnes referred back to the third witness at the beginning to the trial: Sir Frederick Preston, the Home Office analyst, who had testified to finding thirty-two grains of this poison in the deceased's body.

"That is a large dose of antimony, Dr. Bierce?"

"A very large dose. Yes."

"Do the symptoms come on suddenly or slowly?"

"Very suddenly, after some fifteen or twenty minutes."

"Now I ask your considered opinion, Doctor," pursued the other, e-nun-ci-a-ting each word. "Even though the symptoms were sudden, could the deceased have reached the bell-push beside her?"

"Oh, yes. Quite readily."

"Thank you, Doctor. I have no more questions."

Joyce Ellis had her hand at her throat. But, as counsel for the defence rose, the sensitiveness of that courtroom made clear that a climax was rushing towards them for good or ill.

Butler steadily contemplated the witness.

"Doctor," he said, "would you please describe for us the onset of these symptoms?"

Dr. Bierce nodded curtly. "I should expect in most cases a metallic taste in the mouth, nausea, incessant vomiting—"

"Ah!" The syllable struck across like an arrow. "But may I ask whether the deceased had vomited?"

"No, she had not."

"I quite agree with you, Doctor! At the same time, will you give us your reasons for saying so?"

"It is the first active symptom felt by the patient." Dr. Bierce, clipping his words, grew alert and watchful. "The vomiting is violent and uncontrollable. I have never heard or read of a case, where vomiting was present, in which traces were not left. Besides, the digestive organs showed. . . ."

"Exactly! How does this affect the other symptoms?"

"Sometimes," replied Dr. Bierce, with a mirthless little professional smile under his steady brown eyes, "it is the difference between recovery and death. All the symptoms are strongly intensified."

"These symptoms being?".

"Soreness in mouth and throat, congestion of head and face, cramps in arms and legs, intense stomach-cramps. . . ."

"Cramps!" said Butler. "Now I quite agree with you that Mrs. Taylor could have reached the bell if it lay near her hand. But suppose the bell-cord had been hanging down behind the bed?"

"I beg your pardon?"

"Doctor, did you hear the testimony of the witnesses Alice Griffiths and Emma Perkins?"

The question was purely rhetorical. Witnesses at the Central Criminal Court, except on some occasions police-officers, are never permitted in court to hear the other witnesses. While Butler explained what Alice and Emma had said, Dr. Bierce's domed forehead seemed to rise as though he were growing taller in the box.

"You understand the position, Dr. Bierce?"

"I do."

"In order to reach that bell, the deceased would have had to leave her bed and push the heavy bed out from the wall to reach behind. Or she would have had to stand up on the bed, as we have heard. With the intense cramps you describe, do you consider that she could have done this?"

"No, I do not."

"In fact, should you call it definitely impossible?"

"I should call it," snapped the witness, "so unlikely as to be virtually impossible. Yes!"

Butler's big voice rose.

"Then Mrs. Taylor never rang the bell," he inquired, "because she could not reach the bell?"

Without waiting for an answer, Butler sat down.

You could hear, metaphorically speaking, the crash as one part of the Crown's case collapsed. To the spectators certainly, and to the jury very probably, Butler's cross-examination of Alice and Emma had already been left and right jaw-punches to the prosecution. And this seemed to finish it.

Joyce had observed, out of the corner of her eye, the behavior of the beautiful Lucia during that last cross-examination. Lucia had been half-standing up, with one hand pressing the mink coat against her breast, her eyes on Dr. Bierce as though for some telepathic communication.

And Joyce had been conscious, too, of Mr. Charles Denham. Mr.

Denham, who had been so decent to her, was sitting white-faced at the solicitors' table, his fingers playing with the top of a glass water-bottle. At Butler's final question to Dr. Bierce, Denham closed his eyes as though praying.

From that moment onwards, through the afternoon session and most of the next day, the defence seemed to have its own way.

With the police witnesses, Patrick Butler was deadly. Though he pretended immense respect for the judge and the jury, he had no mercy —as usual—on the police. His duellist's attack rattled and confused even so experienced an officer as Divisional Detective-Inspector Wales.

"On your oath did you question Alice Griffiths and Emma Perkins about the position of the bell-push?"

"No, sir. But—"

"You simply assumed the bell-push had always been in the position where you first saw it?"

"Will you let me explain, sir? I think the deceased could have pressed the bell wherever it was."

"Then you presume to doubt the medical evidence. Is that it?"

"Dr. Bierce merely expressed an opinion, that's all."

"So you doubt the opinion of your own witness? Did you, or did you not, proceed on a mere assumption?"

"In a way, yes."

"In a way!" said Butler, and sat down.

Endlessly the witnesses paraded. On the following day, March 20th, Butler opened and closed for the defence. He put Joyce Ellis into the witness-box; and, despite severe cross-examination by Mr. Lowdnes, she made a good impression. Counsel for the defence, producing a key which he said belonged to the back door of his own house, demonstrated that it would fit the back door of "The Priory." Calling witnesses, he showed that the lock was a "Grierson," which had been fitted to nine-tenths of the houses built in London during the 'fifties and 'sixties of the last century. In his closing speech he had never been more brilliant; Mr. Lowdnes could only flounder in his wake.

It was a triumph, or seemed so. Joyce, who scarcely dared to hope, found herself desperately hoping. Until. . . .

Until, with sickening abruptness, the whole effect was wrecked. It was wrecked by the summing-up of Mr. Justice Stoneman.

"Oh, yes," Mr. Justice Stoneman confessed long afterwards, to a few of his cronies, "I felt the girl was innocent. But instinct, however experienced, is not evidence. Many of Mr. Butler's pyrotechnics"—here the learned judge seemed to be doing sardonic tricks, behind closed lips, with his false teeth—"had only an indirect bearing on the matter before us. It was my duty to indicate as much to the jury."

And, with cool and merciless words, he summed up dead in favour of the prosecution.

"God!" breathed Charlie Denham at the solicitors' table.

The summing-up lasted an hour and ten minutes. To Joyce, trying to shrink herself together, it seemed an eternity. Few persons in that room ever forgot the judge's soft voice, his vivid old eyes flashing up and back from the notebook, the long pauses during which his wrinkled face seemed to ruminate in a vacuum.

Without ever saying a word which would constitute grounds for an appeal, Mr. Justice Stoneman intimated that Alice Griffiths, William Griffiths, and Emma Perkins were liars either unintentional or deliberate.

"Of course, members of the jury, I remind you again that you are the judges of the facts. I am not the judge of the facts at all. On the other hand, you may think it difficult to believe that. . . ."

On and on and endlessly on!

In a dulled way Joyce noticed that all this day Lucia Renshaw had been absent from among the spectators. An usher, approaching the solicitors' table on creaky tiptoe, stooped to whisper in Charles Denham's ear. Denham started, looked round, and then, after hesitating, crept out of the court. Patrick Butler—the judge's voice was still droning—sat motionless, head down, elbows on desk, hands over his ears; but even the back of his neck looked murderous.

Once, with suffused violence, Butler made a move to rise. But his junior, seizing imploringly at the side of his gown, muttered some words of which Joyce could only make out, "contempt of court."

"Members of the jury, you will now retire to consider your verdict. Mr. Foreman, if you should want any of the things which have been produced in this case, what I call the exhibits, please let me know."

The jury—with that same self-consciously stuffed and dead-pan look they had tried to keep throughout—were shepherded away. One of the matrons touched Joyce's arm.

"Come below, dearie," the matron said in a commiserating voice which removed the last hope.

And so, at a quarter to four in the afternoon, when sleet stung the glass dome top and the jury had been out for thirty-five minutes, Patrick Butler sat motionless—alone in the front seat of counsels' benches in a nearly deserted court—stared at the wristwatch on the desk in front of him.

Thirty-five minutes!

By ancient legal maxim, the longer a jury deliberated the more omens favoured the accused. Yet Butler didn't believe this, or didn't want to believe it. He wanted a quick acquittal, a burst of applause, the tingle of pleasure that always ran through him.

It was unthinkable, he told himself again, that he should lose this case. He was not thinking of Joyce at all. His pride would be scraped raw, he would explode and do something damned silly, if he lost. Above all, his hatred of Mr. Justice Stoneman gathered in his brain like a red blood clot.

Far across from him the revolving door to the corridor, where a helmetless policeman stood guard, whished once more as someone pressed through. Charles Denham, footsteps clacking on a polished floor in that intense quiet, threaded his way across towards counsels' benches.

Patrick Butler, to keep his hands steady, picked up a yellow pencil and toyed with it.

"Where have you been?" he asked.

"I went out to answer a 'phone call," Denham said in a curious tone. And then, "It may help take some of the conceit out of you."

Butler's fingers tightened on the yellow pencil. The word "conceit" scratched him. He would have affirmed, and seriously believed, that there was not an ounce of conceit in him.

"Meaning what, Charlie?"

"Have you got your car here?" Denham asked.

"Yes. It's parked near the front entrance, about thirty yards down Old Bailey." Butler meant the street, not the building. "Why? What's up?"

"Tell you later," said Denham. His dark eyes never moved. "You've lost your case, you know."

"Like to bet on that, Charlie?"

"You faked a defence," Denham stated, "and old Stony saw through it."

Butler's fingers snapped the yellow pencil in two.

"It might interest you to know," he said in a repressed voice, "that except for two points my defence was as correct as. . . ."

"But don't worry!" the solicitor interrupted. "With what I've just heard, we've got grounds for a successful appeal."

"I never appeal," Butler said. "I never need to."

"God help you, Pat."

"Thank you," snarled Butler. "I prefer to stand on my own feet. What's all this mysterious news?"

"Have you seen the papers this afternoon? Or did you notice Lucia Renshaw yesterday?"

"Who's Lucia Renshaw? —Oh! You mean Mrs. Taylor's niece? What about her?"

"Yesterday," and Denham pointed, "she was in the Corporation seats behind you. This morning. . . ."

There was a sudden stir through the court. The spectators in the public gallery roused up. On the dais behind the chairs of the judge's bench, the Clerk of the Court moved softly across and tapped on an almost invisible door in the panelling. That door led to the judge's private room, and was opened by his clerk.

"See you later," gulped Denham. "The jury are coming back."

Then everything seemed to last an eternity, like a marihuana dream.

Those in the public gallery licked their lips. The footsteps of the jury clumped for half a mile before they assembled and settled down. Mr. Justice Stoneman, as detached as a Yogi, was in his tall chair. The prisoner, half-fainting, was supported into the dock and stood up facing the judge.

When the foreman of the jury rose, the Clerk of the Court was already on his feet.

"Members of the jury, are you agreed upon a verdict?"

"We are."

"Do you find the prisoner, Joyce Leslie Ellis, Guilty or Not Guilty of murder?"

"Not guilty."

A spatter of applause, quickly hushed, competed with the sleet on the roof. Patrick Butler, head down, released his breath with a noise like a sob. Joyce Ellis stumbled and almost fell.

"You say that she is Not Guilty, and that is the verdict of you all?"

"It is."

Mr. Justice Stoneman made a slight gesture. "Let her be discharged," he said.

The usher intoned his summons for the following day: another case, another heartbreak. The judge rose. The court rose. Then, as unexpectedly as a grenade explosion, it happened.

For Patrick Butler, K.C., could no longer control himself. He was on his feet, imperiously, as Mr. Justice Stoneman turned away towards the door of the private room. Butler was transfigured. Clearly, exultant in triumph and contempt, his voice thundered across at the judge.

"How do you like that, you old swine?"

5

TWENTY minutes later, with the collar of his overcoat turned up, Butler emerged from the main entrance of the Central Criminal Court.

He was very tired, somewhat irritable, yet still exultant. He had used—to Mr. Justice Stoneman—perhaps the most outrageous words ever uttered within those walls. And Patrick Butler did not care a damn.

In the robing-room after the trial, when his fellow-counsels (each attended by his clerk) hung up their robes in lockers and put away wigs in leather boxes, not one of them referred to the incident. They murmured congratulations on his victory, one or two of them in a tone reserved for funerals. Butler had smiled back. His words to old Stony, of course, had not been contempt of court; the case was finished. But old Stony, they believed, could make it very unpleasant for him.

Let old Stony try!

Sleet flew at his face in fine needles as he ducked out of the main entrance. The street called Old Bailey, sloping down from Newgate Street on the north to Fleet Street on the south, shone as black as a Venetian canal under scattered lights. He was hurrying down towards his car when someone moved out from the shadow of the building.

"Mr. Butler," said the voice of Joyce Ellis.

Inwardly he uttered a groan of exasperation. The case was over! He was tired! He—

"I wanted to thank you," said Joyce.

Despite himself Butler was touched and concerned when he looked at her. Over her clumsily tailored suit she wore only an oilskin waterproof, whipped back by the icy sleet-gusts.

"Look here, you haven't got a coat!"

Joyce was surprised. "Coat?"

"Confound it, you've got to have a coat! You can't go about without a coat!"

"That doesn't matter!" She brushed it aside, though her eyes grew warm that he should think of it. "It's only . . . Mr. Butler, you promised me something."

"Promised you something, me dear?"

"Yes. I shouldn't remind you, except that it's terribly important to me. You said, if I testified exactly as you told me to testify, you'd answer me one question at the end of the trial. Please don't go away!"

"Well . . . come down to my car and be comfortable, then."

"No!" Her eyes and mouth implored him. "I mean, Mr. Denham's there. He's been wonderful, but—I don't want him to hear. Couldn't we go somewhere and talk for five minutes?"

Again inwardly, Butler raved with exasperation. But good nature won.

"Come with me," he suggested.

Just across the street was an institution which called itself a coffee-house. Once, before the war, its stalls of polished oak—divided into booths for the tables along one side—competed with eighteenth-century prints of old Newgate Prison to exude a Dickensian cosiness.

Now, as Butler pushed open a creaky door, he saw that the place was dirty and unkempt. A solitary electric light burned far at the rear. At the rear there had been a parrot, which was said to resemble an eminent judge and to which the legal gentleman taught Latin tags mixed with profanity; the parrot was still there, old and half blind, and it screamed.

Breathing a mustiness of dried coffee-stains and damp chill, Butler installed his companion in a booth facing him across the table. Some recent customer had discarded a newspaper, crumpled over an empty and fly-blown sugar-bowl. One small headline leaped out at Butler.

WAVE OF POISON CASES
SAYS SUPT. HADLEY

The parrot screamed again. From the rear of the shop, silhouetted against dim electric light, a collarless proprietor shambled forward and looked at them with distaste.

"Two coffees, please."

"No coffee," snapped the proprietor, with a gleam of pleasure in his eyes.

"Got any tea, then?"

The proprietor reluctantly admitted that he might have tea, and shambled away. Patrick Butler looked at Joyce.

"Well, me dear?" he asked as heartily as he could.

Joyce tried to speak, and couldn't.

Butler, studying her furtively, admitted to himself that she had stood the strain of the trial very well. He could remember one client, another woman, whose face had fallen in and whose hands—quite literally—had become a livid greenish-white.

Joyce, though under such intense nervous reaction that she could not keep her own hands still, had not aged or grown ugly. Her eyes haunted him, the large grey eyes with the black lashes. Melting sleet-drops glistened against the tumbled black hair cut in the short bob. Her mouth, to Patrick Butler, was a sensual allure about which he as a sensible man must not think.

Then Joyce spoke quietly.

"You don't really believe I'm innocent, do you?"

Butler looked shocked.

"Come, now!" he urged her in a reproachful tone. "Don't you put your trust in British justice?"

"I. . . ."

"The jury acquitted you, acushla. They believed what you said. You're a free woman, free as air. What more do you want?"

"Is it ungrateful to want something more? *Is it?* I only. . . ."

The tea had arrived, momentarily checking conversation. Two thick white mugs, slopping a beverage like mud-coloured dishwater, were planked down on the table. Meanwhile, Butler had surreptitiously taken out his notecase under the table, fished out its contents of fifty or sixty pounds, and crushed the money into the palm of his hand.

"Now tell me, me dear," he soothed. "What are your future plans?"

"I don't know. I hadn't thought as far ahead."

"We-ell! But you must have money, you know. Of course, there's the legacy from Mrs. Taylor. . . ."

"I can't touch that, I'm afraid. I should see her face every time I spent any of it."

"A sentiment," Butler continued soothingly, "that does you credit. So if you'll just accept this," his clenched hand slid across the table, "from a well-meaning friend who. . . ."

Suddenly Joyce lost all control of her reflexes. There was a crash as her elbow knocked over the white cup, which cascaded its mud-coloured tea down beside the table. Joyce, catching herself up, regarded it with horror as though she had really committed a crime.

"I'm awfully sorry. But please don't offer me money. Please."

"Sure now, me dear, and 'twas only. . . ."

"Oh, stop it!" Joyce cried uncontrollably.

"Stop what?"

"Stop using that fake Irish accent. It's no more natural to you than Cockney or Lancashire. You didn't dare use it in court."

"*Nolle prosequi. So-and-so you!*" screamed the parrot, and sharpened its beak on the bars of the cage. Patrick Butler felt the blood rise in his head. Casually, temptingly, he slid the money inside the crumpled newspaper near her hand.

"I watched you in court," said Joyce. "Sometimes I thought you believed me, and then . . . I didn't know. You're a wonderful lawyer, I know that. But you're really a romantic actor. You were acting and acting and acting."

Now the blood of anger buzzed in his ears.

"Isn't that rather ungrateful of you?" he asked.

"Yes, it is," admitted Joyce, with tears in her eyes. "But, when we first met at Holloway, you *said* you believed me."

"Naturally!"

"Afterwards you said . . . if we wanted to preserve real truth, we often had to tell lies about small things. Then, later, there was that question of the door banging in the middle of the night."

"I never heard that story," he retorted truthfully, "until Alice Griffiths told it in the witness-box."

"But, Mr. Butler, there wasn't any door banging in the middle of the night! It was one of the big shutters upstairs; I went up and fastened it. After the first day of the trial, you told me to corroborate it in the witness-box."

Here Joyce's eyes, frantic with bewilderment, searched her companion's face in vain.

"Alice and Bill Griffiths," she insisted, "are honest people. Why did they tell that lie?"

"You ought to be glad they did, Miss Ellis. It saved your pretty neck."

"Then you don't believe I'm innocent? You never did?"

"I'll tell you," returned Butler, with brutal directness, "exactly what

I told Charlie Denham. You're as guilty as hell. Why don't you be reasonable and admit it?"

It was as though he had struck her in the face. There was a long silence.

"I see," Joyce murmured, and moistened dry lips.

Slowly, because her knees were shaking, she slid along the bench and stood up outside the booth. Without looking at Butler, she buttoned up the oilskin waterproof. Now she felt the trembling through her whole body. Joyce took two steps away, and suddenly turned.

"I worshipped you," she said. "I still do. I always will. But one day, maybe before very long, you're going to come to me and tell me you were wrong." Her voice rose piercingly. "And for God's sake don't say you're never wrong!"

Then she ran for the door.

The glass-panelled door banged. The parrot screamed again. As a draught swirled through the dingy coffee-room, the discarded newspaper flapped up and sank down on the seat opposite Butler. The closely wadded banknotes slid along into coffee-stains. For a moment Butler did not touch them.

Curse and blast all women who made emotional scenes! Butler, though he felt an inexplicable twinge of conscience, could not understand Joyce. He sipped his tea, lukewarm as well as vile, and set down the cup. Angrily he snatched up the despised banknotes. Then he looked up, to find Charles Denham standing beside the booth.

"For the love of Mike," Butler burst out, "don't you start!"

"Start what?"

"How should I know? Anything!"

"Congratulations," murmured Denham, sliding into the seat opposite, "on the verdict."

"There's no call to congratulate me. I told you it would happen."

Despite Denham's calm tone, his dark eyes were glittering as they had glittered in the courtroom, and his nostrils were distended.

"What I began to tell you in court," he went on, "is that there's new evidence. Last night, while Joyce was still on trial, something else happened."

"Oh? What happened?"

"You told me you didn't know Lucia Renshaw, who was in court yesterday. Do you know her husband? Dick Renshaw?"

"Never heard of him. Should I have?"

"Mr. Renshaw," Denham said, "was poisoned last night with another heavy dose of antimony. He died, in horrible agony, about three o'clock this morning. He was probably poisoned by the same person who killed Mrs. Taylor."

The old parrot screamed, flopping about in its cage with demoniac excitement. Patrick Butler, who had taken out a silver cigarette case and snapped on a lighter, sat motionless while he stared at Denham. Then he blew out the flame of the lighter.

"The same person . . . Look here, Charlie! Are the Renshaws your clients too?"

"Yes. Just as Mrs. Taylor was."

"And Renshaw's poisoned too! Do the police suspect anybody?"

"Yes. Lucia Renshaw herself. And I'm bound to admit," Denham averted his eyes, "the evidence looks very black against her. There'll probably—well, there'll probably be an arrest."

Butler smote his fist on the table.

"Oh, bejasus!" he exclaimed in sheer ecstasy. "Do you mean I can go into court and kick the police's behinds *again*? In more or less the same poison case?"

"Pat, not so fast! Don't you see the point of all this?"

Denham smiled. From the moment of Joyce Ellis's acquittal, he had become a very different person from the haggard, haunted young man of the past weeks. He was again his pleasant, quiet, unobtrusive self. Yet about him there was a sense of strain—perhaps a new strain—even when he smiled.

"Joyce," he pointed out grimly, "certainly didn't poison Dick Renshaw. And, in my opinion," he hesitated, "the beautiful Lucia didn't either. We're in the middle of a worse mess than we ever thought. Look here!"

From beside him Denham picked up the crumpled newspaper, flattened it on the table, and indicated again that small headline:

WAVE OF POISON CASES

SAYS SUPT. HADLEY

"Don't bother to read the item," Denham advised. "I've got secret information that isn't printed here. I got it from Dr. Fell."

"Dr. Fell?"

"You've heard, I think, of Dr. Gideon Fell? He was at the trial too.

If you'd ever turned round and looked behind you, you'd have seen him."

Butler was ruffled. He put away cigarette case and lighter.

"Would you mind telling me," he requested, "just what in blazes you're talking about?"

"In the last three months," answered Denham, tapping the paper, "there have been nine unsolved deaths by poison. All in different parts of the country."

"Crimes of imitation, me boy!" Butler was impatient. "It always happens."

"I said in the last three months. Most of them before Mrs. Taylor's death. Now listen!" Charles Denham wagged his head forward, eyebrows intent. "In not one of those cases—not one, Pat!—have the police been able to trace the purchase of any poison to any suspect. You know what that means."

Butler whistled. For the buying of poison, no matter under what disguise or what false signature in the poison-book at the chemist's, is the factor which almost invariably trips up the murderer.

"Come off it, me boy!" scoffed Butler, a little angry that Charlie was again his normal self. "There's no doubt about where the poison came from in Mrs. Taylor's case."

"I wonder!" said Denham.

"What's that?"

"Tell me, Pat. Did you notice anything odd about that trial today?"

"Odd!" said Butler. "The man asks me," he addressed the coffee-room with some violence, "whether I noticed anything odd! Candidly, Charlie, I did. Mr. Justice Bloody Stoneman. . . ."

"No, no, not the judge! I meant the witnesses. In particular, that doctor."

"Dr. Bierce?"

"Yes," agreed Denham, running a nervous hand over his face. "He was trying to tell us something; and the rules of evidence wouldn't let him. But he said, you remember, that Mrs. Taylor's house wasn't healthy. He said it wasn't a good atmosphere for anybody as unsophisticated as Joyce."

Then Denham's tone changed, self-consciously.

"By the way," he added, "where is Joyce? I thought I saw her coming in here with you."

"She did."

"I was waiting in your car. I—I rather hoped. . . ."

"She didn't want to see you, Charlie. She told me so."

"Oh. Well. After all," and Denham smiled and tried hard to laugh, "there's no reason why she should want to see me. None at all." There was a pause. "You got her address, of course?"

"No, I'm afraid I didn't. And if you take my tip, Charlie, you'll keep away from that woman. Unless you want a dose of arsenic in your beer."

"So clever in your foolishness!" murmured Denham, after another pause. "So foolish in your cleverness!"

"Will you tell me," Butler inquired with restraint, "just what this has to do with the sinister poisoning of nine people? And with this woman Lucia Renshaw being accused of killing her husband? Had she any motive for killing him?"

Denham hesitated.

"It's true," he admitted, "that they didn't get on very well. . . ."

"That's not evidence, Charlie. It's merely a definition of marriage. Why do the police suspect her?"

"Because, apparently, Lucia's the only person who could have done it! And yet. . . ."

"What, exactly, do you want me to do?"

"I can't brief you officially, of course. We don't know which way the cat, meaning the police, will jump. But it's only five o'clock now. Could you possibly run out to Hampstead and talk to her before dinner?"

"I can," Butler assured him heartily. "I can, Charlie; and I'll do more than that. Give me five minutes' talk with the lady, and I'll tell you whether or not she's guilty."

"Pat," said the other, after a silence during which he put his head in his hands, "I owe more to you than I can ever pay back. No, wait; I mean that! But this last victory of yours—it's unhinged you! Do you set yourself up as God Almighty?"

"Not at all." Butler looked shocked. "It is merely," he explained with urbanity, as he picked up his hat, "that I am never wrong."

6

THE home of the late Richard Renshaw and his wife, called 'Abbot's House,' was in Cannon Row, Hampstead.

Sweeping up Haverstock Hill and Roslyn Hill, the limousine turned right at the traffic-light opposite Hampstead Underground Station, and up the steep, curving High Street which leads eventually to the Round-pond. But, only a little way up, there is an inconspicuous turning. Making several narrow turns in a short distance, the car emerged into sedate Cannon Row.

And Patrick Butler, jumping out impetuously, got his first shock.

"Good God, Charlie! This is—" And he stopped.

Under a blue-black sky, from which rain or sleet had ceased to fall, the house was set back some forty feet behind a fence of thin overlapping shingleboards painted brown.

Other houses in Cannon Row were mere dim outlines with dim-yellow lights. But this monstrosity, though not overly large, loomed up in whitish-grey blur because it was faced with stucco and built in that style called Victorian Gothic. On each side of an arched front door were two large full-length bow windows, set one above the other to match. Along the roof-edge ran miniature battlements, with a miniature sham tower at one corner.

"This is Mrs. Taylor's house," said Butler, with his memory full of ugly images. "I'll swear those are the same trees tapping the front windows on each side!"

"And why not?" asked Denham.

"Why not?"

"Both houses," said Denham, "were built by Mrs. Taylor's grandfather in the middle 'sixties. One at Balham, which was then fashionable. One here, which is still fashionable. This one," he added, "also has a Grierson lock on the back door."

A raw wind scratched branches in thin tick-a-tack on window-glass. The two houses, at least, were not furnished alike inside. Butler saw this, with relief, when a young maidservant opened the front door.

But the atmosphere of hysteria, blowing out at them, was as palpable as the signs of disarrangement. Kitty Owen, the maidservant, was eighteen years old and would have been pretty if she had not been so thin. Kitty shied back in terror until Denham mentioned their names.

"I'm sorry, sir," the maid gulped. "I thought you was more people from the police. But I'm not sure whether you can see the madam. She's been having hysterics."

"Mrs. Renshaw invited us, you know," smiled Butler.

Kitty, for some reason, started perceptibly. She regarded Butler with a paralyzed look merging into deeper fear.

"I'll go and see," she managed to say. "Will you wait in there, please?"

The doorway she indicated led into a high Victorian drawing room, now richly furnished with somewhat soiled pre-war furniture and a number of good antiques. Shaded lamps shone down on an Aubusson carpet.

In the middle of the room, as though he had just left off pacing, stood Dr. Arthur Evans Bierce.

"Butler!" said Dr. Bierce, at the introductions. "We met in court, of course. I thought you were some relation of . . . but of course you looked different in wig and gown."

Seen close at hand, he exuded that same air—intensified—of curt, no-nonsense friendliness, tinged with the disillusionment of a g.p. who sees state-medicine approaching to wreck his initiative. His narrow bald skull, faintly freckled, loomed up like Shakespeare's. His handclasp was firm and bony.

"You—er—hadn't met before the courtroom?" Denham asked.

"No," said Butler. "I knew what I should get from this witness."

"You saved Miss Ellis's life," the doctor stated. "I am proud to make your acquaintance, sir."

"And I to make yours, Doctor," said Butler, towering with his most impressive eighteenth-century air. "You're Mrs. Renshaw's physician?"

"Hardly." Dr. Bierce spoke dryly. "Mrs. Renshaw, I believe, gets her medical advice from Harley Street or Devonshire Place." His brown eyes, under the sandy brows, grew wary. "But she 'phoned me late this afternoon, in a somewhat frantic state, and asked me to come here as a friend."

"How is Mrs. Renshaw now?"

"I don't know. She won't see me. I think I had better be going."

"Tell me, Doctor. Do you consider *this* house 'unhealthy'?"

"I beg your pardon?"

"My young friend here," Butler referred to Charlie Denham as though the latter were about fourteen, "reminded me of something in your testimony. You said of Mrs. Taylor's: 'The whole house was unhealthy.' Can you say the same of this one?"

"Sir, I—"

This was the point at which Kitty, the maid, came flying in at the door.

"Only one of you's to go upstairs," Kitty reported. "Mr. Butler, please."

Butler hesitated, especially since Dr. Bierce seemed about to speak. But he followed Kitty.

She led him down the main passage, into a lofty back hall where a wooden staircase—ascending first along the left wall, then along the back wall—led up to a number of bedroom doors round a gallery with a balustrade. It was darkish here, due to fuel economy; several times Butler stumbled. Kitty tapped on the rear bedroom door, up the flight of stairs, at the right, and opened it.

"Yes?" said a woman's voice from inside.

Lucia Renshaw, in a heavy negligée of white lace, was sitting in an easy-chair at the far side of a portable electric-fire set against the grate. She rose to her feet, obviously shy and a little dazed.

And Patrick Butler, that cynical bachelor, received the shock of his life.

Vaguely he was aware that he stood in a high-ceilinged bedroom, whose high windows had old-fashioned shutters, and that one lamp burned on a little table between twin beds. At the back, slightly towards his left, he could see the white-tiled pallor of a modern bathroom.

For everything else. . . .

"Mr. Butler?" asked Lucia Renshaw in a low voice.

She had been crying bitterly. But of this there remained traces only in the faint red veins of the iris in her appealing blue eyes. Lucia's hair, heavy and dull-gold in this light, was unloosed and lay round her shoulders from a madonnaesque parting in the middle.

Lucia was rather tall, though to Butler she seemed middle-sized or even small. Such words as 'healthy' and 'wholesome,' though ordinarily they would have made Butler laugh, now struggled through his mind. The colour of her skin, a soft tawny-pink, was thrown into contrast by the white negligée. The thick lace of the negligée did not quite conceal the fact that—in her apparent haste and befuddlement—she wore under it only a brassiere and a pair of step-ins. There were pink satin slippers on her feet.

"Mr. Butler?" she repeated hesitantly.

It is a sober fact that Patrick Butler had to fight to control his voice, like a schoolboy.

"Yes, Mrs. Renshaw."

"They're all against me," said Lucia. "They all hate me. Will you help me?"

"I will do more than that. I will save you."

Butler's very real streak of eighteenth-century gallantry, which underlay all his bombast, saw nothing melodramatic in this speech, or in what followed: Impulsively Lucia extended her hand; and he, with the same gravity, bent over and kissed her hand. "By God!" he thought. "By God!"

"I knew you would," said Lucia. "When I heard you in court yesterday. . . . Court!" She shuddered. "Won't you sit down?"

"Thank you."

She indicated another easy-chair on the opposite side of the orange-glowing electric-fire. With what grace, with what infinite grace in this age of clumsy movement, she sat down! Lucia shook back her heavy yellow hair. Her tawny-pink skin was again in contrast to the white negligée as she breathed deeply.

"I like things to be pleasant!" she said. "I enjoy life! I never lose my temper and be rude to people, even in these times. And now. . . ."

"Your husband is dead. I'm sorry."

"I'm sorry too. But only for remembrance's sake." Lucia looked away, squeezing her eyes shut. "I asked Dick to give me a divorce last night. That's why I was in this room when he died."

Butler did not know why he felt obscurely startled.

"Your husband died in this room?"

"Yes. I. . . ." Lucia hesitated. She also was startled. Her blue eyes, with only a film of tears to mar the perfect beauty of the face, moved round the room. Then she shrank back timidly, as though under a threat.

"I shouldn't be sitting here, should I? But most of the time I've been so *dreadfully* upset and confused I simply haven't known where I was. Shall we go somewhere else?"

"No, of course not!" The fluent 'me dear' stuck in his throat. "What you did, Mrs. Renshaw, was perfectly natural."

"Oh, do you think so?"

"Of course. And if I'm to help you, Mrs. Renshaw, I must hear what happened. You say you asked your husband for a divorce?"

"Yes."

"What did you mean by adding, 'that's why I was in the room when he died'?"

"Sleeping here, I mean." Lucia lowered her eyes. "We'd occupied separate rooms for over a year. But last night I decided to sleep here. . . ."

"When you intended to ask him. . . . ?"

"Oh, not for the reason you're thinking!"

"I wasn't thinking—!"

Both of them stopped, fierily confused; and Butler, for one, was a liar. Yet in his sudden hatred of the deceased Richard Renshaw he could not help asking the question in his mind.

"What was your husband like?"

"That's the extraordinary thing. He was something like you."

"Like me?"

"Oh, I don't mean he looked much like you. Dick was very dark, almost swarthy; you're fair-complexioned and you've got light-brown hair. But his voice, and his way of carrying himself, and one or two gestures. . . ."

God rot the man! Butler, conscious that his wits were not at their best, had the sense to say only:

"Tell me your story, please."

Again Lucia sank back in the chair. Her heightened colour had faded.

"Dick," she went on, "had been away on a business trip. Yesterday afternoon, when I got home, there was a telegram to say he'd arrive by the train that gets to Euston at eleven o'clock. So I—I made up my mind. I told Kitty, that's the maid, to air the beds in this room, and fill the water-bottle, and get things ready."

Butler, while the voice flowed on, glanced surreptitiously round the room.

The twin beds were now trimly made, their yellowish coverlets smoothed out. Just between the beds, but higher up against the wall, hung a rather large ivory crucifix. It surprised Butler, though he could not have said why. Of great antiquity, yellowish-tinged, the crucifix stood out against the brown panelling of the wall.

Underneath it, beside the lamp on the bedside table, gleamed a glass water-bottle. It was an ordinary night water-bottle, round and narrow-necked, with a drinking-glass inverted over the neck. It was only about a fifth full of water. Not until you scrutinized it closely did you see the faint smears on its surface: the dustings of 'grey' powder where the police had searched for fingerprints.

Domestic murder, under the ivory crucifix.

Butler wrenched his attention back to Lucia.

"And of course," Lucia was saying, "Kitty didn't begin to do the room until past eleven o'clock. I'd already got undressed, in my own room down the passage; so I supervised her in here. I told her she'd better change the beds instead of just airing them; and she did. Finally she picked up that water-bottle. . . ."

Lucia, peering past the heavy line of her hair, tried to nod towards the bottle and then faltered.

"Go on!" prompted Butler.

"Kitty took the water-bottle into the bathroom, there. I watched her —you can see the wash-basin is just opposite the door. She poured out the water that was in the bottle, and rinsed it out a couple of times, and filled it with fresh water from the tap."

"And then?"

"She put it on the table, where it is now, with the tumbler over the top. Then I told her she could run along up to bed. But every second after eleven o'clock I'd been getting more and more panicky."

"Why?"

"Because of Dick!" The wide blue eyes opened at him. "All the time he was away, I had been working up my courage to ask for the divorce. . . ."

"Why did you want a divorce?"

Lucia stared at the fire.

"I didn't mind his being constantly unfaithful to me." She paused. "No, that isn't true. We like to say tra-la-la and be so sophisticated, don't we? I *did* mind. But it wasn't because I—I was in love with him. It was the horrible, awful humiliation."

Butler looked at the floor. He could guess, or thought he could, what it cost her to say that.

58   BELOW SUSPICION

"Go on about last night."

"About a quarter to twelve I heard a taxi drive up. I was sitting up in that bed there." She nodded towards the one on the left. "I had to catch him *then*, don't you see? If you bring up something a man doesn't like, he just says, 'I've got too much on my mind; we'll talk about it later!' And you let it go, or at least I do, unless you've got yourself worked up. That's why I was here in his room. After all that time. . . . !"

"How long had your husband been away?"

"Over three weeks. He only intended to stay a few days, really; but they let him open one of his old factories again, and he stayed to oversee it or whatever they do. Anyway, he was back. I heard the front door slam with an angry kind of noise. . . ."

In imagination Butler could hear it, and hear the heavy steps of Dick Renshaw ascending the uncarpeted stairs.

"He opened the door," Lucia went on. Her voice rose. "He stood and looked at me, in a queer kind of way, with his suitcase in his hand and his hat on the back of his head. I was sitting up in bed, with my knitting; Kitty brought me my knitting-bag when she first came into the room. Dick said, 'Hullo, is this a reconciliation?' I said no, it wasn't, and pitched in to talk about the divorce.

"Dick's face got as hard as stone. He didn't say anything. He began unpacking the suitcase, and putting everything away, while I still kept on talking. When he had finished unpacking, he very leisurely undressed and put on his pyjamas; and still without a word. By this time I was scared. Of course, I'd arranged matters with Miss Cannon in case he. . . ."

"Just a moment!" Butler interrupted.

Butler's mind had stumbled on the words, 'Miss Cannon.' 'Miss Cannon of Cannon Row' danced through his brain like a nursery rhyme.

"You'd arranged matters," Butler prompted her, "in case he—what?"

"Oh, in case he hit me or anything," answered Lucia, raising her thin-arched eyebrows in a face so perfectly made up that no make-up was apparent. She did not appear to find the statement unusual, or even notice her companion's boiling rage.

"I—er—I see. Who is Miss Cannon?"

"Oh, Agnes Cannon has been with me since I was fourteen. She was my governess. I don't know what you'd call her—a kind of fixture. She was to come in here, and threaten to ring the police, if Dick got violent."

"And did he get violent?"

"No, it was worse." Lucia shuddered. "He sat down on the edge of his own bed, in pyjamas and slippers, and just looked at me. For a second I thought he was going to . . . make advances; you know. But his eyes changed. He picked up that water-bottle on the bedside table."

Lucia paused, her hand at her breast.

"I ought to explain," she added, "that Dick had one habit; it never varied. He once told me he'd been doing it since he was an undergraduate. Every night, just before he turned in, he'd take a deep drink out of the water-bottle. He didn't use a glass. He just tilted up the bottle and drank till you thought he'd never stop.

"After that, last night I mean, he turned back the bed-covers. But, instead of getting into bed, he sat down and said to me, 'Unless you can get evidence against me, which you can't, just forget that divorce; you know what happened to your private 'tecs when you tried it.' And he kept on talking, not loudly, but about dreadful things.

"All of a sudden—it might have been ten or fifteen minutes later—a funny look came over him. It was as though he had a dry taste in his mouth, and kept moving his tongue round. Dick got up, and went to the bathroom muttering something about brushing his teeth. The next thing I knew, in the bathroom, he was being violently sick. Mr. Butler, I. . . .

"Anyway, I jumped out of bed and cried out, 'What's the matter? What's the matter?' But it only went on and on. Then he staggered back, and fell on his own bed. His eyes were glassy. He twisted on his side, and said—not to me; just to the air—something I can't understand even yet. He said 'O, where hae ye been, Lord Randal, my son?' "

There was a silence.

The words of the old ballad, one of the most subtly terrifying in English, hung in the room as though all the evil of the past were moving here in imperceptible waves.

"Then," Lucia went on, "Dick looked straight at me and said . . . what I don't want to repeat."

"I'm afraid it's necessary. What did he say?"

" 'You've poisoned me, you bitch.' And he rolled over on his face and writhed."

The recital, clearly, was too much for Lucia Renshaw. She sprang to her feet. Putting one hand on the ledge of the old black-marble mantelpiece, she looked down at the electric-fire. Despite her all-too-evident maturity in the white negligée, the words fell from her lips as incongruously as from those of a small girl; and, when she again appealed to Butler, Lucia's expression was that of a hurt child.

"I tried to get a doctor, you know." She spoke as though in protest. "I called out for Miss Cannon; and we 'phoned and 'phoned. Our own doctor was out on a case. We tried to remember the names of doctors in the neighborhood. But we couldn't. Then we began ringing our friends."

"Didn't it occur to you to ring 999 for an ambulance?"

Lucia lifted her shoulders wearily.

"No. At times like that (oh, it's true!) you become completely stupid. We didn't get a doctor until nearly three o'clock. By that time we were all running about, Miss Cannon and Kitty and I, and the front door was open. A policeman came in."

Now terror shone in Lucia's eyes and loosened her firm mouth.

"The doctor hurried upstairs. But it was too late. Poor Dick was in convulsions so bad that Miss Cannon said, 'Couldn't you hold him down? I can't stand this!' Before the doctor could open his bag, Dick gave a moan and—didn't breathe any more. I didn't realize how bad it was until I saw the policeman take out a pencil and notebook."

"They're all against me!" Lucia burst out. "They all hate me!"

"Here's one who doesn't," declared Butler, rising to his feet with all force of personality.

"Do you mean that, Mr. Butler? Do you mean it?"

"Of course." Yet his brain felt dead, or atrophied, because of his very power of sympathy for her. "It was antimony, wasn't it?"

"Yes."

"In the water-bottle?"

Lucia nodded quickly, without looking at him.

"Why do you say they're all against you?" he asked.

"Because they think, don't you see, I'm the only one who could have put poison in the bottle. Or they s-say so."

"Listen to me! Your maid," Butler spaced his words, "rinsed out the bottle and filled it from a tap in the bathroom. Couldn't Kitty herself have introduced the poison then?"

"No."

"Why not?"

"If you put that awful stuff in water, the police say, you've got to stir it and keep stirring it until it dissolves so nobody notices a trace. Anyway, Kitty didn't do anything at all. I watched her." Here Lucia gave him a furtive, shivering glance. "I could say she might have, only...."

"Only what?"

"I forgot to tell you Miss Cannon was here then. She watched Kitty too."

"But afterwards?"

"Kitty put the bottle on the table; I told you that. She and Miss Cannon left the room together."

"But afterwards, I repeat, while you were alone in here?"

"Miss Cannon," said Lucia, "has the room at the end of the gallery. I told her to sit there, and watch my door till Dick got home, and to listen after that in case he—well, you know. Nobody went into this room except Dick himself."

Patrick Butler, the urbane and never-flurried, felt panic tighten his collar and made the chilly room seem too warm. He struck wildly at phantoms.

"Could somebody have crept in here and poisoned the bottle? Through the windows, maybe?"

"Not," Lucia swallowed hard, "without my seeing him. Besides, the shutters of both windows were locked on the inside."

"Wait! Could there have been something wrong with the bathroom water-tap?"

"No. The—the police thought of that."

"All I've got to tell you," Butler assured her in his most lordly manner, "is that you needn't worry. *Don't* worry, do you hear? Leave everything to me. You see, Mrs. Renshaw...."

"Couldn't you ... couldn't you call me Lucia?"

"Would you mind?"

Lucia extended both her hands, and he gripped them hard. There was about this woman, he thought, a beauty and strength of sheer spirit which tingled from her hand-clasp. Even now her face was earnest, almost tender. She was, he thought, an innocent who enjoyed life and even kept on her old governess because Lucia could not bear to part with her. She was....

A sudden knock at the door made them both jump back as though they had been guilty of some indiscretion. More flurry, more near-hysteria, burst in as the door opened.

In the doorway stood a smallish, trimly dressed woman whose eyes also showed the strain of recent weeping. Her soft and fluffy white hair belied her age; Miss Agnes Cannon (of Cannon Row) could have been not quite in her middle forties. The white hair emphasized the roundness of a gentle face, with a pair of gold pince-nez, as Miss Cannon pressed a damp handkerchief against her mouth.

"Mr. Butler?" she asked, and rushed on without waiting for an answer. "I have a message for you from Mr. Denham. He wants you to go downstairs at once."

"Forgive me, but I'm afraid. . . ."

"Please go!" Miss Cannon burst out. "Mr. Denham says it's terribly important. It's about—the police."

7

"WILL you excuse me for a moment?" Butler asked Lucia. "I want to ask you a few more questions later."

And he hurried downstairs, his mind obsessed with water-bottles. He remembered, as a grotesque coincidence, the picture of Old Charlie sitting at the solicitors' table in the courtroom and toying idly with the neck of a water-bottle there. Otherwise Butler's brain was not at its clearest.

Charles Denham, seated on a long sofa in the front drawing room, was smoking a cigarette and blowing slow smoke rings.

"Well?" Butler demanded. "What's up?"

"I admit," said Denham, "I was getting a little impatient. You've had much more than five minutes with Mrs. Renshaw. Is she guilty or not guilty?"

Butler was stunned. "Is she *guilty?*" he repeated.

"Yes."

"Are you off your head, Charlie? That woman is as innocent as a saint out of heaven!"

"You exalt the sex," observed Denham, watching another smoke ring. "Now I love 'em, mind you! I love their ways and their eyes and their lips. But I keep 'em in their place, Pat."

"What in hell are you talking about?"

Butler did not see the slight twitch in Denham's dark-complexioned face.

"The evidence against Mrs. Renshaw," the solicitor said evenly, "is about as black as it can be. Can you think of a defence?"

Butler couldn't. But words seemed to form themselves by instinct.

"Let me ask you just one question, Charlie. Do you think Lucia Renshaw is a complete nitwit?"

"On the contrary. She's a very clever woman."

"Very well. Then if she had poisoned her husband, do you think she'd have been such a fool as to leave all that damning evidence against herself?"

"In a detective story, no."

Butler, opening his mouth to reply, stopped dead. It struck him, like a blow between the eyes, that he had heard exactly these same words somewhere before. Denham watched him out of a smoke-mist.

"Oh, yes," Denham interpreted his thoughts. "We've been speaking in quotations. But what I said just now about Lucia Renshaw was what you said, some time ago, about Joyce Ellis. It makes a difference, doesn't it, when you happen to be emotionally involved yourself?"

His voice poured with bitterness. Twisting round, he squashed out his cigarette in an ashtray on the table behind him. On that table were two very large silver candelabra, highly polished, each with seven branches. Their glitter seemed to fascinate Patrick Butler.

"Who says I'm emotionally involved?"

"Aren't you?" said Denham. "I was trying to find out."

"It seems I misjudged you, Charlie. By the Lord, I think you'd give anything on earth to see me come a cropper!"

"No, no, no!" protested Denham. He weakened, as usual.

"But I won't come a cropper," said Butler. "Not until grass turns red and you've got a beard that winds three times round the Nelson Monument. Why did you get me to come down here, anyway? With a fake story about the police?"

"Not exactly the police," Denham corrected him. "May I introduce Dr. Gideon Fell?"

The presence of Dr. Fell in this room—or, in fact, any room—could have gone unnoticed only by someone wearing mental blinkers. Dr. Fell let out a tentative harrumph to indicate it.

Standing near the white-marble mantelpiece, leaning on one cane instead of two, and with his old black cloak over his shoulders, Dr. Fell dwarfed even Butler as his bulk dwarfed the room. On top of this bulk a large red face, dominated by a mop of greyish hair, beamed down on Butler through eyeglasses on a broad black ribbon. Dr. Fell was so delighted that his red cheeks were bunched up, like his several chins, and it gave him an almost toothy look under his bandit's moustache.

"Sir," he intoned, "I have longed to make your acquaintance. I do not say"—here Dr. Fell made a dangerous wide-sweeping gesture with his cane, flapping back the cloak—"that in your legal tactics there has ever been the slightest whisper of a *suggestio falsi*. No! Since I myself have so often flummoxed the evidence, and cheerfully perverted justice for a good end, I beg leave to consider you only a right-thinking amateur. Sir, I am your well-wisher!"

"Sir," replied Butler, instantly liking him and bowing as he might have bowed to Dr. Johnson, "I am yours!"

"Thankee," beamed Dr. Fell, hanging the crook of the cane over his arm so that he could rub his hands together. "Shall we proceed to business?"

"What business?"

"The murder of Richard Renshaw."

An arrow of distrust shot through Butler's mind, though he continued to smile.

"I know you, Dr. Fell, as an old friend of Superintendent Hadley. Are you here on police business?"

"No," said Dr. Fell, looking unhappy. "At the moment, as often happens, I am in disgrace at Scotland Yard. You see, I am one of those who believe that Joyce Ellis was innocent."

"Good! Then you agree the prosecution didn't consider the evidence properly?"

"Sir," returned Dr. Fell, "*nobody* considered the evidence."

There was a brief silence. Dr. Fell boomed out this dictum with such flat positiveness, whacking the ferrule of his cane on the floor, that Butler and Denham exchanged glances.

"Oh?" smiled Butler. "Not even counsel for the defence?"

"With all respect, sir; not even counsel for the defence. That was only natural. You were seeking the ingenious explanation rather than the true explanation. But . . . Archons of Athens! It did seem to me at that trial, even as an old scatterbrain," Dr. Fell spoke apologetically, "that both sides were looking up into trees for the roots and digging underground for the branches. When I heard Mr. Richard Renshaw had been poisoned afterwards, I can't say I was surprised."

"Weren't surprised? Why not?"

"For one reason," said Dr. Fell, "because I rather expected it."

"You expected Mr. Renshaw to be murdered?"

"Well," argued Dr. Fell, squinting hideously down his nose, "I expected *somebody* to be murdered. Dash it all!" he complained, in the querulous tone of one who is trying to be reasonable, "surely it was at least probable that somebody would be murdered! Er—am I making myself clear?"

"Frankly, you're not. Dr. Fell," said Butler, "what's your interest in this case?"

"Mass-murder," said Dr. Fell. "May I remind you, as I reminded Mr. Denham today, that during the past three months there have been nine unsolved poisoning cases in various parts of the country? For reasons with which I will not bore you, I do not include the case of Mrs. Taylor. But I very much include the case of Richard Renshaw. And that makes ten."

Mass-murder by poison. To Butler it conjured up such a gruesome image that he fought against it.

"Look here! You don't think all these cases are connected?"

"By thunder, I do!" roared Dr. Fell, firing up and rearing up. "It may be, I acknowledge, only my own morbid fancy. And yet I will venture a further suggestion. I will make a guess that all these murders were brought about—or at least directed—by one person and one person only."

"But, my God, why?"

"For pleasure and profit," returned Dr. Fell.

"Just a moment," interposed Charles Denham, leaning forward on the sofa. "Are you suggesting," he hesitated, "a kind of gangster organization to kill any given person for money?"

"No, no, no!" said Dr. Fell with violent emphasis. "An organization of that kind simply would not work in this country."

Dr. Fell, filled with mysterious internal snortings which crept up over the ridges of his waistcoat and threatened to dislodge his eyeglasses, began to take a turn round the room. Then he stopped, and pointed with his cane.

"Hadley knows, if I don't," he continued. "The so-called underworld is too small, too closely knit, too full of narks, too leaky with information! A whisper of this would get to Scotland Yard in three weeks, much less three months. No, you may eliminate the professional criminal.

"*But,*" argued Dr. Fell, again making a hideous face for emphasis, "what sort of group might exist and lie concealed in dead silence? That's what I ask myself; and I reluctantly admit that I don't know. How could there be nine murders without a single clue? How could somebody obtain poison and leave never a record anywhere? How—"

Dr. Fell stopped dead.

"O Lord!" he breathed, puffing out his cheeks. "O Bacchus!"

For Dr. Fell was peering down, like an immense red genie over a microscope, at one of the larger silver candelabra on the table behind the sofa.

"What's the matter?" Denham asked rather sharply.

Dr. Fell did not reply. He picked up the candelabrum, which was one of the perfectly plain type which may be found in any well-to-do home. Turning it over in his hand, he examined it carefully. He peered into the sockets of the candle-holders. He scraped inside with his fingernail, and produced what appeared to Butler only traces of wax gone black with dust.

"Dr. Fell!" said the exasperated barrister, who was preoccupied with Lucia and not inclined to take the learned doctor very seriously.

"Eh?"

"Shall we get back to the man who was poisoned in this house last night? What do you know about it?"

"Only"—Dr. Fell replaced the candelabrum on the table—"that the lady had wanted a divorce for some time. . . ."

"You can't find a motive in that!"

"Sir," replied Dr. Fell, frowning in a ruffled way. "I was not speaking of motive. Finally: I know that her husband returned home and drank from a poisoned water-bottle, and that for some reason Mrs. Renshaw was in his room that night."

"May I ask who told you this?"

"I'm afraid," interposed the voice of Lucia Renshaw from the doorway, "I'm afraid I did." She gave a murmur of a nervous laugh. "I 'phoned him. Wasn't it all right?"

No, it wasn't all right! But Patrick Butler could not say so.

He realized, with angry disappointment, that his sense of intimacy with Lucia was now gone. It would not return tonight. Lucia smiled, with her warmth of personality, on all three guests.

She was now fully dressed, in grey silk blouse and black skirt, grey silk stockings and black shoes. Her hair, done up as though in haste and carelessness, yet emphasized its softness and sheen. If Lucia still felt trapped and terrified, she gave no sign of it. Beyond her in the doorway showed the gentle face and pince-nez of Miss Agnes Cannon.

"It was awfully good of you to come here, Dr. Fell," said Lucia earnestly. "And I didn't ask you because—well, because of the awful trouble I'm in. I'm sure Mr. Butler and Mr. Denham can deal with that. Oh! Isn't Dr. Bierce here?"

"That's four of us," murmured Denham, who had got to his feet.

"He was here, Lucia," Denham added aloud, "but he had to go. Evening surgery."

"Oh, I'm sorry!" Lucia was conscience-stricken. "I didn't want to inconvenience him. You see, I was rather moping and brooding upstairs. Dear Agnes—Miss Cannon here—persuaded me to come down."

Dear Agnes, Patrick Butler thought furiously, deserved a good swift kick with a football shoe.

"But I wanted to talk to you, Dr. Fell," Lucia rushed on, "because you're the one—aren't you?—who knows all about locked rooms."

"Locked rooms!" exclaimed Butler. "There's no locked room here!"

"No, of course not. But how could someone have poisoned that bottle when there wasn't anyone to do it except myself? If I could tell you the circumstances, Dr. Fell. . . ."

And she told him.

Butler, it must be confessed, was growing madder and madder. He concealed this by an air of greater and greater arrogance. As though severing himself from the whole proceeding, he strolled over and sat by an open writing-desk.

All the same, as Lucia's half-breathless account went on—the waterbottle rinsed and refilled, the poison gulped down under the crucifix, Dick Renshaw writhing in his last convulsion—it seemed to throw its evil spell and contaminate this room as it had contaminated the room upstairs.

And Butler noticed, with deep satisfaction, that Dr. Fell was becoming as puzzled and uneasy as the barrister himself. Before the end of the story, Dr. Fell, now piled massively into one corner of the sofa, appeared so struck with consternation that even Lucia observed it.

"What is it?" she asked quickly. "Is anything wrong?"

"By thunder, there is!" wheezed Dr. Fell. "Everything is wrong! Do you know, Mrs. Renshaw, this is not what I expected at all?" He ruffled up his greyish hair, and he appeared to have more chins. "I expected.
. . ."

"What?"

"To take one minor point. About the character of your late husband—"

"I don't want you to think I wasn't sorry for him!" cried Lucia. "I was sorry."

Standing behind Lucia's chair, the fluffy white hair framing her young-looking face, Miss Agnes Cannon spoke suddenly.

"You have no need to feel sorry for him, my dear," said Miss Cannon, in her soft and cultured voice. "I have told you before he was better dead."

"Agnes, you mustn't say that!"

"Dick Renshaw was a bounder and a waster," declared Miss Cannon, though a thin film of tears appeared behind the pince-nez. "He pursued women and he lived above his income." Unexpectedly she added: "He was a spiv and a drone and an eel and a butterfly!"

Dr. Fell blinked at her. "I—harrumph—beg your pardon?"

Patrick Butler was instantly on his feet.

"The term she mentions, Doctor," he said richly, "were framed by our Labour Government to describe any man who works with his brain rather than his hands."

The star of the fanatic sprang into Miss Cannon's eyes; as, on the other side of the fence, it was also in Butler's.

"The Government, young man," Miss Cannon said pityingly, "do not exactly work with their hands."

"No, madam. Or with their brains. I should respect them more if they did either."

"You ought to be jailed for speaking against the Government!" cried Miss Cannon. "We're living in a democracy!"

"Madam," said Butler, closing his eyes, "your remark is such a perfect thing that its beauty must not be spoiled by comment. I accept the definition."

"*Stop it!*" roared Dr. Fell.

"Speaking for myself," continued Dr. Fell mildly, when silence had been restored, "I share the sentiments of Mr. Butler. If necessary, I could express them with a fluency guaranteed to blast the walls. But that is why we must not discuss them now. We feel too strongly to talk sense on either side. And now perhaps (confound it!) may I ask Mrs. Renshaw a relevant question about her husband's death?"

Lucia nodded expectantly, her dark-red mouth vivid against heightened colour, her body bent forward in the chair.

"You told this girl—harrumph—Kitty," said Dr. Fell, "to change the beds. Did you also tell her to sweep and dust?"

"To sweep and . . . why on earth do you want to know that?"

"Indulge me!" begged Dr. Fell. "Did you?"

"I'm not sure whether I told her. But I remember her running the carpet-sweeper back and forth, with the handle of my knitting-bag over her arm in case she forgot it. Yes; and I think she dusted."

"Alas and alack!" Miss Cannon said indulgently, with a bright friendly look to show no offence over political matters. "With all my efforts, I've never been able to make Lucia a good housekeeper. I attend to such things here."

"Ah!" muttered Dr. Fell.

"Kitty did dust, after a fashion," said Miss Cannon, with brisk competence. "But it's a pity I wasn't there longer. Dear Lucia almost *drove* me out of the room."

"Agnes, that was only because I was afraid Dick would be there any minute!"

"Well, Kitty made a bad job of it. There was a great deal of dust today, when I cleaned out the bedroom and the bathroom." Miss Cannon shuddered. "After the police had gone. One could even see marks in the dust."

Dr. Fell sat up suddenly, amid a creaking and cracking of woodwork which endangered the whole sofa.

"What marks?" he demanded.

"Really, sir, I . . . well!" Miss Cannon retreated a little. "I hardly remember."

"Are the marks there now?"

"Not after *I* cleaned, I assure you."

"Then for the love of Heaven try to describe them!"

Every person in that room sat or stood as still as death. Patrick Butler, by the writing-desk, found himself gripping a well-polished and flattish sea-stone used as a paperweight. As a boy in Ireland, the memory flashed through his head, he could throw a heavy stone hard and with uncanny accuracy; he had the knack yet. He would like to throw this one, as a relief for his feelings, at the blackening centre of a mystery.

"I think," Miss Cannon's pale brown eyes narrowed behind the pince-nez, "it was as though someone had scratched in the dust of the window sill. There were two or three marks."

"Shaped like what?"

"Something like the letter 'T' reversed. And perhaps with a little tail to it. I don't know! I'm not sure!"

For a moment Dr. Fell remained motionless. Then, with infinite labour, he wheezed and propelled himself to his feet.

"Mrs. Renshaw," he said in a voice he very seldom used, "I should like you and Mr. Butler to come upstairs with me for a private conference. Believe me, I do not make the request idly."

While Charles Denham and Agnes Cannon remained still, Lucia

led the way out of the drawing room. She walked rigidly and did not speak; it was as though her mouth would tremble if she attempted speech.

On the stairs Dr. Fell asked to be taken to Dick Renshaw's bedroom. Silently Lucia opened the door and pressed the electric-switch just inside.

The muffled lamp glowed again on the bedside table. Two oblongs of orange-yellow colour stole into the electric-fire. With scarcely a glance at the room itself, Dr. Fell carefully closed the door and faced Lucia and Butler.

"Ma'am," he said to Lucia in a heavy voice, "please accept now the fact that I am a bumbling old duffer. I suffer from, as it were, a certain absence of mind. I am just as apt to lift my hostess's best Wedgwood-china tea-pot and drop it on the hearthstone under the impression that there is a table there. But you had better hear these things from me than from Chief Inspector Soames."

"Just a minute!" Butler was beginning, when Dr. Fell's gesture cut him short.

"So I want to speak to you," the doctor went on to Lucia, "in the presence of your counsel and with his permission. For your own sake don't lie to me. The police have only begun to work. They are endlessly patient to track down a lie." Dr. Fell's face grew lopsided with supplication. "Mrs. Renshaw, do you have any antimony in your possession?"

"No!" Lucia said in horror.

"Did you ever buy it, or try to buy it? At any time in the past?"

"Never!"

Instinctively Lucia had taken hold of Butler's arm; and the current of intimacy wound them together again.

"That in itself," Butler interposed dryly, "is a stone-wall for the defence. You couldn't convict Satan himself unless you could show he had access to poison."

"Sir," retorted Dr. Fell, with a shade of wonder, "is it possible that even you don't realize the danger of the situation?"

"Naturally I realize it! But, in the remote chance that they did arrest Lucia," Butler glanced at her soothingly, "I mean to get her acquitted."

"And suppose you did? Would that solve your problem?"

Butler realized, with surprise, that he was still gripping the stone paperweight from the writing-desk downstairs. He looked at it blankly, as he looked at Dr. Fell, and dropped it into his side-pocket.

"Suppose," continued Dr. Fell with fiery emphasis, "you devised an explanation—as you or I probably could!—of how the poison got into the water-bottle. Suppose you secured Mrs. Renshaw's acquittal in a blaze of triumph. Don't you see the police might have still another charge against her?"

"Another charge? What charge?"

"The murder of Mrs. Taylor."

8

FOR about ten seconds Lucia Renshaw did not seem to understand.

Then her slim hand, with the pink fingernails, slid from Butler's arm as though her whole body had gone nerveless. She backed slowly away from Dr. Fell, an oddly crouching gesture for so tall and graceful a woman.

She backed into one of the twin beds, started to sit down there, suddenly looked round in horror until she saw it was not the bed where Dick Renshaw had died, then sat down and supported herself with the palms of her hands flat on the bed.

"Mrs. Taylor?" Lucia almost screamed. "Aunt Mildred?"

Dr. Fell nodded.

"But that's s-silly!" protested Lucia, with the air of a child who stretches out its hand towards fire and is unsure whether the fire will burn. "It's ridiculous! It's all finished and done with!"

"It is never done with, I fear. After Joyce Ellis, you were the principal suspect from the beginning."

"How do you know that?" Butler asked quickly.

"My dear sir!" grunted Dr. Fell, between petulance and distress. "I was on the inside of that affair from the beginning. Didn't I tell you they threw me out of Hadley's office when I tried somewhat bumblingly to explain what I really did mean? Then Joyce Ellis was acquitted. Somebody turned the police's attention straight back to you."

Now Lucia's voice was almost a whisper. "Who turned their attention back to me?"

"Mr. Butler did," said Dr. Fell. "He proved, to the satisfaction of a jury, that the locked house was not really locked at all. He proved that an outsider must have got in. He proved many things even more damaging to you."

(And I did it with a fake defence. Joyce herself kept telling me, in private, that the back door was locked all night.)

"Shall I outline the case, Mrs. Renshaw, as it might appear to the police?" said Dr. Fell.

Butler did not look at Lucia, who had raised her head. Yet he was strung up to alertness.

"Before I let you ask any question, Dr. Fell—which side are you on?"

"Side?"

"Are you running with the hare or hunting with the hounds? You're either for us or against us. Which is it?"

"Look here," said Dr. Fell, rubbing his forehead under the tumbled hair. "This whole affair is too tangled for an unqualified 'yes' or 'no.' If I can get a few things straight, I am on your side with a bang. But perhaps I had better go." His eyes wandered up to the crucifix on the wall. "I am much disturbed."

"No!" cried Lucia. "Please! Patrick! Make him tell us!"

Butler shrugged his shoulders. Dr. Fell studied Lucia, who in a hypnotized way had been incredulously murmuring "Principal suspect" and "Kill Aunt Mildred?" as though she had walked through a valley of snakes without ever seeing one. Dr. Fell cleared his throat.

"Did you tell the police, today, that you had wanted a divorce?"

"Yes!"

"Is it true, as Miss Cannon said, that your husband lived above his income?"

"Dick never talked to me about money. But I think he was in debt."

"H'mf, yes. Were you—confound it all!—were you entirely dependent on him for support? Had you any money of your own?"

The blue eyes opened wide. "No. Not a bean. I never had."

"Then, if you simply up and left him, you would have no means of financial support?"

"No, I—suppose not. I never thought of it. Besides, Dick wouldn't have allowed me to leave him."

"Now we know," persisted Dr. Fell, trying to cover his embarrassment by looking fierce, "that you and your husband were Mrs. Taylor's only relations. To be strictly accurate: you were her only relative. And her heiress."

Lucia's body grew rigid. But she did not reply.

"Tonight, before Mr. Butler came downstairs, I had a word with young Denham about Mrs. Taylor's will. You inherited three properties: Mrs. Taylor's home, called 'The Priory'; this house, called 'Abbot's House,' and a third property called 'The Chapel.' Curious flavour of religion about those names, isn't there?"

Lucia merely gave a jerk of her head, as at some irrelevant question, and scarcely seemed to breathe.

"In cash and securities, with all taxes deducted," said Dr. Fell, "you inherited fifty thousand pounds. That sum would free any woman from dependence on her husband."

"Dr. Fell! You don't think I'd . . . oh, no!"

"On the afternoon preceding Mrs. Taylor's death during the same night," pursued Dr. Fell, "I think you paid an unexpected call on her?"

"Yes! But . . ."

"It was not your habit to pay calls at Balham, was it?"

"N-not exactly. But I went when I could. She was old and lonely."

"During your talk with her, Mrs. Taylor was already mentioning her craving for Nemo's salts, and protesting that there weren't any in the house? Do you remember hearing your aunt talk about it?"

Lucia hesitated. "She did say something, yes. But I didn't pay any attention to it."

"You see," rumbled Dr. Fell, again making motions of distress, "Dr. Bierce can testify that she did talk about it. By the way, did you know about the antimony which was kept in a tin in the stable."

"Don't answer that question!" snapped Patrick Butler.

"But I did know about it," Lucia whispered. "Bill Griffiths, the coachman, told everybody about it. To warn them."

"Let us take the morning after Mrs. Taylor's death," continued Dr. Fell, with his voice in—deliberate?—imitation of Butler's courtroom manner. "We know, now, that the key to the back door was not in the lock of the back door. We know it was lying inside the door, on the floor of the passage. Mr. Butler proved—"

"Wait a minute!" Butler exclaimed. "That wasn't—"

"Wasn't what?" Dr. Fell asked sharply.

(*I can't tell them it wasn't true. I can't tell them it was a lie I invented myself, and put into Joyce Ellis's mouth. I can't tell them the key was really in the lock all night!*)

"You were saying, sir?" intoned Dr. Fell with polished courtesy.

"Nothing at all. Sorry."

"Therefore," Dr. Fell turned to Lucia Renshaw, "we have a clear case. Someone—someone from outside—had only to take a pencil, and push the key through the lock from outside. Then the door could be opened, and locked afterwards, with another key. Mr. Butler proved. . . ."

(*God Almighty, where is this leading? What was in that glance Lucia gave me just now?*)

". . . that it was a key to a Grierson lock," said Dr. Fell. "Isn't there a Grierson lock on the back door of this house, Mrs. Renshaw?"

"I don't know! I don't know!"

"Well, unfortunately there is. That provides you with a key. Of course, if you could prove your whereabouts on the night of the 22nd of February, that would be different. Where were you then?"

"Here! In this house!"

"Can you prove that by any witness?"

"No. Dick went away on his trip the day before, the 21st, and—" Lucia stopped suddenly, her eyes more horrified, her pink fingernails pressed against her cheeks. "Dick's dead," she said. "I forgot."

"Could you prove your presence here by a servant, for instance?"

"No. In this part of the world, Thursday is the servants' day off; and they don't get back until late at night."

"Miss Cannon's testimony, then?"

"Poor Agnes is . . . well, she's a paid companion. Dick wanted to get rid of her. She was away on Thursday night too." There was a silence. "But I couldn't have killed *Dick*," Lucia cried, as though seizing at a straw. "Somebody said it only a minute ago! I didn't have any poison!"

"Ma'am, there is another piece of evidence I am bound to tell you now. It was not presented at the trial; because the police, quite rightly, believed it immaterial to that case."

"Well?"

Dr. Fell began to wheeze as though that vast bulk had been running.

"Bill Griffiths, the coachman, testifies that more than four table-spoonfuls of antimony were taken from the tin. That's over twice the amount Mrs. Taylor swallowed. The murderer was keeping another heavy dose in reserve."

Then Dr. Fell did not give her time to comment, even if she had wished to comment.

"You said a moment ago, Mrs. Renshaw, that your husband 'wouldn't have allowed you to leave him.' Why not?"

"If he couldn't have me"—Lucia's golden hair gleamed as she looked at the floor—"nobody else was going to have me."

"Were you afraid of him?"

"Horribly!"

"In your statement to me downstairs, and probably to Mr. Butler as well, you quoted Richard Renshaw as saying: 'Unless you can get evidence against me, which you can't, just forget that divorce; you know what happened to your private 'tecs when you tried it.'"

"Yes," Lucia agreed in a whisper. Still she did not look up.

"What did he mean by those words?"

"That's the part I'm ashamed of. That's the part I'm really and horribly ashamed of." Lucia's breast rose and fell under the grey silk blouse. "But what can you *do*? I hired a firm of private detectives to—you know—follow him."

"Yes?"

"In about a week they wrote to me and said they had to give up the case; but they wouldn't say why. I hired another firm. Before long a man came round to say *they* had to drop it. Finally I coaxed the truth out of him."

"Well? What was it?"

"One of their operatives, or whatever they call it, was so badly smashed up with brass knuckles that he's still in hospital."

It was as though a fist smote through the human lives of this affair, or a catapult released more evil forces than they had dreamed of. But Dr. Fell did not seem surprised.

"Then you could never get free from your husband. Or thought you couldn't?"

Lucia spoke miserably. "That's what I thought, yes."

"And so, for real independence, the poison was as necessary as the fifty thousand pounds. And you killed your husband as you killed Mrs. Taylor. That, I fear, would be a rough outline of the case against you."

Silence.

Lucia, sitting on the edge of the bed with each hand out a little way to support herself, seemed to be staring at her crossed ankles. They did not see her eyes, but they saw two tears fall from her eyes. Then the light ran along her hair as she lifted her head. The heavy-lidded blue eyes regarded her companions with numb appeal.

Though Patrick Butler had never any doubt about her innocence—and, as he would have said, he was never wrong—his belief was strengthened, and upheld and made happy, by Lucia's expression now. His heart went out to her in love, and in pity, and in as much humility as he was ever able to feel.

But Lucia was looking at Dr. Fell. "Is that what you think of me?" she asked wonderingly. "Is that what you really think of me?"

"No, no, no!" spluttered Dr. Fell, making such mesmeric passes that his cloak flew around him.

"Then why do you—?"

"Dash it, didn't I explain? That is the charge as it might be brought by the police." His tone changed. "But with one part of it I do agree. These two deaths, Mrs. Taylor's and Mr. Renshaw's, are interlocking factors of the same crime. They depend on each other. One murderer is responsible for them both."

"But—what do you think?" asked Lucia. "You said, when you'd got certain things straight, you'd know what to believe about me. Tell me!"

"My dear young lady!" Dr. Fell looked dumbfounded. "I haven't asked you a single question about the matter which interests me most!"

"You . . . what?"

"No, no, no, no!" he assured her gravely. "Only two questions over-whelm and overshadow everything else. By thunder, they do!"

"What are they, then?"

"You were present," said Dr. Fell, screwing up his face, "at the first day of the trial. You heard the testimony of Alice Griffiths, Mrs. Taylor's maid. She said that you and Mrs. Taylor, when you paid a call there 'had words' about religion. What did she mean by that?"

Lucia, obviously still stunned with shock, could have been no more puzzled than Patrick Butler.

"About religion?" Lucia echoed.

"Yes!"

"But I can't remember . . . wait!" There was a curious, quick shift and gleam in Lucia's eyes. "I believe Aunt Mildred did say something about joining the Roman Catholic Church."

Dr. Fell was taken aback. He blinked at her, holding hard to his eyeglasses on the black ribbon.

"You're sure of that?" he persisted, with a kind of panting effect. "You're sure Mrs. Taylor used the term 'Catholic Church'?"

"Well, that's what I understand. Aunt Mildred was nice, but she had such a queer sense of humour—like calling Dr. Bierce 'Ambrose'—and every time she made some kind of joke she'd leer and show her teeth like a wolf. I said we belonged to the Anglican Church, of course!"

"My last question," said Dr. Fell. He looked at her steadily. "Do ladies nowadays still wear garters?"

(*The old boy's off his chump! Or is he?*)

"Why—" Lucia was beginning, as though in a startled rush of words to answer. Then she stopped. "We really don't, you know," Lucia said dryly, "unless we can't get a suspender-belt. It hasn't been done for some time."

"Not even," said Dr. Fell, "red garters?"

It was at this point that Patrick Butler made a fierce shushing gesture.

For some time Butler had been conscious of a sense, purely animal, that someone was watching or listening. It grew more intense because he seemed to be excluded from the conversation. Glancing towards the door to the gallery, where lights now burned, he noticed that the keyhole was obscured. Feeling at once intensely curious and yet foolish, like a man in a farce, he edged across and threw the door open.

Outside, bent over to listen, stood nobody more alarming than Kitty Owen, the maid. Kitty was not at all discomposed as she straightened up.

"Yes, Kitty?" inquired Lucia, as casually as though the maid had tapped at the door. Lucia rose to her feet. "What is it?"

"I was looking for your knitting-bag, ma'am. Can I come in and see if it's here?"

"Yes, of course."

Kitty straightened her lace cap. What was the look she gave Lucia, as she sidled past into the room. Dislike? No. A sense of superiority? Perhaps. Butler, conscious of being obscurely disturbed, tried to analyze it.

All this time Lucia had never looked at him.

"Kitty," she explained to the air, "is so fond of knitting. I don't like it, really. She carries that bag about like a treasure, and finishes all the things I start. But she mustn't carry books there, Miss Cannon says. Have you found it, Kitty?"

From the other side of a chest-of-drawers, where it had evidently fallen, Kitty picked up the large dull-green knitting-bag.

"Yes, ma'am. I'll finish the sweater, if you don't mind."

"Very well, then. Run along."

Kitty ran. But, as she paused in front of Butler, she turned up her vivid dark-brown eyes in the same look of astonishment and fright she had given him at the front door.

"You do remind me of Mr. Renshaw!" Kitty said, and the door clicked softly after her as she hurried out. Lucia, now standing in the middle of the room, had the dangerous poise of a woman near breaking-point.

"I'm sure," said Lucia, "you'll excuse me if I don't hear any more about how guilty I am. Dr. Fell—"

She stopped abruptly, not finding him in his proper place. All that could be seen now was what looked like a huge black tent, topped with a mop of shaggy hair, as Dr. Fell stood between the beds and blinked down at the water-bottle on the bedside table.

Moving over to one side, Butler again looked at that infernal bottle. It contained little more than an inch of water, full of microscopic beads that gleamed under the light, but still deadly.

"Ma'am," grunted Dr. Fell without turning round, "did your husband drink as much water as is gone from this bottle?"

"No, no! The police took away a lot, to analyze. That's how I know it was antimony. The Chief Inspector told me this afternoon. And that is the last question I answer, tonight or at any other time."

Butler took a few steps round and faced her. "Listen, Lucia. . . ."

"I should be glad, Mr. Butler," Lucia said quietly, "if you did not intrude in my affairs any longer."

Butler, though feeling the full slap in the face, thought he could understand it. She was growing hysterical, of course. Any woman would do the same.

"Listen to me, please." He spoke gently. "There's not a particle of direct evidence against you for the murder of Mrs. Taylor. It may look bad, of course. . . ."

"Yes. And who made it look bad?"

Butler's heart sank, though he kept an expressionless face. "I really don't understand you."

" 'Mr. Butler proved,' " Lucia mimicked. " 'Mr. Butler proved.' I thought if I heard that just once more, I should begin screaming. You've put me into rather a pretty corner, haven't you?"

"It was my professional duty to defend my client."

"By attacking me?"

"Are you under the impression that I attacked you?"

"Didn't you? Didn't you get your witnesses to tell lies?"

"You—you should know better than to ask that question, Mrs. Renshaw. As a matter of professional ethics. . . ."

"I hate you!" flared Lucia, and her eyes brimmed over again. "You're against me too!"

"Oh, don't be such a fool!"

"How amusing!" breathed Lucia, with a woman-of-the-world's lightness, and her eye on a corner of the ceiling. "So now I'm a fool!"

"I beg your pardon. But it might interest you to know that I broke an unwritten law by even coming here."

"How interesting!"

"It is, rather." Butler gritted his teeth. "This work is done by a solicitor. Counsel's advice is taken only by a solicitor. I came here because—I don't know!—altruistic purpose—"

"Oh, get out!" screamed Lucia.

Patrick Butler bowed stiffly. In a blind rage, but with a sick sensation in his heart because Lucia had never seemed so desirable, he went out and closed the door with murderous care. Slowly walking downstairs, he saw the rear hall only as a blur of dim lights and luxurious furniture.

But over one chair, he noticed, lay his overcoat and hat. Slowly he put on the overcoat, as though his back and shoulders hurt him. As he went forward into the passage leading to the front, he saw Charles Denham—also in an overcoat, and holding a neat bowler hat—hesitating near the front door.

"Had enough for one evening?" Denham asked quietly.

"Eh? Oh! Yes."

"Like Dr. Bierce," said Denham, opening the front door, "I don't seem to be wanted here. It's half-past seven, Pat. I need my dinner."

"What I need," said Butler, "is about sixteen drinks."

The sharp-edged air, with a tang of damp, closed round them as they stepped outside the door. Denham shut the door and looked quickly at his companion.

"So you've seen through Lucia already?" he asked.

"That woman is as innocent as you are!" Butler shouted.

"Oh, granted." Denham spoke placidly. "But let's face it, Pat. She's completely selfish; and she has no more heart than. . . ."

His gaze wandered out to the hard asphalt paving of the road beyond the thin board fence. Butler saw the look.

"That's a lie!"

"I thought she'd appeal to you. But aren't you going to have a hard time defending her?"

On either side of the house, meeting the board fence at the front, ran two low stone walls spiky with dead rose-branches. Near the front of the left wall some boy with a decorative sense had placed an empty tin which might have contained Nemo's salts. Butler saw its faint glimmer by the light of a street-lamp.

"I'll defend her, all right," he snapped. "And I only hope Mr. Justice Bloody Stoneman is on the bench again!"

"But it's a pity, isn't it?" murmured Denham. "Don't you prefer your clients to be guilty?"

"Look here, I only said. . . . !"

"Where's the credit—or the fun—in defending somebody who's innocent?"

That was the moment when Butler, adjusting his overcoat, found in his inner coat-pocket the smooth, polished stone from the writing-desk. He took it out and weighed it in his hand. He wondered, in a kind of abstract fury, whether he could throw the stone and hit that tin on the fence.

"Between ourselves, Pat: how do you intend to defend Lucia?"

"I don't know."

"Not a ghost of an idea?"

"Not yet, no!"

Charles Denham began to laugh.

Butler, still eyeing the tin on the fence, swung towards him. "What's so damned funny about it?"

"I apologize it. It isn't funny. But the one client you know to be innocent is the one client you can't get acquitted!"

Patrick Butler threw with all his weight behind it. The tin, squarely struck, banged and flew wide; the stone clattered away into the road. From somewhere a dead shrubbery rose the squall and snarl of a cat.

That night Butler got drunk. At eleven o'clock, when he was sloshing down watered whisky at the Blue Dog Club in Berkeley Square, Lucia Renshaw was undressing to go to bed in her own home. Lucia's bedroom, full of mirrors, showed multiple reflections as she sat down to take off her stockings.

The stockings were rolled a few inches above the knee, and fastened with small, round garters coloured red. Before removing them, Lucia stared thoughtfully at her own reflection in a full-length mirror.

9

WELL, he was finished with Lucia Renshaw! Finished with the whole case! Finished and fed up!

When Butler came downstairs to breakfast on the following morning, with a bad headache, he had made that decision overnight. The whisky had told him that he wouldn't accept snubs or insults from anybody: he was Patrick Butler, by God—the woman could seek counsel's opinion elsewhere. Mrs. Pasternack, his ancient housekeeper, was waiting in the dining room.

"Good morning, Mrs. Pasternack."

"Good morning, sir. I've taken the liberty of. . . ."

"Mrs. Pasternack," said her employer, with pain jumping above his eyes, "I have nothing on my appointment book today. I don't even want to talk to my clerk. I'm out if the 'phone rings. That's all, thanks."

Mrs. Pasternack hesitated; but she knew him.

"Very good, sir."

Butler's home was an old, narrow, sedate house in Cleveland Row, facing across towards what used to be the Stable Yard Museum. Mist shrouded the dining-room windows on a raw morning. Since it was past nine o'clock, all electric light and heat and gas had to be turned off, and the little eighteenth century dining room seemed to wear a frosty rime.

There were two sausages on Butler's plate. They would be chiefly full of meal instead of meat; his gorge rose. Pouring out tea, which was at least hot, he glanced idly at the few letters beside the plate. He picked up the topmost letter, a grey envelope addressed in block capitals with a pencil.

He opened it, and read the brief message which was also in block capitals.

STAY OUT OF THE RENSHAW CASE.

THIS WILL BE YOUR ONLY WARNING.

Butler sat up. His jaw thrust forward; a smile, pleased and wicked, curved his mouth and warmed his inner being.

"Well, well, well!" he murmured cheerfully.

The telephone was in the dining room. Gulping down the tea and pouring out another cup, Butler carried the cup to the 'phone, where he looked up Lucia's number in the book and dialled it.

"May I speak to Mrs. Renshaw, please?"

"I'm afraid not," replied the unmistakable voice of Miss Cannon. "Who is calling?"

"It's Mr. Butler, me dear," announced that gentleman, in broad Dublin. "And fetch her to the 'phone now, wid no more nonsense."

At the other end of the line there seemed to be some kind of scuffle.

"Patrick," breathed Lucia's voice. It was as tender and intimate and personal as a touch. It poured with apology and penitence. "I was thinking of ringing you. To tell you what an awful beast and ungrateful wretch I was last night!"

"Say no more about it. You were upset."

"If I can ever make it up to you—!"

Butler's heart was singing.

"You can," he assured her. "You're having lunch with me today."

There was a pause; then more faint noises as of a scuffle, with a mumbling voice in the background.

"Oh, I can't," Lucia answered in the tone of a woman who means, "Please insist!"

"Why can't you?"

"Well! With—Dick being dead. . . . !"

"You hated the swine, and you know it. Wear your best dress in honour of the occasion. Meet me in the foyer at Claridge's, near the entrance to the little brasserie under the stairs, at half-past twelve."

Vividly he could see Lucia as he heard the yearning note in her voice.

"Perhaps I could," she admitted.

"Good! And one other thing." His eyes gleamed. "You told me last night about a firm of private detectives you hired. One of their men, who was watching you, got badly smashed up by a person or persons wearing brass knuckles. Was it your husband who gave this man the beating?"

"Good heavens, no! Dick—wasn't the type."

"I thought not. He'd get somebody else to do his dirty work. Well,

I may be able to find out something from this firm of private detectives. Will you give me their name and address?"

Lucia's voice hesitated. "I don't remember the address; it's in Shaftesbury Avenue. It's just called *Smith-Smith, Discretion Guaranteed*. You could find it in the 'phone book. But why do you want it?"

"I've just thought of a line of investigation. Claridge's at half-past twelve?"

"Claridge's," breathed Lucia, "at half-past twelve."

Butler, as he put down the 'phone, was so happy he could have danced for joy. If he did not actually dance, it was because he had conformed (outwardly) to custom ever since he had been called to the Bar. But he ate the unspeakable sausages with every evidence of relish, he ate buttered toast, he swilled tea. Mrs. Pasternack, watching him through an open door, judged the moment propitious when he had finished.

"If you'll excuse me, sir." Mrs. Pasternack glided in. "I've taken the liberty of asking the young lady to wait in the library."

"Of asking—*what?*"

"Sir, the young lady," replied Mrs. Pasternack, very slightly accenting the final word. Mrs. Pasternack was far from being a moralist. But those ladies whom she designated as "persons," at this hour of the morning, were more likely to be leaving Mr. Butler's house than calling there.

"Who is she?"

"A Miss Joyce Ellis, sir."

Hell! Flinging down his napkin petulantly, Butler got up like a schoolboy in a rage. Wasn't he ever to hear the last of the infernal girl? And yet . . . she was attractive, in a way. It surprised his aching head to remember that she had appeared in his dream last night. Perhaps she had come to apologize for her conduct at the coffee-room.

"I'll see her," he told Mrs. Pasternack.

Across the passage was his little front library, whose walls bore almost as large a collection of works on crime as the library of Dr. Gideon Fell. White mist, at the windows, turned all books dingy; it darkened the andirons and changed the leather chairs into hollows of shadow.

Joyce, sitting beside a little table and idly looking through *The Trial of Adelaide Bartlett*, rose to her feet as he entered.

"I'm sorry to bother you," said Joyce sincerely. "I know it must be a nuisance."

Butler was his heartiest.

"Nuisance?" he scoffed. "Faith, now, and how could you—" He stopped dead, because Joyce's eyes were fixed on him.

"I don't care what you say to me," the eyes told him, as clearly as though she had spoken aloud, "I don't even care what you do to me. But stop, stop, *stop* using that fake accent."

The rush of bitterness which filled Patrick Butler, surprising him, was directed against himself. Perhaps he was acting again; he didn't know. But the bitterness was jagged-edged, stabbing. He drew a chair near her and sat down.

"I'm pretty much of an ass, don't you think?"

"No!" Joyce said sharply. Her eyes softened. "That's one of the things that makes you so . . . that's one of the things that makes you yourself."

"Ah, well, to the devil with it!"

"I only came here," Joyce said quietly, "because I know what you're doing. And I think I can help you."

Butler sat up straight, all posing gone.

"You know what I'm doing?"

"Yes. There was an account last night in the papers about Mr. Renshaw being poisoned."

"But even so—!"

"Mr. Denham," Joyce put down *The Trial of Adelaide Bartlett* on the table, "Mr. Denham came out to Holloway Prison. He knew I'd have to go back there to pick up the few little things I'd left in my—cell. He thought I might have told a matron or somebody where I was going."

"But when did Old Charlie do this? He was with me until dinner time!"

"After he left you. And, as it happens, the Chief Matron has a sister who keeps a lodging-house in Bloomsbury; she recommended me by 'phone, and Mr. Denham found me at the lodging-house." Joyce hesitated. "Mr. Denham—"

"Here, what's wrong with Old Charlie!"

"Nothing!" Joyce assured him hastily. "He talked to me; people often do." Joyce made a wry mouth, but it was a beautiful mouth. "Anyway, I know you're going to defend Mrs. Renshaw, and I think I can help you."

"How?"

Joyce leaned forward. She was still wearing the clumsily tailored suit and yellow jumper of yesterday, though with no outer coat. But she had gone to the hairdresser; and about her skin clung a flavour not so harsh or antiseptic as that of prison soap.

"You want to know," said Joyce, shaking her sleek black hair, "the motive for these murders."

"Naturally!"

"I lived for nearly two years at Mrs. Taylor's," continued Joyce, and picked at the arm of the leather chair. "I liked her. I think everybody liked her. But somebody like myself will go on and on, never noticing little things. And then, all of a sudden—!" She stopped. "You see Mr. Butler, you're not really observant."

More than the throb of a headache shot through Butler's brain. His hands tightened on the arms of his chair.

"Besides," Joyce went on, "you're too—too healthy. That's why. . . ."

"I see. You interest me very much. Then I am not observant?"

The tone of his voice made Joyce Ellis look up quickly.

"To the whole bench of high-court judges, all twelve of them sitting in a row," pursued Butler, "you could give quite a fascinating lecture on the subject of observance. Forgive me, Miss Ellis, if it does not interest me."

Then Joyce cried out at him. "Oh, won't you ever listen to anybody?"

"On occasion, of course."

"Don't you even want to hear what I have to say?"

Butler got up coolly, glancing at his wrist-watch.

"Some other time, perhaps. If you'll excuse me, I have a number of appointments this morning. I know you'll understand."

"Of course," said Joyce. And, as he made a movement towards the bell: "Don't bother to have anyone show me out, thanks."

Perversely, his conscience smote him. Or perhaps it was because, he told himself, she did have a remarkably fine figure.

"Perhaps," he suggested, "if you could have dinner one evening. . . ."

Joyce whirled round at the door.

"I don't intend to see you," she told him in a thin, light voice, "until I can tell you the name of the real murderer."

Butler laughed outright. "More power to you! But do you think," he asked quizzically, "you can find the solution before I do?"

"I can try," said Joyce. She moved softly across the old polished boards of the passage, and was lost in white mist with the closing of the front door.

It seemed to him, as he stood in the dim room under the walls of old books, that he ended every meeting with her either by cursing her or admiring her—sometimes both. The idea of Joyce as a detective, solving anything, greatly amused him. But the idea of Joyce, and everything connected with Joyce, was swept out of his mind when he met Lucia Renshaw for lunch.

Butler arrived at Claridge's more than half an hour early, just in case it should occur to Lucia to be half an hour early too.

Since by Government order it was not yet time to turn on electric lights, the big foyer at Claridge's had been illuminated by tiers of candles, many reflected in mirrors. They mellowed and softened the walls to a dream-like scene out of the eighteenth century.

But the electric lights were on again when Lucia, half an hour late, hurried through the revolving-doors, up the few marble steps, and greeted him with a face of distress.

"I couldn't get a taxi!" she explained. Then she regarded him with real reproachfulness. "Why are you laughing?"

"I wasn't laughing. Honestly."

"But you were!"

"I was only thinking about Dr. Fell. First about a silver candelabrum," he nodded round the foyer, "and then about that grotesque question: 'Do ladies nowadays still wear garters? Not even red garters?'"

"Patrick," observed Lucia, after a slight pause, "that's not very funny."

"I know it isn't. I was simply wondering what in sanity's name he was talking about. Shall we go in?"

The little brasserie, with its red-leather upholstery and its circle of Swedish hors d'oeuvres, was so crowded that they had to wait for a table. All this time, and during lunch, Lucia made small-talk with a brightness which (her companion could guess) concealed sheer terror. Arrest seemed imminent; the minutes crawled. Her attractiveness, the blue eyes and fair hair set off by a blue costume under the mink coat, drew strength and vitality from that very fear. And how he admired her courage!

They were sitting side by side. Not until the coffee had arrived, and they had both lighted cigarettes, would Lucia refer to any of the tortures in her mind. For some time she had been furtively studying the red leather upholstery. Then she spoke abruptly.

"This Dr. Fell. He's got an awfully big reputation, I know. But he's feeble-minded or something!"

"No, Lucia. I'm afraid not."

She twisted round to look at him. "But you heard the stupid kind of questions he asked!"

"Yes. There were times when I thought he was crackers. But let's face it, which I sometimes won't: Gideon Fell is nobody's fool."

"I even heard," exclaimed Lucia, "that he got into an awful flap about a silver candelabrum; and it was only one of the ordinary candelabra in the drawing room!"

"Yes," agreed Butler. Puzzles, like doubts, gnawed at him. "The reason Dr. Fell got so interested, as far as I could see, was that one of the candle-sockets wasn't clean."

"But it was clean!"

"I beg your pardon?"

"Kitty," Lucia assured him rather breathlessly, "told us about it this morning. It upset Miss Cannon, because poor Agnes wants everything spick-and-span. We looked downstairs, and every socket-holder was highly polished."

"It wasn't highly polished last night, Lucia. I can testify to that. Somebody must have—"

Butler paused. His headache had gone; his wits were alert. That word 'somebody' was beginning to lurk in his mind like a masked face.

"Never mind," he said. "I've got two pieces of news for you."

"Oh? Good news?"

"First of all, you're having dinner with me tonight."

If this was not what Lucia expected, she did not show it. She showed neither hesitation nor coquetry. Putting down her cigarette on the edge of the saucer, she looked full at him in a way that dazzled him.

"I'd love to," she answered, "if you'll let me make a suggestion. I—I think I understand you well enough to know you won't be shocked. Could we dine and dance at some thoroughly disreputable place?"

Butler was delighted.

"By George, we can! And we will!" But a busy barrister, whose life is fairly circumspect, has a limited knowledge of places that can be called thoroughly disreputable. "That is," he added, "if you can think of one."

"I know of one," Lucia said quickly. "I've never been there, but they say it's terribly amusing. You don't," said Lucia, disregarding grammar, "you don't know who you're dancing with."

"How do you mean, you don't know who you're dancing with?"

"Never mind!" Lucia brushed this aside, with a quick deep breath. "You'll see! Have you got pencil and paper?"

He gave her a pencil and the back of an old envelope.

"I can't remember the name of the club," Lucia went on. "But here's the address." She wrote down 136 Dean Street, underscoring it, and then handed back envelope and pencil. "It's in Soho. And afterwards"—Lucia's woman-of-the-world's air contrasted oddly with the childish innocence of her mouth—"are you game for a real adventure without even asking what it is?"

"Am I!" exclaimed Patrick Butler of the County Antrim. "Am I! Just try me and see! Tell you what—I'll send the car round for you tonight. . . ."

"No, no, no." Lucia spoke in a low voice; her eyes were eager. "You couldn't take a limousine into that district. No formal dressing, either; wear your oldest clothes. I'll meet you there at eight o'clock."

Their conspiratorial intimacy had increased; Lucia touched his hand.

"If they do arrest me," she breathed, "I'm going to have some fun first!"

"That was the second piece of news I had for you," said Butler, and leaned closer. "I told you last night you weren't to worry."

"Why not?"

"Because now I know how to prove your innocence."

"I wish you'd tell me about that, Mr. Butler," struck in a new, heavy voice from close at hand.

Lucia jumped as though she had been stung. Butler too felt a twinge. Standing by their table, looking down with an expressionless face, was Superintendent Hadley of the C.I.D.

Hadley, even in his ancient raincoat, did not look at all out of place here. He was tall and square-shouldered; his hair and cropped moustache, the colour of dull steel, gave him the air of a retired military man. Patrick Butler hesitated between arrogance and friendliness.

"I didn't know a man of your position," he said, "would condescend to follow people." His hand closed over that of Lucia, who was trembling. "Mrs. Renshaw, may I present Superintendent Hadley of the Criminal Investigation Department?"

"Oh, I didn't follow you," said Hadley. He did not add that Lucia had been under what the C.I.D. call "observation" for two days. "Mind if I sit down for a moment?"

Butler beckoned a waiter, who fetched a chair. Hadley sat down opposite them, and put his bowler hat on the table.

"I don't in the least mind telling you where I stand," Butler went on, "because I believe what Dr. Fell believes. Have you seen him, by the way?"

"Saw him this morning," grunted Hadley, with a shade of wrath in his face. "He was about as comprehensible as usual."

"He believes," Butler stated, "that there's a murder organization which can operate with poison and never leave a clue."

"Lower your voice," said Hadley, without taking his eyes from the others'.

"This lunatic group," Butler insisted, "operates under some kind of 'cloak.' I don't know what. I can't for the life of me," he clenched his fists, "see how it can be deeply concerned with an ordinary candelabrum and a squiggly mark in dust and a woman with red garters. But I'll bet I can tell you who was the head of the whole group."

"All right. Who's the head of it?"

"I said, 'was' the head of it," Butler corrected, conscious of the bombshell he was about to explode. "The head of it, who was poisoned so that someone else could take his place, was Mr. Richard Renshaw."

Lucia upset her coffee-cup.

It was a small cup, having little coffee in it, but it clattered harshly against the hum of talk in the restaurant. Lucia's cigarette, on the edge of the saucer, sizzled and died.

"A—a criminal?" she cried incredulously. "That's impossible!" Then, with a curious but startling irrelevance: "Dick always chose my clothes, you know."

"You observe," Butler smiled at Hadley with his easy manner, "that Mrs. Renshaw knows nothing about it. That's why Dr. Fell asked all the queer questions last night: to prove she knew nothing about it." Then Butler's voice changed. "Find the person who took Renshaw's place as head of the murder-group, and you'll find the poisoner. What do you say, Mr. Hadley?"

The muscles tightened down Hadley's lean jaws.

"We get information, Mr. Butler. We don't give it. At the same time. . . ."

Hadley's fingers drummed on the table-cloth.

"At the same time," he went on, "I'll admit this much. Renshaw kept three separate banking-accounts under three different names." His glance at Lucia was opaque. "If you do happen to be innocent, Mrs. Renshaw, you'll be a rich woman."

(*Good God, I was right!*)

Butler's fist crashed on the table. "Why don't you follow that lead, Superintendent?"

"H'm. How would you follow it?"

"A man from a firm called *Smith-Smith, Discretion Guaranteed* was bashed about by two wide-boys in Renshaw's pay. Smith-Smith, or whoever he is, must know the boys concerned. Trace it back from there to the middle of the Murder Club!"

There was the flicker of a smile on Hadley's hard face.

"It's an odd thing, Mr. Butler. But we've already thought of that. Smith-Smith, whose real name is Luke Parsons—well, he's discretion guaranteed, all right. We couldn't get a word out of him."

"Do you want to bet *I* can't?"

"I see," remarked Hadley, eyeing him up and down. "Are you thinking of jumping into this thing yourself?"

"With both feet. Yes."

"Bit risky, isn't it?"

Butler was really surprised. "Do you honestly think," he inquired, "I'm afraid of these scum? As a matter of fact, I've been threatened already."

"*What's that?*"

"Oh, yes. With a note straight out of Sexton Blake. 'Stay out of the Renshaw case. This will be your only warning.'" Butler spoke dryly. "I've had a good deal of professional experience with crooks, Superintendent."

"You've got a lot of them turned loose, if that's what you mean."

"That's exactly what I mean," Butler agreed amiably. "And there isn't a thimbleful of intelligence in the whole lot of them."

Hadley's jaw tightened still more.

"Will you tell me the good of intelligence," he said, "against a straight-bladed razor across your face? Or a potato full of safety-razor blades?"

"I'll worry about that when I meet it."

"Were you ever in a real roughhouse? Do you know how to use your fists?"

"No," Butler answered contemptuously. "I never bothered to learn."

"You never bothered—" Hadley stopped.

Then he leaned forward across the table, leaning his elbows on it. Hadley's hair and moustache had a steel-grey edge against the gaudy restaurant with its chattering crowd.

"Listen, Mr. Butler. These are post-war days. The whole East End has moved slap round Piccadilly Circus. Leave this kind of work to us. I'm warning you, now! Because. . . ."

"Because?"

"Because I can't spare the men to protect you!"

For a moment Butler looked at him, past the smoke of a cigarette which had burned nearly to Butler's mouth.

"And who the devil," he inquired quietly, "ever asked for your protection? Or would take it if you offered it on a plate? —More coffee, Lucia dear?"

Half an hour afterwards Patrick Butler, in all his pride, was sauntering up the stairs towards the agency listed as *Smith-Smith, Discretion Guaranteed.*

10

"YES?" said the girl with the horn-rimmed spectacles, her bun of hair outlined against a dingy window with fading gilt letters.

It was a dreary, grimy building in Shaftesbury Avenue, up one flight of stairs. Patrick Butler observed that the office could contain only two very small rooms of which this was the outer.

Butler had already prepared his plan of attack. But, seeing that the door on his left was very slightly open, he somewhat altered the plan. Assuming his most winning smile, he sauntered across broken linoleum to the bun-haired girl by the window. That door on his left could only lead to the office of Mr. Luke Parsons, alias Smith-Smith.

"Good afternoon," said Butler. "I wonder if I could have a word with Mr. Parsons?"

The girl's attempt at the proper reply was almost pathetic.

"Have you an appointment?"

"No, I'm afraid not." Butler raised his voice. "But I think he'll see me. My name is Renshaw."

From the adjoining office Butler could have sworn he heard the sharp metallic squeak of a swivel-chair. Red buses were grinding and bumbling into each other beneath the windows; he could not be sure. Yet there was no mistaking the quiver of the girl's arm, the quick upturn of her eyes behind the spectacles, as she reached out for the 'phone.

"Don't bother to do that," Butler said quickly, and patted her hand. "I'll just go in and see him."

And he sauntered across and opened the door.

He had hoped, perhaps, for some faintly startling effect. But he got more than he could possibly have anticipated.

In an even dingier room, behind a flat-topped desk facing the door, sat a lean middle-sized man whose old-time police-moustache was too black for his age and too big for his face. His jaw had dropped. His face was the colour of a tallow candle. He sat there petrified, with one leg twisted round the leg of the swivel chair.

The room was a grey blur, shaken by traffic vibrations against the two windows on the right. Butler allowed a slight pause before he pretended astonishment.

"Great Scott, what's the matter?" Then he simulated realization. "Stop a bit! You didn't mistake me for my brother, did you?"

From somewhere in the direction of Mr. Luke Parsons, whose eyes bulged among their wrinkles, issued a sound like, "Brother?"

"Yes. My brother Dick. He died two days ago, poor fellow."

"O-er!" breathed Mr. Parsons, untwisting his leg from the swivel chair.

"I've been living in the States for the past six or seven years." Butler closed the door. "I thought perhaps. . . ."

"You don't look like him; that's fact," said the man with the bald head, still fascinated. "But that voice! And the way you—" He stopped. "Oh, ah; you're his brother. The States, you say?"

"Yes. I took the first plane when I heard of Dick's death."

"Now there's a place," said Mr. Parsons bitterly, "where firms like mine have got *rights*. How does the Yard look on a private firm here? Like *dirt*. I've got no more rights than"—his finger stabbed in the general direction of the people in Shaftesbury Avenue—"than any of them."

"That doesn't matter." Butler lowered his voice. "I have a little business, of a strictly private nature. . . ."

Even the police-moustache was galvanized to a quiver.

"My dear sir!" murmured Mr. Parsons, with a bad imitation of a bank-manager soothing a rich client. "Sit down! Sit down!" He hastily bustled out with a wooden chair, and sat back again. "If you'd give me the facts, now?"

"It's a little difficult to begin."

"Of course, of course! It often is. There's a lady in it, perhaps?"

"In a way, yes."

"Painful but natural," the lean old bald-head assured him, with a commiserating shake of the head. "And you know our motto, sir: Discretion Guaranteed. Now if you'd look on me as a sympathetic friend, eh?"

"The fact is, I've been in business in the States."

"Ah. May I make so bold as to ask the nature of it?"

Butler played a leading card.

"The same business Dick organized here," he replied, fixing his eyes on his companion's. "But I think our 'cloak' is better established."

For a moment he thought he had gone too far.

Mr. Parsons's face was again the colour of a tallow candle, while the swivel-chair squeaked and cracked. In this greyish room (electricity and heat again off) it was so cold that each could see the steam of his own breath.

And Patrick Butler, for the first time, began to feel he had stepped across into an eerie borderland from which he would not soon emerge. What was terrifying old walrus-moustache? A suggestion of wholesale poisoning—that might well do it, yes. But Mr. Parsons had blenched only when he heard mention of the organization's 'cloak.' What cloak, in sanity's name?

"If you'll excuse me," said Mr. Parsons in the genteelest of voices, "I don't want nothing to do with it."

"Look here," Butler said sharply, "I don't think you understand me."

"No?"

"No. I don't want to involve you in my affairs." Then he laughed. "You may remember, some time ago, that my brother had a little trouble with his wife?"

The bulbous eyes were wary. "Did he?"

"Naturally, Dick got a couple of brisk lads to—excuse me!—operate on one of your men. I want to know where I can find those two, and take them back to the States with me. That's *all* I want."

"Sorry. Dunno anything about it."

"If," Butler said suddenly, and made a feint of reaching for identification papers in his inside pocket, "if you doubt I'm Bob Renshaw...."

"No, no, no! If you were dark instead of fair, I'd think I was seeing his ghost."

"We make pretty fair profits in my business." Taking out his note-case, Butler laid a hundred-pound note on the desk.

"I dunno what you're talking about, so help me!"

Butler laid another hundred-pound note on the desk. Despite the cold room his companion was sweating.

"I might," a low hoarse voice admitted, "give you an address where you *might* find a certain two people. No names in this office. Not ever! And I don't even say you *would* find 'em. Only you might."

"If you're playing a trick, of course. . . ."

"My God, Mr. Renshaw, would I dare to play a trick?"

Butler pushed the notes across the desk. Tearing half a sheet off a memorandum pad, Mr. Parsons printed an address in block capitals, folded the sheet, and shoved it into his companion's hand. Butler put the slip of paper in his pocket, and stood up.

"Tell me, Mr. Parsons," he said, "why do you dislike our business so much?"

And suddenly Butler had a vision of Luke Parsons, the shabby suburbanite, with his squeezed semi-detached house and his bit of garden.

"If my wife ever saw. . . ." he blurted out.

"Saw what?"

"Ah, I was wool-gathering!" murmured Mr. Parsons, with a ghastly heartiness. "Wool-gathering, that's what I was!"

"You understand, I think, that our little transaction remains confidential?"

"Oh, naturally, sir! You may trust me to the hilt!" breathed Discretion Guaranteed; and reached for the telephone as soon as the door had closed behind his client.

Patrick Butler noticed nothing of this. Hurrying downstairs, he did not open the slip of paper until he had partly emerged from the doorway into crowded Shaftesbury Avenue. Then he stared at the address for so long that grim-faced pedestrians jostled him back into the doorway.

The mist and soot-smell of London was in his lungs, but a colder chill lay at his heart. From his inside pocket he took out the envelope on which Lucia Renshaw had written the address at which he must meet her at eight o'clock tonight. Both addresses were the same: 136 Dean Street, Soho.

"Taxi!" he bellowed, without much hope of getting one. "Taxi!"

To describe his state of mind, during the next few hours, would be merely to sum up with his repeated word, "Nonsense!" Lucia Renshaw could *not* be mixed up in this business, whatever it was. He had made his decision; he simply knew. And so Butler went home, fighting shadows.

In his little library, at tea-time, Mrs. Pasternack had kindled a great coal fire under the Adam mantelpiece. Facing the fire stood two easy chairs; and beside one of them was his old dictaphone.

It was coincidence, pure coincidence, that Lucia had given him that same address!

Patrick Butler sat down, and fitted a new wax cylinder to the revolving mechanism. Lounging back in the chair after he had turned on the starting-switch, he watched the cylinder revolve noiselessly before—with a sharp plop—he pressed the button under the speaking-tube.

Then he spoke to it in a fierce and challenging voice.

"Notes," he said, "for the defence of Lucia Renshaw."

The cylinder continued to spin, while he scowled.

"What in hell—no; strike out the 'in hell'—is the 'cloak' for this Murder Club? Aside from murder, what's their racket? It is, obviously, a new one. It cannot be drugs, or white slavery, or anything so dull and stale. Because: not only did it upset the experienced Luke Parsons, but he knew it would shock his wife beyond words. Why?"

Butler released the speaking-button, but plopped it down again savagely:

"Why, at lunch-time, did Lucia Renshaw say: 'Dick chose all my clothes'?"

Again a silence. Then, with more fury:

"Lucia Renshaw, from the first, showed a fondness amounting to passion for—for P.B." (This would have to be taken down by a secretary; he couldn't say 'for myself'; he squirmed even as it was.)

"Was this," he went on, "because P.B. bears a strong resemblance, in voice and general appearance, to L.R.'s late husband, Dick Renshaw? Has she unconsciously transferred her affections to another man who looks like him?"

This, Butler remained clear-headed enough to see, was the crux of it all as far as he was concerned. This was why he raged.

He had fallen for Lucia Renshaw, he told himself, past all doubt or hope. He could see her image from last night: in the negligée, stretching out her hands to him. And the image was so vivid that it hurt him. But he was not going to be anybody's substitute or anybody's rival, even a dead man's! He was going to be. . . .

"Tea, sir?" interrupted the voice of Mrs. Pasternack, accompanied by a rattle as she wheeled in the tea-wagon.

"Oh, to blazes with the tea!"

"Very good, sir."

"Mrs. Pasternack, she is not guilty."

"No, sir."

"Thank you, Mrs. Pasternack. And I am never wrong."

He was in this same mood when he set out on foot, at a quarter past seven, to keep his rendezvous with Lucia.

The mist had thinned a little, though it was still bitter cold, as Butler circled Piccadilly Circus and again went towards Shaftesbury Avenue. At the London Pavilion he saw a depressing sight.

At each side of the theatre doors, and then bent back along the side of the building, stretched an endless three-abreast queue of those waiting to get into the cinema. They did not speak. They did not move. They waited patiently, dull-eyed in the aching cold, for the hour or hours before they could scramble inside for some escape—any kind of escape!—from grey life.

Butler, who would not have joined any kind of queue if his life depended on it, eyed them as he passed. But why shouldn't they wait there? What else had they to do? They couldn't entertain at home, because they had no food or drink to offer guests; they couldn't be entertained for the same reason. Besides, the question of transportation. . . .

"Transportation!" he exclaimed aloud.

Into his mind had come an idea which might (just possibly might) smash the whole case against Lucia Renshaw.

Striding blindly along the street, he examined this idea until, in the upper and darker region, he turned left into Dean Street.

Dean Street, narrow and slatternly, was partly lighted behind shutters and a few half-drawn blinds. Though a part of the so-called 'Wicked Square Mile,' there was little noise except murmurings from a pub and the sound of a consumptive hand-organ. The wheezy music rose with a rattle like strings.

> "She was a poor little dicky-bird,
> 'Tweet, tweet, tweet,' said she. . . ."

A number of pavement-nymphs, uglier than Butler had ever seen them, were ranged at one crossing like fielders in a cricket-match. Beyond them, two tall Negroes talked quietly together. He saw nobody else. The grinding of the hand-organ dwindled to a faint tinkle as he strode on.

Then, with a sense of uneasy shock, he discovered Number 136.

Behind an iron railing and down three steps into a shallow area, there was a long and grimy plate-glass window with the word BILLIARDS in enamelled letters. By bending down, he could see that the place contained three tables and was pretty well filled. Over a glass-panelled door by the window, very clearly, were the enamel figures 136.

"But this can't be—" he began. Then he paused, and looked round him.

True, there was a door at street-level close to 136 on the right. But its peeling paint, its nailed-up look, seemed to indicate it had not been opened since before the war. There was another door on the left, in similar condition. All upstairs windows were dark.

Lucia had spoken of some place, apparently a club, where you could dine and dance. And Lucia, the fastidious, wouldn't suggest a club where you entered by way of a sleazy billiard-saloon? Yet it was just the place to find two alleged tough-lads who. . . .

Butler glanced at his wrist-watch. He had more than ten minutes before it was time to meet Lucia. And he was not conspicuous; it had been no trouble at all to find a disreputable suit, and his greasy overcoat and soft hat both dated from 1938.

He sauntered down the three stone steps, and opened the glass-panelled door.

The room breathed a redolence of beer, though nobody was drinking it. A dramatic click-click of billiard balls, a dramatic exclamation, greeted him out of a clatter of talk. The three tables, set lengthwise to each other down a deep room, had no overhead canopy lights. Three pale yellow electric-bulbs hung on short cords from the ceiling, drawing shadows round nondescript men in faded gaudy shirt-sleeves.

Then Butler spotted another door.

It was well down the room on the right, a little beyond the end of the third table. Butler sauntered towards it.

Nobody noticed him, or so he thought. Only one table, the first towards the front door, was being used for billiards; they played snooker at the second; and at the third—so strongly has lingered the influence of the American G. I.—they played American pool.

That other door, in the right-hand wall beyond the third table, had a key in it. Also, it was unlocked. Butler discovered this when he leaned unobtrusively with his back to the door, hands behind him. It could not lead to any cupboard, because there was a line of light under the sill. Butler slipped the key out of the door and slipped it into his pocket.

At the pool table, its narrow end towards him and a few feet out to the left, the last ball thudded and dropped into the far right-hand pocket. The man who held the cue, a sleek-haired young man in a mustard-coloured suit, laughed and straightened up and turned round.

"Finished?" inquired Patrick Butler.

"All yours, chum," the sleek-haired one said amiably. His mustard-coloured suit was so new and brash that it shouted, 'Thirty guineas; all mine. Like it?' He handed the cue to Butler, who took it.

"Anybody been asking for me tonight?"

The sleek-haired one's eyes narrowed. "I seen you before," he stated.

"Name of Renshaw," said Butler. "Bob Renshaw."

The sleek-haired one, sensing a kindred spirit who wanted to place a bet, lifted his voice above the blatter of talk and the cold smoke-mist.

"Anybody looking for Renshaw?" he shouted. "Bob Renshaw?"

There was a silence so brief that it might have gone unnoticed. Yet through it, as through a sudden rift in smoke, you might hear the louder *click-click* against green felt. A buzz of talk drowned it out, with one or two absentminded negatives. If Patrick Butler sensed the wave of danger that flowed through that room, he gave no sign of it.

"Bad luck," sympathized the sleek-haired one. "Alone?"

"Yes."

"Well, 'ave a smack at it anyway," suggested the sleek-haired one, jerking a thumb towards the pool table. "Easy as kiss-your-'and, after snooker."

"Thanks. I think I will."

The pool balls, vividly coloured and each with a number, thudded out on the table as Butler pushed up the pockets. He circled the table, gathering up the balls and racking them in their wooden triangle. Then he removed the triangle, its point towards his original position on the side near the unlocked door. He would stay on that side of the table, he decided.

Nine minutes until he must meet Lucia! Only nine minutes!

And, while he waited for some reply to 'Bob Renshaw,' he wanted to think about his new idea of the defence of Lucia Renshaw. . . .

Bending down to sight along the cue, with the white cue ball gleaming ahead, he broke with a clatter that sent the bright-coloured spheres rolling wide.

"It's not as good an idea as I'd thought," he said to himself, his original enthusiasm cooling. "It can't help Lucia with regard to the death of Dick Renshaw. But it does prove she couldn't have killed Mrs. Taylor."

(*Don't get too immersed in your thoughts, now. Keep steady.*)

"Balham, where Mrs. Taylor lived, is in South London. Lucia lives in North London. I don't know how many miles they are apart, but it's a devil of a distance. How did Lucia get there and back—at that time of the night?"

Butler, never moving or raising his head, saw the table as a green blur in front of him.

"The Renshaws' don't have a car. Old Mrs. Taylor died between ten o'clock and midnight, probably closer to midnight. No taxi-driver would have taken her so far. If she went at all, she'd have had to use one of those drive-hire-with-chauffeur cars; and there'd be a record. But there won't be a record, because she never went at all.

"That'll prove it at one go! Now if I could only think of a way in which Renshaw's water-bottle could have been poisoned, the case will be wide open. It's so simple a puzzle that the explanation ought to be simple too. Only three persons, Lucia and Kitty and Miss Cannon, were in that bedroom. Practically speaking, we can exclude Miss. . . ."

Here Butler's musings stopped abruptly, with a jar and start.

Something was wrong in the billiard-saloon.

He himself had not been trying to play. He had been merely potting at anything in sight. A green pool ball rebounded from the far cushion, with a noise he could hear distinctly, and spun back to him across a vast, intense silence.

No billiard-click, no voice or foot-shuffle or cue-rattle, stirred in that room. No sense, even of breathing or movement. Only malignancy, fastened on him like the ray of a burning-glass.

To Patrick Butler it seemed that he was alone. Briefly he raised his eyes.

11

IN A SENSE he was alone, yes. Of all the men who had been in that
room, only two remained.

A dirty Venetian blind, its shutters closed, had been lowered across
the front window. Another Venetian blind masked the glass panel of
the front door. The three ceiling-lights, yellow and watery, illumined
only cold smoke-haze and two deserted tables.

On a bench under the front window there sat, with knees crossed
idly, a lean man in a buff-coloured eyeshade which evidently designated
him as the proprietor. On the opposite side of the room from Butler,
a little way down towards the front, the second man leaned negligently
with his back against a rack of cues on the wall.

The second man, who had his hands in his pockets, wore a much-
darned and patched black jersey of the sort used in fighters' training
camps. He was bigger than Patrick Butler, much broader, and so heavily
muscled that his paunch hardly showed. He needed a haircut, and he
had a flat nose.

The silence lengthened. Neither of the two men as much as glanced
at Butler.

" 'E ain't much good at that game, is 'e?" inquired the man with the
eyeshade, as though referring to somebody on a distant planet.

"No," said the other, in thickened bass. " 'E ain't much good at that
game, is 'e?"

"I mean, 'e ain't no good at that game."

"Ar. 'E ain't no good at that game at all."

A small coal of rage burned in Butler's chest. He had heard this sort
of talk often; it was merely that of the ten-year-old boy in the adult
body. And he had come on a peaceful mission.

"I think," he said clearly, putting down his cue on the table, "you're
the two men I wanted to see."

Again there was a silence. Then the man in the eye-shade suddenly rocked back on the bench and began to laugh. Two of his teeth—the front ones—were gold teeth. But he stopped laughing almost immediately.

" 'E wants to see us," observed Gold-teeth sadly. " 'E wants to see us, Em."

"Ar."

"Now why would 'e want to see us?" jeered Gold-teeth.

The man called Em straightened up to his full height and breadth. The rack of cues rattled behind him. Deliberately he drew his left hand out of his pocket, and fitted on his right hand a heavy pair of brass knuckles. Over this—while darting a little eager glance at Butler—he drew a very thin black glove, almost shapeless.

Then Em admired his handiwork. That glove would steady hand and wrist when the fist cut and crushed.

"Now what would 'e do," asked Gold-teeth with interest, "if you was to sort of caress 'im with that?"

"I expect 'e wouldn't like it."

"No, 'e wouldn't like it. But what could 'e do about it?"

"Why," said Em with satisfaction, " 'e couldn't do nothink, could 'e?"

"No, 'e couldn't do nothink. Nothink at all."

Patrick Butler stood negligently by the table, with seething rage inside him and an agreeable smile on his face.

Fear crawled through him, up from his stomach and through his arms. What overrode the fear was his simple belief that people like these were beneath contempt. If they could not be ignored, they ought to be killed.

Idly he looked at the pool balls nearest him. They were of a neat size and weight, each balancing nicely in the hand. With a throw of—yes; about twenty-five feet—you could smash a skull to pulp. So Butler continued to smile. And one of the pool balls was already concealed in his right hand.

"Of course," said Gold-teeth, prolonging the agony, "you don't want to be too 'ard on 'im."

"You seen me work before, ain't you? Am I all right?"

"Oh, ah! Sure you are. But we don't want him to call us names, now do we?"

" 'E won't call anybody no names."

"But 'e might not think it was nice, see what I mean? 'E won't call nobody no names; but wot might 'e call us if he could talk?"

Patrick Butler spoke in his courtroom manner.

"I call you bastards," he said pleasantly. "What do you propose to do about it?"

The pause, this time, was as startling as the stab of a dagger. Both Gold-teeth and Em looked at him full in the face. Then the whole scene exploded.

"Do it proper, Em!" Gold-teeth said viciously.

Patrick Butler's arm whipped forward. And he threw to kill.

The ball, a vivid red colour, crashed into the cue-rack half an inch from Em's head. One cue, splintered in half, flew against others; they toppled and rained down, clattering from the rack and banging the floor in thin echoes, over the shoulders and at the feet of Em himself.

(*I was nervous. I missed him. No more throwing to kill, Pat Butler! But it got something out of my system.*)

Over across the dim room, beyond the tables, Em's face was that of a cruel small boy swollen rather than grown to manhood. He did not seem to realize what had happened until the fallen pool ball rolled past him.

"I'll-do-yer-fer-that," Em yelled. And again he plunged forward.

(*No landing in jail, fool! Get him where . . . now!*)

Butler did not miss with his second throw. The ball, a green streak, whacked the shoulder at the junction of the right arm. Em spun sideways and staggering amid fallen cues, fell on his back. His arm and black glove were as helpless as a sponge. He tried to move his arms and legs feebly, like a life-sized black beetle.

"Now for you, Goldy," said Butler.

It was Gold-teeth he really hated. But Gold-teeth, sitting on the bench under the window, had nipped his hand behind the Venetian blind and rapped sharply on the window for help. A pool ball crashed into the Venetian blind, whose loose flaps absorbed the shock without breaking the window. Goldy, snatching back his fingers and showing his front teeth like a jeering rabbit, ducked to safety under the line of the first table.

For a few moments the place was as eerily silent as a room in Pompeii. Butler, in overcoat and soft hat, had begun to sweat. Just a little behind him, on his left, was the unlocked side-door. Its key was gripped in his left hand. That side-door led—God knew where.

The front door, its Venetian blind trembling, opened softly. Four men, so nondescript that Butler could not have described them, entered just as quietly.

"Spread out," came the gloating voice of Gold-teeth. "Keep down below the tables. Use the moleys when you catch 'im."

The moley was an extraordinary potato, its surface jagged with the edges of safety-razor blades. They ground it into your face, twisted it, and—

" 'E's for it," called Gold-teeth tenderly. " 'E's for it now!"

For about five seconds Butler fired at the newcomers as fast as he could snatch up pool balls. Missiles, yellow and red and blue, streaked down the room like tracer-bullets in an air raid. Another cue-rack toppled and clattered down. One of the newcomers, hit below the belt, screamed and doubled up. Em, who was trying to struggle to his feet despite a broken shoulder, slipped on the fallen cues and lurched on his face.

Butler—with one last glimpse of rebounded pool balls thumping and dancing round the floor with maniacal life—darted out the side-door and closed it behind him. His hands were shaking so much that he almost dropped the key. Running feet pounded inside. He locked the door just in time.

And now he knew where he was.

A narrow passage, lying parallel with the depth of the billiard-saloon, stretched away on his right to a street door. That street door beside the front door of 136, which from outside had seemed nailed-up or deserted since before the war!

On his left, as he stood in the passage, a flight of steps went up to a landing with a lighted doorway. From that doorway drifted the strains of dance music. . . .

Lucia's club. The battered-looking street door was its real entrance.

Butler instantly raced up the stairs. The part of prudence would have been to get to blazes out of here by the street door. But he had promised to meet Lucia. And Patrick Butler, the Irishman, still had a little score to settle with Gold-teeth.

Dance music blared louder on the landing. A glance inside the dim-lit doorway told Butler why Lucia had said, "You don't know who you're dancing with." The dancers, both men and women, all wore masks of black or white or pink. Some were domino masks, but most added a length of cloth which hid the whole face.

On the landing by the door, a young man of Spanish appearance sat behind a table on which lay an open ledger and a number of masks. Butler straightened up and assumed his lordliest manner.

"A mask, please," he said.

"Yes, sare!" The young man jumped up, giving him a quick vivid look, and yanked open the desk drawer which served as a till. "Eet weel be one pound, sare!"

(Bang went the faint thud of a fist on the door below. Gold-teeth and his playmates were in a mood for no less than murder.)

Very deliberately Butler selected a black mask, inspecting it. Then he dropped five pounds on the table.

"You haven't seen me, understand?" he demanded impressively.

"No, sare. No!"

Butler hurried into the dance-room. After three paces he stopped and turned round. The young man with the black Spanish eyes, as Butler expected, had instantly and softly started downstairs to turn the key and admit Gold-teeth and the flood of wasps.

Just as softly, while the young man's back was turned, Butler darted back to the dance-room door only long enough to exchange his black mask for a pink mask underneath the pile on the table. Then he hurried back among the jumbled crowded dancers.

This so-called club was hot and frowsty, not large and not much cleaner than the billiard-saloon below. Along two walls ran a line of bare tables, with dancing-space between. An old, dim, rickety spotlight, fastened at one corner of the ceiling, shifted its colours to red, yellow, purple—like slow-floating missiles—and turned the masked faces to a nightmare.

Yet the club exhaled a sensuality which went straight to Butler's head. Women in masks, as has been known even in England for three hundred years, are women in a yielding mood.

Butler, trying to move without stumbling between the dancers and the right-hand row of tables, whipped off hat and overcoat.

(On with the pink mask, now; they'll look for a black one. Where can I find a dancing partner? Where . . . O benevolent Providence!)

At the back of the room, and surprisingly enough alone at a table, sat a woman whose face was covered by a long white mask, her hair by a white scarf wound turban-fashion. The very dim light concealed the fact that her black velvet gown, cut low in front, was old and shabby.

Butler strode up to her. He threw his wrapped hat and coat under the table. All his theatricalism went into a great Gallic bow.

"*Mademoiselle*," he intoned, "*Je vous ai remarquée. Votre beauté, c'est comme un fleur dans un puisard. Vous permettez?*"

Without further ceremony he took her hand, yanked her to her feet, and whirled the startled woman out into the throng of dancers.

(*Where is Gold-teeth now? Where is he?*)

Yet Patrick Butler could not be unconscious, in any sense whatever, of the woman he held in his arms.

"Your beauty," he continued in the same fluent French, "intoxicates and maddens me. Your breasts burn. Your body is a. . . ."

"Patrick," murmured the hesitant voice of Lucia Renshaw, "I don't think that's very nice."

Butler's step stumbled on the music-beat, so that he almost fell over her feet.

"Good God! You're not—"

"Of course!" The blue eyes regarded him strangely through the eye-holes of the mask. "Didn't you know who I was?"

"Good God, no!" said Butler, hastily relaxing his tight hold. "I apologize! I thought. . . ."

"Oh!" Lucia was silent for a moment, while the music throbbed and the blank mask-faces leered in changing lights. "Is that how you treat any woman," she asked sharply, "when you think she isn't—quite nice?"

"Frankly, yes."

For a moment, if he had noticed it, the blue eyes were furious. But their expression changed.

"It's all right, isn't it," asked Lucia in an indifferent voice, "if you tell me those things in French? That's not the same as in English, is it? And, even if you wanted to tell me those things in. . . ."

This was the point at which Gold-teeth appeared in the doorway, now with half a dozen ugly-tempered friends spreading out on either side.

It was the same doorway through which Butler had entered, though he and Lucia were now at the far end of the room. Yet—and this was what startled Butler—he saw Gold-teeth in a new guise.

There would be no mistaking the bony face with its detached sneer. But gone was the eyeshade of the billiard-saloon. Whatever Gold-teeth had been wearing downstairs, Butler could swear he had not been wearing the suit of soiled evening clothes which adorned him now.

And—there were no gold teeth.

As the misty beam of light melted from violet into yellow, the man's face sprang out. He smiled, like the proprietor of this club—which he probably was, too,—and his front teeth were ordinary teeth.

He did not move. Neither did his companions. Their eyes moved slowly, carefully, patiently round the room. They carried moleys full of razor-blades. Butler thought of Lucia's face. Instinctively he pressed her closer again.

"That's better," Lucia murmured in the same casual voice. "As I was saying a moment ago—"

"Lucia!" He spoke sharply. "Why did you want to come to this club?"

"But I told you! Sometimes I—I just want to go to some disreputable place. Not to do anything I shouldn't, of course," Lucia added hastily, "but just to be there and watch. I expect most women do. But it's really awfully dull, isn't it?"

"Yes," agreed Butler, with his eye on Gold-teeth.

Gold-teeth, now without his dental gold, had moved forward and was walking among the dancers like a good host, examining each in turn.

"Why didn't you tell me," Butler whispered, "that the entrance to this place wasn't through that billiard-room?"

Lucia's eyes widened behind the mask. "But you didn't go. . . . My dear! There are two entrances here, without going through that billiard-room!"

"Two entrances? Where?"

"One is over there." Lucia nodded towards the well-guarded doorway he knew only too well. "There's a flight of steps that goes down to a passage."

"Yes, I've seen that one. Where's the other?"

"Just like the first. Only. . . ."

Again Lucia nodded. The second doorway was in the same wall as the first, but at the opposite end of the wall. Butler saw it clearly: two staircases descending parallel, but with a twenty-foot breadth of wall (as well as the orchestra platform) between them. All guards were concentrated near the first doorway. At the second doorway. . . .

"Lucia, who's at that second doorway usually?" he whispered. "Another Spanish-looking ticket-seller?"

"Yes. Look! You can see him now."

"For God's sake don't point!"

He felt the sudden twitch of nervousness which ran through her.

"Pat, what's wrong?"

"Nothing. Just follow my lead."

Gold-teeth, slowly, was coming straight towards them.

Butler did not abruptly swing his partner and press through the crush in another direction. That was what Gold-teeth was looking for. That was what all enemy eyes, carefully alert, were looking for: some betraying sign of panic. Butler steered Lucia straight towards Gold-teeth.

(*We can't get out that second doorway. One man might do it, but not with Lucia. Those bruisers would run across too quickly and intercept. Got to beat the beetle-wits some other way. Got to. . . .*)

Butler, surging with his partner in erratic steps, bent close to the ear of a man in a black mask.

"Cops," he muttered, with a slight movement of his head towards the men in the first doorway. "Better clear out."

Nothing happened. The black mask merely stared at him and drifted past. Butler did not expect him to make a bee-line for that second doorway. But the seed was being sown, in a place full of wide-boys with hair-trigger consciences. The word would whisper and ripple and spread. . . .

"Cops," muttered Butler to another, always indicating the first doorway. "Better clear out."

Gold-teeth was now ten feet away.

Bang went the cymbals in the orchestra. The four-piece dance band crept their way into a famous song whose heavy beat and macabre power pluck at the nerves and heighten the senses. The piano player, bending close to a microphone, sang with hollow softness:

> *Through the smoke and flame*
> *I've got to go where you are . . .*

A new intimacy shivered through the masked dancers. One man and his partner, a girl of about sixteen, bumped past oblivious, their mouths locked together. Yet the whisper and rustle, "Cops, better clear out," crept like the snake-shuffle of feet.

"It's—it's rather warm in here," Lucia murmured. "Don't you think we'd better leave?"

"We're going to," said Butler. "Cops. Better clear out."

"Pat, what is wrong?"

"In a minute or so I'm going to do some damned queer dance-steps," he whispered. "Will you follow me even if I have to drag you by the hair?"

"Yes!" whispered Lucia. He could feel her breathe. "Yes, yes, yes!"
They were now beside Gold-teeth, just behind him.

> Ain't no chains can bind you,
> If you live I'll find you . . .

With infinite joy, in the dim crimson light, Butler launched a vicious kick at Gold-teeth's shins; then he and Lucia, dodging, melted behind two other pairs of dancers as the light changed.

Gold-teeth's cry of pain and rage, uncontrollable, shrilled up like the effect of a dentist's needle under a tooth. At the same moment Butler swept close to another black-masked man.

"Cops," he muttered, with a same nod. "Better clear out."

And something snapped like a fiddle-string.

Black-mask, whoever he was, stopped dead and dropped his hands from his girl. He whispered something to her. He whipped round and hurried for that second doorway with such quickness and fluent movement that he had a long start before anybody noticed him.

Gold-teeth, his hand raised above the crowd, was pointing frantically. There was a sort of silent explosion among the watchers near the first doorway. Unobtrusively but swiftly they moved out and along the wall, past the little orchestra platform, towards the second doorway. . . .

"Now!" said Butler.

Gold-teeth's men wouldn't nab the fleeing black-mask on the dance floor, and risk starting a riot. They would nab him about half-way down the stairs—and discover they had got the wrong man.

For about twenty seconds, now, that first doorway would be unguarded.

12

BUT not entirely unguarded.

Gold-teeth, who was seldom at a loss and never missed a trick, instantly was elbowing his way back to the first doorway—just in case.

Butler, sweeping Lucia in front of him and using his right hand as a stiff-arm in case someone cannoned into her, followed Gold-teeth in a fast, crazy zig-zag. Imprecations rose behind him.

"Pat, what are you *doing?*" demanded a now-frightened Lucia.

"We're clearing out ourselves. Just as you suggested."

"But my coat! My handbag!"

"Not your mink coat?"

"No. An old one. But my handbag's got—got a key in it. For the real adventure."

"*Real* adventure?"

"You promised me," Lucia's eyes were appealing, "that after we went to this place you'd go with me on a real adventure!"

"All right; but never mind the key. Keep quiet, now!"

Gold-teeth, reaching the first doorway, had whipped round. His little eyes were eager. Two fingers of his right hand touched the end of a closed straight-bladed razor in his left sleeve.

Butler and Lucia, the former abruptly altering the pace to normal, danced straight up and to the side of Gold-teeth, while Butler spoke softly but passionately in French.

"—*et je t'adore,*" he concluded; and deliberately stumbled all over Lucia's feet. Lucia gave an involuntary exclamation. Butler pushed her away from him, slightly jostling Gold-teeth as he stepped back.

"Mademoiselle," he bleated in an agony of apology, "*je vous demande pardon! Mille pardons, je vous en prie!*" In the same humility and tenderness he turned to Gold-teeth. "*Et vous, monsieur, sale chameau et fils de putain. . . .*"

With his left hand, in a noble Gallic gesture, he removed his mask. With his right he hit Gold-teeth full in the mouth.

Somewhere far behind him, a woman screamed.

Whether this was due to his own action or—as was more probable—to a violent commotion at the opposite doorway, Butler could not tell. He was far too much occupied.

The razor, snakelike, had been open in Gold-teeth's hand an instant before Butler hit him. Gold-teeth, staggering backwards across a narrow landing, turned his heel on the topmost step. He pitched backwards, with a face of ludicrous surprise above the blood, and rolled down the stairs like a wooden doll.

The Spanish ticket-seller, jumping to his feet behind the table, suddenly decided he had no interest in this matter. He sat back again.

"Hitch up your skirt," Butler said to Lucia, "and run down like hell after me. If they've had the sense to send men outside and cover this front door. . . ."

They hadn't.

Stepping over Gold-teeth, who lay momentarily stunned at the foot of the stairs, they raced towards the street door. It was unlocked, as usual for the club upstairs. Outside Dean Street lay in chill and half-mist, with not even a noise of commotion from the other entrance beyond the billiard-saloon.

They had discarded their masks. A shivering woman in thin evening clothes, a disreputably clad man without hat or overcoat, hurried in the direction of Shaftesbury Avenue.

"You needn't look for a taxi," Lucia told him, trying in vain to keep up with his long steps despite her good height. "Your car's parked very close to here."

"My car?"

"Yes. I decided, for the real adventure," Lucia hesitated, "we'd better have a car. Just after you'd left home I 'phoned your chauffeur. . . ."

"Where's the car now?"

"Just off Cambridge Circus. Behind the Palace Theatre."

"God bless you!" Butler's nerves were still twitching. "But I've got to find a telephone."

"What for?"

"To ring—preferably Superintendent Hadley, but anybody will do."

They found a public telephone-box only a few yards from where

Johnson, Butler's chauffeur, stood beside the long limousine. Butler
sent Lucia ahead to the car. As usual nowadays, the glass-panelled telephone-box had no light; and, also as usual, its 'phone directories were
ripped to rags. But it required little light and no directory to dial White-
hall 1212.

Butler returned to the car in three minutes. He found Lucia in warm
grey-upholstered gloom, sitting back in a corner and smoothing back
her yellow hair. Butler got into the car, and Johnson slammed the door.
Butler and Lucia looked at each other.

The hot, fuggy atmosphere of the dance-club still enclosed them. Its
images were there. Butler, not yet feeling any let-down, was as nerv-
ously alert and strung-up as though he could never sleep again.

"Feeling—safer?" he asked.

"Oh, yes!" Lucia's smile was broad enough to show fine teeth. But
she hesitated again. "It was awful, I suppose. But there was a kind of
horrible fascination about it. I wouldn't have missed it for worlds!"

"*Chérie, je—*" Butler stopped, his throat choked up, in sheer admiration and strength of sympathy. It was exactly what he felt himself.

"*Tu dis?*" inquired Lucia, lowering her eyes.

"What's that?"

"I noticed," said Lucia, "that once or twice you used the familiar *tu*
instead of the formal *vous*. In speaking to me, I mean."

"Which would you rather have me use?"

"Oh, the familiar. Of course."

Patrick Butler moved sideways, put his arm round Lucia, and kissed
her mouth for so long that he lost count of time. It was obvious, from
answering gestures of the mouth, that Lucia shared his own sentiments.

He did not now think about any spiritual quality, on which he had
commented so forcibly and lyrically last night. He was entirely concerned, and very eager, about other aspects of Lucia. For, if this sort of
thing went on very long, it was clear that. . . .

"No! Don't!" said Lucia. She began to struggle, and pushed him
away. "I mean, not here! Not now! And, since they're going to arrest
me. . . ."

"They're not going to arrest you," said Butler, trying to control his
breathing. "By the way, have I neglected to mention that I'm in love
with you?"

"You did rather neglect it, yes." Lucia, whose white scarf round the neck had become disarranged, tucked its ends back into the low-cut bosom of her gown. "Still, there's heaps of time to. . . ."

What stopped him was something Lucia would not have understood, and which he did not understand himself. Why was it that—even while he was kissing Lucia—there had at once sprung into his mind the image of Joyce Ellis?

To the devil with Joyce! *He* wasn't interested in Joyce. He hadn't even thought of the woman since he had seen her this morning. These infernal tricks played by the imagination. . . .

"Besides," Lucia was saying, with a sidelong look, "we're going on a little journey."

Butler shook himself awake.

"Not that it matters a hang," he said, "but where are we going?"

Lucia fended him off by reaching forward and tapping on the glass panel behind the driver.

"Your chauffeur has instructions," she said.

The car slid into gear and moved away. Lucia, though her eyes still shone and there radiated from her an aura as palpable as a touch maneuvered to keep Butler away from her.

"What—what did they say about your 'phone-call?"

" 'Phone-call?"

"To Scotland Yard!"

"There was a Flying Squad car in Old Compton Street. They'll have got to Gold-teeth's club," he snapped his fingers, "like that. They'll have nabbed the only two men we want, Gold-teeth and another called Em. We were talking today, you remember, about two men hired by your husband to put an operative from Smith-Smith in hospital?"

Lucia sat very still, her mouth partly open. Any mention of Dick Renshaw seemed almost to hypnotize her, and Butler hated this. Noiselessly the limousine eased round Cambridge Circus, and down the long stretch of Charing Cross Road, while Butler told her about the night's events.

"You can bet a fiver," he concluded, "that they're the same two men. They were ready for me; they knew I was coming. That's why there was so much personal malice in it. The ordinary hired thug does his job as impersonally as a butcher chops meat. These beauties. . . ."

Again, in imagination, he saw Em fitting on the knuckles and Gold-teeth's far-away look of pleasure.

Lucia was staring at the floor.

"What will happen to them now?"

"Tomorrow morning," Butler said grimly, "I appear before the beak and charge 'em with felonious assault."

"But—Pat!" Lucia's voice was warm, with pleasure and pride in it. "You did most of the assaulting, didn't you?"

"Technically, yes. That's why the charge may be difficult to establish. But the actual charge doesn't matter. We've got to hold 'em and hammer 'em about something else. What do they know about the head of the Murder Club?"

"Can you . . . can you prove they do know anything about the head of this Murder Club? Even if it really exists? Can you prove they know anything about it?"

"No! And, actually, maybe they don't know."

"Who," Lucia spoke thoughtfully, "could have told them you would be in the billiard-saloon tonight?"

"In my opinion, a large-moustached rat named Luke Parsons, alias Smith-Smith of 'Discretion Guaranteed.'" Butler's anger simmered, and yet his imagination was full of black doubts. "The trouble is, that large moustached-rat was really scared white. He didn't want any trouble. Oh, no! Not any kind of trouble! Why should he warn two nobodies, like Gold-teeth and Em, that he'd just betrayed 'em? He wouldn't have warned anybody. Unless. . . ."

"Unless what?"

"*Unless,*" replied Butler, whacking his fist down on his knee, "*he warned the head of the Murder Club.*"

There was a silence, while Butler remained blind to everything about him.

"I've been on the wrong track!" he declared. "I am never wrong, believe me, when it comes to the guilt of a given person or the issue of a trial. This time I wasn't wrong; I only started on the wrong track. Instead of following Gold-teeth and Em, I should have concentrated on the large-moustached rat named Parsons.

"Lucia, he knows who the head of the Murder Club is! He's cornered and mesmerized by the head of the Murder Club! That's why he turned the colour of a tallow candle when he thought he heard Dick Renshaw's voice in the outer office! That's why. . . ."

"What on earth are you talking about?"

"Wait!" groaned Butler. "Let me think!"

"Pat, dear!"

"Eh?"

"Will you listen to me?" Lucia begged softly. There was a tenderness in her voice, a submissiveness, which moved him deeply because he had never (quite) expected to hear it there. Lucia stretched out her arms. "Will you come here for a moment, please?"

It was an invitation he had no wish to disregard, though it definitely did interfere with thinking. After a time Lucia spoke in a muffled voice, her head against his shoulder.

"I was thinking," she murmured, "about your Inn. I'm stupid about those things; Charlie Denham told me. But don't you belong to one of the Inns of Court?"

"Yes, certainly! Why do you ask?"

"Well . . . Are they going to like it, Pat, if you testify in the police-court tomorrow about a Soho brawl where you were concerned? Mr. Denham said—"

Barbed jealousy, of anybody or anything, stung him. "When did you see Charlie Denham?"

"Today. After lunch. Anyway, he said that at the trial yesterday you got up and deliberately called the judge an old swine."

Butler shrugged his shoulders. "I called the old swine an old swine," he pointed out simply.

"But mightn't your Inn disbar you? And now you've got a brawl in Soho; and what would happen if you did something awful to this man at the detective-agency, on top of all the rest of it?"

Now this, of course, was quite true. Yet it had never even entered Butler's head to do anything else. He stared at her.

"Don't you understand?" he demanded. "I'm doing this for you!"

"I know that, dear!" Lucia was crying. "I know! And I love it. Especially when you take chances and—" She swallowed hard. "But don't you understand that sooner or later—Mr. Hadley said so at lunch—you're going to get *hurt*?"

"I didn't get hurt tonight, did I?"

"No, dear. But you were awfully lucky!"

Patrick Butler looked at her. He looked at her again. Sensing the change, Lucia glanced up. Very carefully and deliberately Butler removed his arms from round her. He edged across and sat in the opposite corner of the car, with all the arrogance of a Roman emperor.

"It would appear," he observed offhandedly, to the glass panel in front of him, "that I am lucky."

Lucia's voice was conscience-stricken. "Darling! Wait! I didn't mean. . . ."

Butler waved his hand.

"This evening," he continued in his courtroom voice, "two gentlemen attempt to put me in hospital. By the merest luck, a whim of chance ha ha, both these gentlemen are themselves in great need of medical attention. You and I, in a night-club devoted to spivs and amateur prostitutes, are cut off by several more than two of them. Yet by blind luck we walk out as free as air."

"Pat! Please listen to me!"

Then Butler's tone changed.

"Where the hell are we, anyway?" he demanded. "What are we doing here? Where are we supposed to be going?"

Looking out the side windows and the back window, he became again conscious of a world outside.

They were crossing Westminster Bridge towards the Surrey side. The avenue of tall lamps threw trembling reflections deep in the water, as though, someone had written, the ghosts of suicides were holding up torches to show where they had drowned. Through the rear window of the car, far behind, Butler could see the great clock-tower, with its illuminated face, towering grey-black above grey-black Parliament roof-ridges.

The shock and clang of Big Ben, on the quarter-hour after nine, quivered in vibrations as well as sound. It roused Butler to an icy courtesy.

"May I again ask, Lucia, where we are going?"

Lucia, white-faced and shrinking back, regarded him with eyes of hurt and reproach. Then she turned her face away.

"To Balham," she muttered. "That is, if you still want to go."

"Ah," said Butler. Even his eyebrow-raising was overdrawn. "By Balham, I presume, you mean Mrs. Taylor's house?"

"No, I don't!"

"Then will you be good enough to explain?"

Even Lucia's movement, as she turned her shoulder farther away, said, 'I hate you!' But she replied in a light, lofty tone.

"You heard last night, I think, that I inherited three houses. One at Hampstead, Mrs. Taylor's at Balham, and the third is at Balham too. It's a little place. It—it's never been lived in, really."

"And this," asked the astounded Butler, "is what you call an 'adventure'?"

No reply.

"At a time when I should be after Luke Parsons, and working in your interest, you want us to explore a potty little house that's never been lived in?"

"You beast!" flamed Lucia, whipping round for a brief and tearful look at him. "You may find more than you think!"

You may find more than you think.

That sentence, from Lucia, was vaguely disquieting. Mist, almost invisible, hovered over the black Thames. Westminster Bridge was like a swept, lonely dance floor.

Patrick Butler, already forgetting how furious he had been, now felt contrition and wished to apologize. But he was really in love with Lucia; his pride blared at him; and his usual fluent speech would have been thick in his mouth. So he folded his arms and stared straight ahead. Lucia also stared straight ahead. There they sat like a pair of dummies, while the car hummed through dismal Kensington and Brixton.

Unspoken recriminations hovered in the air during that long drive. Butler, meditating dark thoughts of suicide, had his black world broken unexpectedly.

"*Look out, you fool!*" yelled the muffled voice of the chauffeur.

Brakes screeched faintly; the heavy car skidded and stopped dead; both its passengers were flung forward.

On the left they could see the red-white-and-blue enamel of an Underground Station sign which said, 'Balham.' On the right towered what looked like the arch of an overhead railway bridge. In the middle hung a traffic-light, green. A lean figure in an Inverness cape and an old tweed cap, someone who carried a doctor's medicine-case, had been concentrating across the street against the green light.

As though by a simultaneous impulse, Butler and Lucia turned to each other.

"I didn't mean it!" Butler said.

"Neither did I!" said Lucia.

There would have been more to this, no doubt, if the lean figure in the old cap had not strode towards the car to exchange words with the chauffeur. Butler picked up the speaking-tube.

"Control yourself, Johnson," he warned the chauffeur. "This is a friend of ours." Then Butler opened the door and called: "Dr. Bierce!"

The figure halted by one side-light. They saw the harassed dark-brown eyes of Dr. Arthur Bierce, with hollows of fatigue beneath them.

"Get in, won't you?" Butler invited. The doctor complied, and the car pulled over to the kerb beside the Underground Station.

Dr. Bierce lowered himself on one of the pull-out seats facing them. When he removed his cap, the freckled bald skull again loomed up. He sat there with his medicine-case in his lap, his lower lip drawn down, curt yet kindly, just now on an edge of nerves.

"Then you decided to come here after all!" he said.

"To come here—" Butler, astonished, broke off and turned to Lucia. "Did Dr. Bierce know about this?"

"No!" said Lucia. "I didn't tell anybody! Did I, Ambrose?"

Dr. Bierce grimaced.

"You may have heard," he said to Butler, "that the late Mrs. Taylor called me 'Ambrose.' After Ambrose Bierce, that very fine writer." The doctor's bony fingers tightened round the handle of his medicine-case.

"Bierce's stories," he added, "were grotesque and often horrible. But they were never morbid."

"That is what I wanted to talk to you about," pounced Butler, very much counsel for the defence. "That's why I ventured to stop you here."

"Oh?"

"We've met only twice, Doctor. Once in court, and once at Mrs. Renshaw's last night. But it did seem to me, in court, that you knew much more and were hinting much more—about Mrs. Taylor—than the rules of evidence allowed you to say."

"Yes," Dr. Bierce agreed curtly.

"At Mrs. Renshaw's, then, I asked you why you said that Mrs. Taylor's house 'The Priory,' was unhealthy. We were interrupted before you could answer."

"Yes." The lean face grew more stern.

"Now tell me. Shouldn't you say that Richard Renshaw was on very friendly terms with Mrs. Taylor? On far closer terms, for instance," he nodded towards Lucia, "than her own niece was?"

"Naturally," agreed Dr. Bierce with the same curtness. "Evil always attracts evil."

There was a brief silence.

"You won't understand, Doctor, if I refer to a group which operates under some fantastic cloak," Butler continued. Dr. Bierce looked at him quickly. "But I think," Butler said, "that Mrs. Taylor was high up in its councils, probably next to the head of it. I think the head of it was Dick Renshaw. And that somebody poisoned them both to assume control."

"Good!" the doctor said tensely, and slapped his hand on the medical bag. "Then why don't you go along to 'The Priory,' now, and make sure?"

Patrick Butler blinked. "To Mrs. Taylor's house?"

"Naturally! Isn't that where you're bound for?"

"No, no, no!" interposed Lucia. "We were going to the other place, the. . . ."

"There is somebody in the house tonight," said Dr. Bierce.

The words were commonplace enough, yet they had the sinister ring of an understatement in a ghost story.

"But that's impossible!" protested Lucia. "The servants left weeks ago. The electricity's been cut off. The house is all locked up."

"All the same," said Dr. Bierce, "somebody is moving from room to room with a paraffin lamp. Wait! Don't think about burglars or murderers. I think I can tell you who it is. Dr. Gideon Fell."

Lucia let out an involuntary cry. "Dr. Fell?"

"Yes. He was certainly there last night, very late, rummaging the house for evidence of a certain kind. The policeman who found him there, and thought he was a burglar, told me so today. Didn't you get my message?"

"What message?"

"My dear madam," Dr. Bierce spoke somewhat testily, "you weren't in between lunch-time and six o'clock, I know that. But I left a message," Dr. Bierce snapped bony fingers beside his ear, to stimulate memory, "with a certain Miss Cannon."

"Agnes never told me!"

"Well! I thought you might be interested. Because I'm fairly sure he's there tonight."

"Why are you sure?"

"Because I saw the lamp. And he told the policeman," added Dr. Bierce, "that he would be doing an experiment to prove who really poisoned Mrs. Taylor."

Butler sat up straight. Lucia, who had been bending forward with her golden head in the dingy light from the Underground Station, suddenly crouched back.

"The house isn't very far from here, is it?" Butler demanded.

"No, no, no!" Dr. Bierce pointed. "Under the arch of that railway bridge; turn right up Bedford Hill Road. And—if I may go with you?"

Butler gave quick instructions to the chauffeur. The car hummed into life.

"Doctor," persisted Patrick Butler, "one thing I want to know very much. What was Renshaw's business? I mean his official or outward business? Lucia here can only talk vaguely of 'factories.' "

"Darling, that's all he ever told me!"

"I don't know his official business," Dr. Bierce retorted dryly. "For all I do know, he may have an office in the City and the useful title of 'Agent.' " Here a sardonic smile, music-hall-Scottish in its dourness, pulled down Bierce's lips. "But I can tell you something about the gentleman, from remarks let drop by Mrs. Taylor. I can tell you how he started life."

"Well?"

"He was an ordained clergyman," answered Dr. Bierce.

13

AT THE top of Bedford Hill Road, on the edge of the Common, the Victorian-Gothic battlements and sham tower of 'The Priory' loomed vaguely whitish against a black sky. Not a light showed anywhere.

Though the house was exactly like the one at Hampstead, it had not the same "feel" as Lucia's home. Its grounds were larger, behind a low stone wall, but they were ill-kept. It repelled you; it had the chilly stare of someone, much too respectable, who cuts you dead in the street. The trees shielded its bow-windows rather than gracing them.

The limousine had been parked a little way down the hill, lights extinguished. Butler, Lucia, and Dr. Bierce—in that order—moved softly up the stone-flagged path to the front.

"A parson!" Butler kept muttering. "Look here!" Then he remembered the ivory crucifix on the wall of Renshaw's bedroom.

"Where else but the Church," softly asked Dr. Bierce, "could he have used that voice of his? Except on the stage—or at the Bar."

"I know I'm like him, curse it!"

"S-h-h!"

"Did you know about this, Lucia? About the past?"

There was no reply. And Butler insisted. "Did you?"

"No. I didn't *know* about it." Lucia pressed the white scarf round her neck. "But once or twice I thought it might be. Just little things. And you're not like him." She pressed Butler's arm. "You're not like him at all; you must know that."

"Try the front door!" suggested the misleadingly harsh voice of Dr. Bierce.

The front door, though in Mrs. Taylor's lifetime secured by lock and bolt and chain, was not now secured in any way. It opened, on dense blackness, when Butler turned the knob. But he knew what he would meet. A faint scent of damp stain and decay was mingled with the ineradicable tinge of the perfume worn by dead Mrs. Taylor.

"Anybody got an electric torch?"

Dr. Bierce was prompt. "I always carry one. Here!"

Inside, as at Hampstead, was the same passage, with two rooms on each side of it, leading to a large rear hall. But, whereas at Hampstead the drawing room had been the first door on the right, here the entrance to the front bed-sitting-room was on the left.

Butler was drawn there as compellingly as though hands pushed him. The others followed, Dr. Bierce closing the front door. The beam of Butler's electric torch touched the open doorway to Mrs. Taylor's room; then it moved to a little table near by.

On the table stood an old-fashioned lamp, a white globe painted with flowers on a white china. Butler picked up the lamp and shook it.

"There's oil inside," he said, as the splashing rose loudly in stillness. "But the lamp's stone cold. There's nobody here tonight!"

"I tell you, I saw the light! Dr. Fell. . . ."

"He couldn't be walking about in the dark, could he?"

Handing the electric torch back to Bierce, Butler took the globe off the lamp, kindled the wick with a pocket-lighter, and replaced the globe. Its pale whitish light, with a tinge of the unearthly, drew round them the atmosphere of the 'sixties in the last century.

As though to defy bogles, Butler strode through the doorway into Mrs. Taylor's bedroom. He did not turn round, or hold up the lamp, until he reached the middle of the room.

He was now facing the dead woman's bed, with its scrolled and pointed wooden headboard a dull brown, its white bell-cord hanging. Its head was set against the inner wall of the passage. Its mattress had been stripped of bedclothing. But it was wicked; it was leering. He would not have been surprised to see fat Mrs. Taylor, with her painted face and her dyed hair, sitting in a pink nightgown and looking at him.

Butler glanced round. The rays of the lamp, a disembodied pallor with small flower-shapes, dimly showed him the horsehair furniture mingled with a few easy-chairs, the clutter of marble-topped tables, the mantelpiece with its clock, the little bathroom built in the deep alcove between this room and the room behind it. The shutters were closed on the bow-window at the front. Nothing was changed since Butler last saw it.

"Pat!" Lucia, who had followed him into the room on tiptoe, glanced quickly at the bed and away from it. "If Dr. Fell's been here, he's gone now. What are we *doing* in this house?"

"God knows. Wondering if it's haunted, I suppose."

Dr. Bierce, as a man of science, seemed to twitch his nose with skepticism.

"Some kind of experiment—!" he began.

"But what kind of experiment?" Butler swept the lamp round. "Everything's the same. Everything is. . . ."

And yet it wasn't. Butler stopped abruptly.

"Who," he demanded, "who put that water-bottle on the bedside table?"

"Water-bottle?" echoed Lucia.

"When Mrs. Taylor was poisoned, there were only two important things on that bedside table besides the electric lamp. One: a tin containing poison. Two: a glass with a spoon in it. There certainly wasn't a water-bottle. But look at it now!"

On the bedside table, which was at the left of the bed as you faced it, stood a (dead) electric lamp with a fringed yellow shade. Beside it was a water-bottle—rather like the one in Dick Renshaw's bedroom—over whose top a glass had been inverted. The bottle was half full.

"It's like. . . ." Lucia's voice trailed away in a gulp. "Well, you know what it's like! But why should it be here?"

"I don't know. Old Madame Taylor, so far as I ever heard, didn't own a water-bottle at all."

Butler approached the bedside table. The pale light of his lamp turned his companions' faces into the pale masks of strangers, yet all were as absorbed as though they feared the bottle might explode. Patrick Butler picked up the glass and inspected it. It was clean and polished. Putting down the glass, he picked up the bottle. He sniffed at its contents. Experimentally he lifted it towards his mouth. . . .

"*For God's sake don't do that!*" exclaimed a wheezy voice, so close at hand that Butler almost dropped the bottle.

They had been too absorbed to hear even the elephantine approach or cane-tap of Dr. Gideon Fell. Dr. Fell, who was too big to go through the doorway by frontal approach, stood sideways there and held up a very small lamp with a cylindrical glass shade. The little flame shone on a distressed pink face, eyes peering over disarranged eyeglasses on the black ribbon.

"Or, if you must meddle with it," wheezed Dr. Fell, with even deeper distress, "I beg of you not to drink the water. It's poisoned."

Butler set down the bottle hastily.

"Thanks, I won't. Excuse me, but is this your experiment to show who really poisoned Mrs. Taylor?"

Dr. Fell frowned. He maneuvered sideways through the door, his shovel hat on his head and his cane hung over one arm beneath the back-flung cloak.

"Mrs. Taylor?" he repeated. "No, no, no! My dear sir, you have got the facts backwards. My experiment, if I can dignify it by that name, is concerned with an important point in the poisoning of Richard Renshaw."

"And—have you cleared it up?" asked Lucia.

Dr. Fell gave her a vaguely benevolent look and bow, like an absent-minded Old King Cole, and nodded to Dr. Bierce. Peering down the mountainous slopes of himself, he managed with some difficulty to extract a large gold watch from among the ridges of his waistcoat. He blinked at it.

"By thunder, it can be cleared up now!" he said, replacing the watch with agony. "That bottle has been on the table for well over twenty-four hours, which gives a good margin. Let us see, now!"

"What is it?" cried Lucia.

Dr. Fell picked up the bottle. Holding it near the pale globe-lamp in Butler's hand, he advanced his own tiny yellow-flamed lamp so that the bottle was brightly lighted between them. The water was crystal-clear; the glass surfaces shone. Dr. Fell studied the bottle, tilting it back and forth.

"Well?" prompted Butler, conscious of heat and excitement without knowing why. "What do you see?"

Dr. Fell let out a gusty sigh of relief.

"Nothing, I am glad to say. Absolutely nothing!"

"But the poison. . . ."

"My dear sir!" said Dr. Fell, who was startled and bewildered. "Poison? This experiment had nothing to do with poison!" And he put the bottle, as well as his little lamp, on the bedside table.

Patrick Butler closed his eyes, counted slowly to ten, and opened his eyes again.

"Just a moment," he said in a voice of such authority that Dr. Fell blinked. "Let's get one thing straight. Sometimes these cryptic remarks of yours sound like mere hocus-pocus, and sometimes they sound feeble-minded."

Dr. Fell looked guilty.

"But the man who solved that Vampire case, and the poisoning at Caswall Moat House," Butler went on, "is no fool. His remarks aren't mumbo-jumbo."

"They aren't," Dr. Fell assured him. "They aren't, really."

"In my opinion," said Butler with the same hammering tone, "you see some link between two pieces of evidence; the link would seem obvious if you pointed it out. But your mind darts off to some other aspect of the case. And you've quite sincerely forgotten what we're talking about when we ask questions about that link." Here Butler assumed his eighteenth-century manner. "Sir, will you accept a challenge here and now?"

"Sir," intoned Dr. Fell, rearing up and adjusting his eyeglasses, "I shall be delighted."

"Then prove my judgment is correct. What is the Murder Club? How does it work? What are the clues to it? And above all," Butler's wild curiosity reached frenzy, "under what cloak does it operate? Can you—or will you—tell us that now?"

Dr. Fell, whose huge goblin shadow covered the door as Butler raised the pallid lamp, looked back at him with clear eyes and without absent-mindedness.

"I can," repeated Dr. Fell, "and I will. You deserve to know the deadliness of the enemy you are fighting."

"And that is?"

Through the dead and silent house, making Butler's nerves jump, clove the strident ringing of a telephone-bell.

"That 'phone," said Lucia abruptly, "has been cut off for weeks!"

Dr. Fell shook his head.

"By some fortunate accident or even design: no. That's how I have been able to keep in touch with Hadley. Will you excuse me for a moment?"

Butler was in despair.

(If he tries to get away from me, if I don't hear this story within the next few minutes, I'll follow him as I mean to follow Luke Parsons.)

Dr. Bierce, cap in one hand and medicine-case in the other, was contemplating the wooden bedstead with a strange expression Butler could not read; it reminded Butler of a face, perhaps out of history, which eluded him. Lucia, biting her lip in perplexity as though she wanted to know the truth and yet didn't want to know it, seemed about to speak. Then she sent a startled glance at the door.

In the doorway stood Miss Agnes Cannon.

"Well!" said Miss Cannon, with a sort of mild and fizzing hauteur. She continued with the same words Dr. Bierce had used: "Then you decided to come here after all."

Colour tinged Lucia's cheeks.

"I did," Lucia said, "but no thanks to you! Why didn't you give me Dr. Bierce's message?"

Miss Cannon, wearing a trim buff-coloured coat and with a blue scarf over her head with a knot under the chin, continued to fizz like a human Bromo-Seltzer as she drew off her gloves. She glanced slowly round the room, and seemed emotionally moved.

"Mildred Taylor!" she said. "In this room died one of the finest and noblest characters I have ever known." Then, abruptly, she answered Lucia's question. "You are a *child*, Lucia. You will not allow me to do my duty and take care of you. If anyone came here, I decided that it should be myself."

"What on earth," cried Lucia, "do you think you can do here?"

"I flatter myself," said Miss Cannon, flashing her pince-nez, "that I am a woman of the world. I know human nature and its ways." Her glance at Butler, though casual, was charged with significance. "You did not even inform me where you were going, or with whom."

"Oh, Agnes, stop it!"

Miss Cannon opened her handbag, threw her gloves inside, and closed the bag with a snap.

"Nor did you know," her voice quivered, "nor did you know, when you rushed home to dress for dinner, that the police had searched the house this afternoon? No, you did not know it."

For a second Lucia seemed to stop breathing. "Did they search my room?"

"Among all the rest. Obviously."

"What were they looking for?"

"They did not inform me. However, they had a search-warrant. I compelled Chief Inspector Soames to produce it."

Lumbering footsteps sounded in the passage. When Dr. Fell entered sideways and loomed up over them, radiating energy like the heat of a furnace, Miss Cannon seemed to melt away into a dim corner. Dr. Fell's expression was grave as he peered at Butler.

"Look here," he began abruptly, dropping his academic manner. "I'm afraid I've got bad news for you. That was Hadley. The police raid on a certain Love-Mask Club was a fiasco."

"How do you mean?"

"One of your enemies, the man you described as Em, had already gone after a doctor to set some compound fractures. The other, whom you described as Gold-teeth, got away before the squad-car arrived. Both are still at large."

Butler laughed. Dr. Fell, holding firmly to his eyeglasses, surveyed Butler with refreshed interest and something of awe.

"I myself," he declared, "am not now of a corporeal shape to wreck billiard-rooms and carry on in Soho night-clubs as you and Mrs. Renshaw seem to have done. . . ."

"Lucia!" cried Miss Cannon.

"But Hadley," Dr. Fell waved her aside, "asks me to convey to you a very grave warning. Gold-teeth means to put you on a morgue-slab."

"Somehow," Butler told him dryly, "you fail to curdle my blood. So the cloth-heads are still at large, eh?"

Dr. Fell's face grew more red. "If you had heard Gold-teeth's record, as Hadley read it over the 'phone, you might be more careful. Have you got a firearms license?"

"No."

"Well, run along to Scotland Yard in the morning; Hadley will arrange it without trouble."

Butler's eyebrows went up. "Do you honestly think," he inquired, "that any gentleman would trouble to use a revolver-bullet against that type? It should be either ignored or stepped on."

"For God's sake, listen! The first time you met, Gold-teeth regarded you as a mug. . . ."

"I took the same opinion of him. A trifle lower, maybe."

"But he doesn't think so now. He won't give you a chance; he'll get you behind your back, when you're not looking. My dear sir, what can you do?"

"Before I met him," Butler retorted calmly, "I hadn't the slightest idea what my tactics would be. I haven't now. But there will be something."

"Pat," cried Lucia, "suppose they're after you *tonight?*"

"Well, suppose they are? Don't be alarmed, my sweet," said Butler, and openly patted her cheek—to the pink consternation of Miss Cannon.

"We are now, I hope," Butler continued, putting down the white-globed lamp on the bedside table and letting his raw curiosity boil up again, "going to hear something really relevant. Dr. Fell, do you propose to tell us about the Murder Club?"

"Yes," answered Dr. Fell very gravely.

In the midst of a silence, while the others instinctively moved back, he sat down on the edge of the heavy bed. His hand, held forward on the crook of the cane, supported its ferrule against the floor.

"I admit," Butler burst out, with unaccustomed humility, "that my wits aren't up to everything. I know this crowd have developed some entirely new kind of racket. . . ."

"*No!*" said Dr. Fell in a voice like a pistol shot, and rapped the ferrule of his cane on the floor.

"It isn't new?"

Dr. Fell rolled up his big head, with its grey mop of hair, and scrutinized Butler with a twisted-up look in which the wisdom of an elderly man mingled with the spirit of a young one. But he lowered his head again.

"I have often told Superintendent Hadley," he went on, "that his best course would be to shut himself up for fifteen hours a day and read history. He has answered me, not without reason, that this would leave him no time for anything else. Yet there is no crime, not even a trend in crime, which does not recur again and again.

"*New?*" thundered Dr. Fell. "This cloak-for-devilry, which you are pleased to call a racket, is as old as the Middle Ages."

The dim white lamp, amid so many shadows, turned the room with its yellow-striped wallpaper to a dusky reality of the Victorian era. Time ceased to exist. Mrs. Taylor, if her ghost still leered under the dyed hair, might have been dead for nearly a century. But Dr. Fell was drawing them back to a time many centuries before this.

"I am not digressing," he said, "if I refer to the peasant of the Middle Ages. Any schoolboy knows that his life was hard and intolerably dreary. Church and State, or so it seemed, combined to oppress him. Lords of both rode past on their fine horses, to halls full of meat and drink. He must somehow find a penny, or its measure in barter, to get drunk at the ale-house. He could be hanged for small offences, snatched off to foreign wars; live at best by scratching in the earth.

"His only solace lay in the churches, bedight and gleaming like a vision of heaven, golden with candles like the gold out of coffers. Yet, even then, terrors and portents lurked behind every hedge. God existed, but He was aloof and terrible. What did He do for the children of misery?"

Dr. Fell paused, and made an inconsequential gesture.

"Let it go!" he said. "It is only a brief vision, tinged with comedy if we consider the thing called progress. Let us look at the intolerable dreariness in the life of the average man today.

"I hasten to say, since Miss Cannon is about to speak, that this is not a question of what Government is in power. It is the result of a world cataclysm. No Government outside Utopia could have brought a cure-all by this time. But look at your average man!

"His scale has risen, no doubt! He does not starve, though he gets just enough food to keep his body going. Even if he has money, he cannot buy anything. There is nothing to buy. He stands in long queues for cigarettes, when he can get any. Even newspaper-advertisements jeer at him, carolling that So-and-So's Custard is noblest, but that he can't get any because so many people want it.

"He is stifled in crowds, hammered to docility by queues, entangled in bureaucratic red-tape, snubbed by tradesmen with whom he must deal. His nerves, frayed by five years of war and air raids, are scraped raw by reaching for something which isn't there. Haven't you ever observed those long theatre-queues, blank-faced as sheep, waiting in the cold to lose themselves for a time in the sugar-candy nonsense of a motion picture?

"And what is his state of mind then?

"Well, let's look back to those withered—but all too familiar—figures in the Middle Ages. To many of them, in their dreary lives, the Lord of Lords was a cold enigma. But there was another God, just as authentic and far more exciting. *He* had power too. *He* could dispense rich gifts. *He* would reward the faithful against Church and State. And so they could. . . ."

Dr. Fell paused.

"Could—what?" asked Lucia, who was gripping the footboard of the bed.

"They could worship Satan," replied Dr. Fell. "Then, as well as now, in sheer lust for excitement."

The silence seemed to stretch out unendurably, tautened by the un-canny look of four faces in that queer light.

"Will you face the fact," said Dr. Fell, "that cycles return?"

It was Miss Cannon who answered first.

"Really, now!" she said in a high, thin voice. "If you ask us to treat seriously a whole lot of foolish nursery tales. . . ."

Dr. Fell closed his eyes.

" 'No doubt you have read'—I quote Mr. Machen—'of the Witches' Sabbath, and have laughed at the tales which terrified our ancestors, the black cats and the broomsticks, and the doom pronounced against some old woman's cow. Since I have known the truth, I have often reflected that it is on the whole a happy thing such burlesque as this is believed.' "

Dr. Fell opened his eyes. The corners of his bandit's moustache were drawn down. He spoke heavily.

"Ma'am," he asked Miss Cannon, "do you know what the Black Mass really was?"

"Well! I—"

"No fiction writer has portrayed it with accuracy, except Huysmans in *Lá-Bas*. Only the Church has dared to speak out and tell the details; and I shall not be more prudish than the Church. The Black Mass, which was celebrated on the body of a naked woman for an altar, began with the ceremony of—"

Two voices spoke out sharply, one after the other.

"Really," said Miss Cannon, "one is or likes to be broad-minded. But good taste is always good taste."

"The Anti-Christ!" exclaimed Dr. Bierce, like a man praying. "Let it burn and be destroyed!"

And now, as Butler looked round, he realized of what Arthur Bierce reminded him. He should have seen it long before. Bierce, whatever his background, seemed less a physician curing bodies than a seventeenth-century Scottish Puritan curing souls. Even his appearance, the narrow bald skull dominating brooding brown eyes and a thin ascetic's face, stood out in the gloom like the colours of an old painting.

Butler noted this vaguely, in a daze of revelation. He glanced at Lucia.

"Witchcraft!" Lucia said, and shivered. "The worship of Satan! But —nowadays?"

"Nowadays," assented Dr. Fell, "more than ever."

"Why?"

"Because the world is in chaos. Because, after the late affair of Adolf Hitler, many persons believe that decent standards of behaviour cannot exist. Horrors no longer offend. As for religion, observe that politics have taken its place. We have seen little girls, fifteen years old, screaming-drunk in Leicester Square. Decent men are gleeful about trickery and deceit, because their lives compel them to be. This will all change, I grant you! Meanwhile, there is the witch-cult."

"Widespread?" demanded Patrick Butler.

"Not widespread, no. But profoundly evil and doubly dangerous. Because it contains the avid thrill-seekers and the potential murderers."

"Murderers?" screamed Lucia.

"Don't you understand?" Dr. Fell asked quietly. "The witch-cult has always been the cloak for the wholesale poisoner."

14

"YEARS ago, you know," continued Dr. Fell, apparently not conscious of any sense of tension in his listeners, "Inspector Elliot and I believed we had found a witch-cult in that Crooked Hinge affair. We hadn't; it existed only in one person's mind. But now, by thunder, the reality has come home with a vengeance! Er—shall I explain how I discovered it?"

"Yes, yes, yes!" Lucia kept repeating in a low voice. She wheeled out one of the old horsehair chairs to face Dr. Fell, and sank into the chair. Miss Cannon, still flustered and evidently shocked, hovered near her.

Dr. Fell blinked at Patrick Butler.

"Last night, at Mrs. Renshaw's home," he said, "I told you about my belief in an organization which distributed poison. But I couldn't, for the life of me, think how it worked silently with every tongue mute.

"Archons of Athens, what a scatterbrain!" added Dr. Fell, knocking the heel of his hand against his forehead. "I had forgotten history, which no criminologist should ever do. For, immediately afterwards, I saw on the drawing-room table a very large silver candelabrum with seven branches."

For a moment nobody spoke.

"But all you did," protested Butler, though he saw many dangers sweeping near, "was scrape some pieces of wax out of one holder. The wax had gone completely black with dust."

"Oh, no!" said Dr. Fell. "Not dust! As I found immediately afterwards, Miss Cannon here is too good a housekeeper to let any dust settle. And the underside of a blob of wax, when you scrape it off, will not be black too. Did you ever in your life see *black* candles, of a size to fit those large socket-holders? You didn't; they aren't made except privately. They were black candles—"

"For the Black Mass," supplied Dr. Bierce, with savage quietness.

"I might inform you," said Miss Cannon in a high voice, "that the candle-sockets were *quite* clean. I saw them this morning."

"So I was informed by Hadley. He saw Mrs. Renshaw during lunch." Dr. Fell looked at Lucia. "In other words, Mrs. Renshaw, someone in your house cleaned out those sockets during the night. I repeat: in your house. Don't you find it coming closer to home?"

"I don't know what you're talking about." Lucia spoke from a dry throat. "Really and truly I don't."

"We-ell," mused Dr. Fell, resuming his narrative with an offhand gesture, "just after the dazzling illumination brought by the candles, I was handed more information which, as you may have noticed, made me jump."

"What information was that?" struck in Arthur Bierce, who stood over in shadow with his fists clenched. "I—er—I had left the house after meeting you. What information?"

"On the sill of one window in Mr. Renshaw's bedroom," answered Dr. Fell, "somebody had drawn a few little designs in the dust. Miss Cannon kindly informed me that each design looked like 'an inverted "T," and with perhaps a little tail to it.' H'mf, yes."

"Unfortunately," said Miss Cannon, "the marks in the dust are gone."

"Fortunately," said Dr. Fell, "the police had photographed them when they first went over the room."

Reaching into an inside coat pocket which must have contained enough old letters to stuff a shoe-box, Dr. Fell produced a crumpled glazed photograph. He held this before Lucia's eyes, inviting her to look.

"They're just as Agnes said!" protested Lucia. "The little tail is an extension, a slight extension of the vertical line."

"Do you make anything of them? Hey?"

"No!"

"This is the correct way of viewing the photographs," said Dr. Fell. "But now look at them upside down!"

He reversed the photographs, and Lucia cried out.

"Why . . . they're crosses! I mean, they look like Christian crosses!"

"Aha!" grunted Dr. Fell, and stuffed the photograph away in his pocket. "On a wall of that room, we remember, was an ivory crucifix. Someone looked at it, when the poison was poured, with derisive mockery. Some one drew in the dust, as comments, drew several times in quick hatred, the first symbol of all devil-worship—the reversed cross of Satan!"

Whack went the ferrule of Dr. Fell's cane on the floor.

" 'When the poison was poured—' " repeated Lucia.

"Yes. A very important point."

"Then, last night"—Lucia's blue eyes sought new dangers—"you asked me two questions you said were very important. You asked whether I'd quarreled with Aunt Mildred Taylor about religion. And I still say she was talking about the Catholic Church!"

"Are you sure?" Dr. Fell asked softly.

"Dr. Fell, I'm positive! She had an awfully queer look about her, as I told you. But what she actually said was, 'What joy you'll know, my dear, when you're converted to the old religion.' "

"The old religion!" Dr. Fell glowered with satisfaction. "That's better! I thought as much!"

"You don't mean to say. . . . ?"

"It is the name given by many adepts to the Anti-Christ and his worship," said Dr. Fell. "As for the second important question I asked you, and was satisfied of your innocence when it seemed to puzzle you—listen!"

Dr. Fell gave a half-chuckle which had no mirth in it. He raised his old greyish head, heavy with the weight of learning, and looked in turn at each of the four persons who surrounded him.

"Let me repeat a little story," he said. "You all know it. It has been printed in half the schoolbooks, and read by most of the nation, with this curious additional fact: that neither the writers who prepared it, nor the readers who memorized it, ever had the slightest idea what it really meant.

"The story goes that during the reign of Edward the Third, in the fourteenth century, a certain Lady (most versions identify her as the Countess of Salisbury) danced at a court-ball given by the king. While dancing, she dropped her garter and was overcome with confusion. King Edward instantly picked up the garter, fastened it on his own leg with the words 'Honi soit qui mal y pense' and on this incident founded the Order of the Garter, the highest of knightly Orders in all Europe."

Dr. Fell puffed out his lips under the bandit's moustache, making a wry and satiric noise.

"Now the interest of that little tale lies not in whether it is true or partly legendary. But centuries of repetition have made it lose its point."

Here Dr. Fell made a still more satiric face.

"It took very much more than a dropped garter, believe me, to shock a lady of the fourteenth century. In fact, the incident would have caused only mild embarrassment under Queen Victoria. Any child today can translate '*Honi soit qui mal y pense*' as 'Evil to him who evil thinks.' Where on earth could there have been any suggestion of evil?

"But King Edward knew. He knew what overcame Lady Salisbury and terrified the guests. His quick thinking, as Miss Murray has pointed out,* probably saved her life. For the garter, then used as cord or string or lace. . . ."

Lucia Renshaw rose to her feet. With the same unconscious grace of movement, she stepped back a few paces with the palms of her hands pressed to her face under the eyes.

"Go on!" said Patrick Butler.

"The garter," said Dr. Fell, "was the mark of the witch-woman. It designated the creature, skilled in lechery and murder, who stood out against the lurid sky of the Middle Ages. And the red garter, above all, meant the head of a group, or coven; high in unholy councils, closest of all to the person, usually a man, who towered over them in the role of Satan."

A deeper chill had settled on them, as though the globe-lamp itself contained no heat and dead Mrs. Taylor had joined the group.

"Yes, you can look at me!" Lucia spoke clearly and defiantly. "I've been wearing the beastly things, at one time or another, for over a year. I was even wearing them last night."

Dr. Fell exhaled a deep breath.

"Ma'am," he growled, again distressed, "I'm glad you told me that. In your dressing-table drawer, the police found. . . ."

"Yes, of course! That's why I was so frightened when Agnes said they'd searched the house. They were searching for—"

"No, no, no, no!" Dr. Fell grunted testily. "They were searching for something more important, I assure you, than five gaudy sets of red garters. But why did you lie to me last night?"

"Because I didn't know what they meant! You made it sound so horribly mysterious and important that I shied away from it by—oh, call it instinct! Dick made me do it, you know."

"Your husband made you wear the garters?"

---

*Margaret Alice Murray, *The God of the Witches* (Sampson Low, Marston & Co.), pp. 71–76.

"Yes! It seemed to be some kind of joke. But with something underneath it. Often he'd say, 'Is my dear wearing her adornments?' He always called them 'adornments,' and he always laughed. I could never tell when he was going to ask about it."

Lucia moistened her lips.

"I—I said, you remember," her glance strayed towards Butler, "that Dick always chose all my clothes. That was as close as I dared to hint at it. But I didn't know what it meant! I swear I didn't! Pat, dear!" She started to put out her arms to him, but dropped them. "Don't you believe me?"

"Of course I do." Butler's laugh rang in the ugly room, without any response. "So will everybody else. What do you say, Miss Cannon?"

Miss Cannon, who had removed her pince-nez to dab at her eyes, regarded him in a nearsighted way.

"I say," she replied in her most genteel voice, "that if I hear any more of these improprieties I shall leave the house. I consider the whole subject improper and unfit for discussion."

"One moment!" said Dr. Fell very sharply.

Lucia made a slight gesture which begged Butler to go over and stand beside her. He did so, unobtrusively touching her arm. Now he saw Dr. Fell's wide-open eyes, a clear grey, undimmed by time or vast quantities of beer.

"Your husband, Mrs. Renshaw, had been an ordained clergyman. That," said Dr. Fell, "was discovered very quickly by routine police-work. Did you know it?"

"No. Not until tonight. Dr. Bierce told me. But I had (how can I explain it?) vague kinds of suspicions. . . ."

"Did you suspect—as I firmly believe—that he was the head of a witch-cult?"

("So I was right!" thought Butler.)

"No!" cried Lucia. "Never! All I ever thought . . . well, there are all kinds of funny religious cults that haven't any harm in them. Like worshipping trees or the sun or something."

"Did your husband ever initiate you into any rites necessary for entrance to the witch-cult?—There is no need to blush like a schoolgirl, Mrs. Renshaw. If he had, believe me, you would have remembered."

"I don't remember. That is, no."

"Did he ever hint at it?"

"*Must* I answer that question?"

"My dear lady, you need answer me nothing. Walk out of the house, as Miss Cannon wants to do; go your way in peace. I am only, as I told you, an old duffer who wants to help you."

Butler, whose hatred of Dick Renshaw had reached a new height or depth, jogged Lucia's arm in intimation that she ought to reply. Dick Renshaw surrounded them and clouded them as with black wings.

"Maybe"—Lucia interlocked her delicate fingers—"maybe I only think of it as a hint because of what I know now. But once he said to me," she hesitated, "he said, 'My dear, you are only Venus in appearance; at heart you are the curate's aunt.' I said, 'And maybe you're the wrong man.' That was one of the times when he hit me. Oh, can't we stop this!"

"In just a minute. I don't like it, by thunder! Did you know that only an ordained clergyman can celebrate the Black Mass?"

"Dr. Fell, I never even heard of the Black Mass, except in one or two supernatural stories where they never said what it was about." Evidently despite herself, curiosity struggled in Lucia's gaze. "What do they do?"

"You never knew," persisted Dr. Fell, ignoring the question for an explosive one of his own, "that its rites were being celebrated here?"

Again two voices snapped out, one after the other.

"Here?" exclaimed Miss Cannon.

"In this house?" demanded Dr. Bierce.

Bierce, his fists clenched, walked slowly round to the other side of the bed and faced Dr. Fell.

"Not in this house," said Dr. Fell, letting his eyes rove round the dingy room still faintly exhaling Mrs. Taylor's perfume. "But very close to here. In a little building belonging to Mrs. Lucia Renshaw."

Again, as Miss Agnes Cannon shrank back, Dr. Fell turned to Lucia.

"I think I told you," he went on, "that I spoke to Mr. Charles Denham about Mrs. Taylor's will. Mrs. Renshaw inherited three houses, 'The Priory,' 'Abbot's House,' and a third called, 'The Chapel.' "

"Well?"

"Someone has pointed out, Dr. Bierce, our grotesque way of naming houses. We put up a little box of a villa, with no tree within a hundred yards; we call it, 'The Elms,' and nobody thinks twice about the name. This house is not a priory. No monk ever entered the 'Abbot's House.' But—fine irony, by thunder!—this place called 'The Chapel' really is a chapel."

Bierce's high framework of bones seemed to stand out beneath the skin of his face. With a violent effort he controlled himself.

"If you tell me it's a Nonconformist chapel," he said thickly, "I tell you at once that you lie."

"No, no! I mean a private chapel, one attached to a great house torn down long ago. But it was consecrated. It can be, and is being used for the worship of Satan."

On Bierce's lips, it seemed to Butler, there trembled again those words, "Let it burn and be destroyed!" But the physician only pointed to the bed and said in the same harsh voice:

"Mrs. Taylor?"

"In my opinion, sir, she was the chief assistant to the head of the witch-cult, Richard Renshaw."

"And she went to the rites at this—chapel?"

"My dear sir," said Dr. Fell, "you yourself testified at the trial that she could have walked to China and carried her own suitcase. She was no invalid."

"And, when she thought anyone was hiding something from her, she would ransack the whole house for it. The damned woman," snarled Bierce, emphasizing the adjective in its literal sense, "insisted on sleeping alone here, except for a companion-secretary at the very back of the house. If she went out by the front door, not a soul would know of it."

"Yes."

"Dr. Fell, what is your interest in the—chapel?"

"Confound it, don't you see?" Dr. Fell was again distressed and exasperated, as at another obvious point. "We are not investigating a case of Satanism. We are investigating a case of wholesale poisoning. As for the chapel. . . ."

He moved his head round to look at the rest of his companions. He added: "I am taking you all there tonight."

Somewhere in the dark house there was a heavy crash of glass.

All four of them remained motionless. The sound, it seemed to Patrick Butler, had come from fairly close at hand.

"Have you still got your electric torch handy?" he asked Dr. Bierce. "Good! Give it to me!"

The physician brought the torch from the chair where he had put his cap and medicine-case. Lucia took a step forward.

"Pat, what are you going to do?"

"Oh, just have a look round."

"Pat, be careful!"

"Careful? Careful of what?" asked the puzzled Butler, and hurried out into the passage.

For, in leaving that room, it never occurred to him that there might actually be a burglar or a prowler. He merely wanted to be alone for a few minutes, in the dark, shut up with his thoughts so that no facial expression might betray them; and he closed the door after him.

Casually he flicked the beam of the torch round the four doors in the passage, one on each side, and along the faded yellow wallpaper. Then he strolled down the passage.

During the past half-hour he had been in more (unacknowledged) anguish than at any time before. He felt like striking his fist against the walls in helpless sickness of heart.

Satanism. The flesh and the devil. Black candles burning at a human altar, under a reversed cross. Red garters and laces and strings, withered with the evil of the past. The garter, in one Irish superstition, was supposed to possess magical power. And, he remembered from Pepys's Diary, it was a very old custom to fight for the bride's garters at a wedding. . . .

Wedding. Lucia. The chapel.

It was to the chapel, unquestionably, that Lucia had been taking him that night. He remembered Lucia at Claridge's: "A real adventure!" Lucia at the Love-Mask Club: "My handbag's got—got a key in it." Lucia in the gloom of a speeding car: "You may find more than you think."

Wait a minute! Was it possible the Black Mass would be celebrated there tonight? Was that why Dr. Fell wanted them to go?

All he knew about this ceremony was that it ended in promiscuous eroticism to whose image he closed his mind quickly, as he might have closed a door.

Nonsense! It wasn't possible!

Lucia was not guilty of anything, particularly of murder. His absolute conviction of this, as he had time to think back on everything, grew still and steady. If he had been compelled to address a jury:

"Did you ever hear," he would have said, "any woman answer more clearly and reasonably and honestly the questions Dr. Fell asked her a few minutes ago? Those infernal garters were a device of Dick Renshaw; and may his soul toast on a griddle at this moment!

"And even suppose she did invite me to this chapel? Her own words contain an explanation, though she never put it forward as an explanation. She had believed her husband of being some kind of parson, perhaps a bogus parson, and, as she said, 'There are all kinds of funny religious cults that haven't any harm in them.'

"That's it exactly! To explore this third house belonging to her ('It's never been lived in, really') might produce evidence in the case of Renshaw's murder and at the same time be a harmless adventure which would appeal to Lucia. It's so easy, when you understand it! It's so. . . ."

Patrick Butler stopped in his tracks, listening.

Where was he, anyway?

His finger had slipped off the button of the electric torch; he must have been in the dark for many seconds. He had become so immersed in silent speech that he hadn't noticed where he was going.

To judge by the freer air, the hardwood floor, the feel of a small rug under one foot, he must be in the large rear hall with the gallery round it. Butler had the momentary panic of one roused out of a dream. It would not be pleasant to meet dead and damned Dick Renshaw, as though meeting his own image in a mirror.

Somewhere close at hand, a footstep creaked.

"Who's there?"

"Who's there?"

The two challenges whipped out together. Butler pressed the button of the torch and swung it upwards. Someone, facing him from a comparatively short distance, did the same. The two beams of light crossed above a table, and just between two silver candelabra exactly like those at Lucia Renshaw's. What Butler saw was the large and reassuring figure of a policeman.

"Oh, ah?" said the law, who carried a bull's-eye lantern. "And who might you be, sir?"

"My name is Butler," smiled the other. "I'm here with Dr. Fell, who's in the front room. Er—I think I have a card with me."

He found the card and handed it across the table. The policeman accepted it stolidly, gave it a quick glance, and handed it back.

"Butler," said the law, as though he found the name familiar but sinister. "Do you know the back door's wide open, sir?"

"That must have been Dr. Fell! I'll see to it. I heard glass smash somewhere out here. . . ."

"That was the prowler, sir."

"Prowler?"

"He run into a big glass-vase thing on a pedestal inside the back door. Then he saw my light, and he cut and run for it. We've had instructions to look out for him."

"How do you mean, instructions?"

"Just instructions, sir. And I'd be a bit careful, too. His two front teeth was gold."

15

"THAT'S the chapel, eh?" muttered Dr. Bierce.

"But I keep telling you," Lucia persisted, in a low voice, "I haven't got the key! I left it in my bag at that night-club."

"Never mind. My own key here," said Dr. Fell, fishing out a large iron key with a cardboard label attached, "I obtained one from the Town Hall. Like my other information about it."

Agnes Cannon and Patrick Butler said nothing.

They stood at the edge of the Common on its eastern side, almost at the southern end. The Common, by day a dull greenish-brown vastness, now by night was black and empty, edged by a few far-away street lamps or bare trees.

The chapel, middle eighteenth-century, would have caught attention without rousing curiosity. Narrow, small, built of dark-grey stone, it had a peaked roof like a church without a spire. No shred of glass remained in its pointed mullioned windows, from damage older than the blitz. One large window, boarded up inside with wood turned greyish-black, faced the watchers; the narrow side was towards the pavement beyond a high yew hedge.

On either side of the chapel, each perhaps a dozen feet from it, stood two very respectable suburban houses with front rooms dark to save fuel. The white mist was rising again. Whatever you touched was as cold as a toad.

Dr. Fell's voice, rolling ahead of them, became the only path through an opening in the hedge and round the side of the chapel to the left.

"About two hundred years ago," the voice was a rumbling whisper, "most of *that* side of the Common was the estate of a baronet named Fletcher. A covered passage connected the house with this chapel. Hence the door, here at this side—is anything wrong back there?"

"Nothing at all," replied Butler, at the end of the single-file line. "Lead on."

He had only brushed his back against another hedge. But he thought he felt Gold-teeth's hand on his neck.

Lucia, just ahead of him, was wearing Butler's coat; he had insisted she put it on. So intense was the sense of sympathy between them that Lucia, as though hearing his thought, turned round.

"Pat," she whispered, "what did happen back there? When the glass smashed and you went out to look?"

"I've told you a dozen times: nothing," he lied.

"Don't you trust me?"

. "A policeman found the back door open, that's all. Dr. Fell later admitted *he'd* left it open, didn't he? The policeman fell over a glass vase on a pedestal. End of episode."

Ahead of them a key grated in a lock. The arched and pointed door opened in the side of the withered little chapel. All scrambled inside, even to the bulk of Dr. Fell, who now held Dr. Bierce's torch. As Dr. Fell locked the door behind them and put the key in his pocket, Miss Cannon spoke in a curious tone.

"Why, this is an ordinary chapel," she said as the light roved. "The pews are broken down and it's in a dreadful state, but it's nothing but an ordinary chapel!"

"True," agreed Dr. Fell. He added, as though irrelevantly: "Sir Thomas Fletcher, the original baronet, isn't in the *Dictionary of National Biography*, but his son Harry, who was mixed up with that curious devil-worshipping society known as the Monks of Medmenham, has an inch or two of print. Come with me."

Butler, so deep in his own thoughts, never remembered where Dr. Fell led them. It was growing late, Butler reflected. His vitality must be ebbing. Or Gold-teeth would not have been in his mind at all. Gold-teeth, face to face and in light, would be no problem at all. Here. . . .

Somewhere, under a window, a large trap was being raised in the floor. They were descending, one by one, a staircase just wide enough to accommodate Dr. Fell. Bierce, last in the line, closed the trap after them.

(Wake up, you fool!)

Different, all different! The staircase was carpeted in some soft, deep material. On the right, covering stone, were hangings of another soft, heavy material. In brief gleams of the light, carpet and hangings seemed a deep red. On the left of the narrow stair, the banister was of some black lustrous wood resembling ebony.

But over all distortion-glimpses, which showed little, the room down here was full of a stale smell of incense—sweetish, and mixed with another fainter scent which Butler could not place until he remembered the Erlington case. It was the breath of marihuana.

At the foot of the short staircase, on what might have been a newel-post, stood a heavy bronze group or statuette—only a shadow-mass—which must have weighed forty or fifty pounds.

They had all reached the floor of the low, oblong room when there was a click like that of a switch. From the centre of the ceiling sprang up the light of a human eye.

An inverted glass bowl, large but dim-lighted, had been painted to represent that staring eye. It was whitish, though faintly blood-shot; its iris was red, its pupil black. Though it stared down, like an eye probing consciences, it did not illuminate the room except to trace the red and black of the hangings. Both ends of the red-carpeted room lay in shadow.

"Dr. Fell," Lucia was looking round in a kind of fascination, "that light is electricity, isn't it?"

"Oh, yes. Just as the walls behind these hangings are concrete."

"But who—?"

"This chapel, not a very good real-estate investment, was bought by Mrs. Taylor's grandfather. Mrs. Taylor inherited it from her father. Unto the third generation."

Bierce was looking behind him, at the bronze statue-group on the newel post of the ebony staircase. Patrick Butler followed his glance. The bronze represented a nymph in the arms of a satyr, after the realistic Italian school, every feature and muscle a-quiver with mimic life.

"Dr. Fell, you've been here before!" Miss Cannon almost screamed at him.

"Oh, yes. This morning."

"Then why do you drag us here now?"

"Because every inch of this room must be searched. Haven't I kept telling you that through all history the witch-cult is the cloak of the poisoner?"

"But I don't see—" began Lucia.

She removed Butler's coat from her shoulders, because it was now too warm, and threw it to him. Dr. Fell, an immensity partly silhouetted against the staring gleam of the eye, pointed at Lucia with his cane.

"Let us suppose, for the sake of argument," he said, "that you are a member of the cult. You are either, at the beginning, a thrill-seeker or a half-believer. But you come here, and breathe this air. Braziers burn in corners, herbs mixed with—"

"Marihuana?" Butler asked quietly.

Dr. Fell nodded. "Whose first and most important effect, as our newspapers or fiction-writers seldom tell us, is not to make you run amok. It is to remove all of what are called ordinary inhibitions.

"Down there"—Dr. Fell pointed to darkness at the end of the room—"candles burn at the altar. You grovel before Lucifer. You do acts of less than human decency; you have reached the pit, and therefore are exalted to a kind of infernal ecstasy. What things are not possible to the Lord of Flame? Now look there."

Again he pointed. Midway down the line of each red-and-black curtained wall, on either side of the rows of black gold-embroidered cushions which served as pews, stood a broad cabinet whose carvings made it seem half open.

"Confessional boxes," said Dr. Fell.

"You mean they confess their. . . ." Lucia stopped.

"They creep in, masked, not to confess their sins. To confess their desires for sins. They speak to the head of the cult, Satan's representative, who can grant all.

"On the ordinary, or even extraordinary, sins we need not dwell. They are easily provided. But suppose a woman wishes her husband dead? Or a husband would be rid of his wife? Or an old dotard with money lingers on and refuses to die?

"We had two problems to face," Dr. Fell went on, "in the case of nine poisonings in six months. First, how could a cult hide in such secrecy? And Satanism gives all the answers. Its members are outwardly respectable because, to join at all, they must be at least faintly well-to-do. They wear masks, of course. But masks may slip, in a moment of frenzy—"

"Masks!" Butler interrupted with bitterness. "Masks again! Always masks!"

"And so it will be," Dr. Fell retorted, "until we snatch the mask from the present head of the witch-cult."

"Your second problem?" asked Bierce, whose hatred and disgust surrounded him like the odour of this muffled room.

"How was it," asked Dr. Fell, "that in nine cases the police could trace no poison to any person concerned in the matter?"

"I am professionally interested in that, thank you."

"Let us suppose, then, that you are an architect living, say, at Oxford. What matters, much, in this lean and embittered world? Why should you put up with your wife, when the joy of Satanism is in your vitals?"

"I have never," said Dr. Bierce, twisting up his mouth, "been able to afford the luxury of a wife. But grant it! What happens?"

Again Dr. Fell pointed towards the grotesque confessional box.

"You whisper your desire," he said. "And all is planned, prepared, blue-printed for you. On a certain day you will go to, let us say, a city such as Wolverhampton. You will be given the street, the address, and the name of a certain quite innocent chemist. There, with a carefully prepared story, you will buy the poison called aconitine.

"And you will get it, never fear! You sign the poison-register with the real name of a man living in that city. You return from your journey. Your wife, after some time, is poisoned. . . ."

"With aconitine?"

"No!" groaned Dr. Fell. He seemed a vast cloak flapping against the staring bloodshot eye-light. "That is the whole secret. She will be poisoned with arsenic."

"Arsenic?"

"All is prepared, you know. You return here and whisper again to Satan's deputy. For your aconitine, which you pass through the grill, you exchange the arsenic. Some other would-be-murderer, a little pleasant woman from London, has bought arsenic in Leeds. With so many others it is subtle, deft, sleight-of-hand exchange. No suspicious poison —that is, one which couldn't be used for simple domestic use as well, and which many do buy—is ever used. When your wife dies of arsenic in Oxford, who will search for you buying aconitine in Wolverhampton?"

There was a silence. Lucia's head was bowed, and she trembled.

"Of all the ingenious new devices—!" exploded Butler.

"New?" Dr. Fell repeated wearily. "My dear sir, it was used by John Eachard's Satanist-cult in 1746. Can you wonder if I show no surprise?"

Arthur Bierce looked round wildly.

"But what, in the name of the true God, are we looking for?"

"Records," said Dr. Fell. "Don't you see that with such a complex organization in the hands of one man . . . Richard Renshaw had three bank-accounts, with a total of six figures . . . there must be records enough for a filing-case? They must contain names, dates, places. But where are they?"

Bierce spoke dryly. "Renshaw had an office in the City, I daresay?"

"Yes."

"Possibly even with the title of 'agent'?"

"Quite right," grunted Dr. Fell. "But the police found nothing there. This afternoon," he looked pointedly at Lucia, "they searched his house: not for garters. For two nights"—here Dr. Fell extended grubby hands, palms upward—"I have been ransacking Mrs. Taylor's house without effect. There is only one conclusion. The records must be here."

There was an interruption. Miss Cannon, who had been looking in a vague way at the bronze nymph-and-satyr, suddenly ran up the carpeted steps and disappeared through the open trap.

"Let her go," growled Dr. Fell in a quiet voice. "She has seen enough."

"But I haven't?" asked Lucia.

With only a grunt for a reply, Dr. Fell lumbered round to survey the room again. Then he began to walk down what might be called the aisle of the red-and-black chapel.

With their eyes growing accustomed to the streaky illumination, the others followed him. The soft red carpet gave no more whisper of sound than the heavy velvet curtains. The low roof was supported by pillars and carved beams of that wood which resembled polished ebony. On either side of the aisle, the piles of black gold-embroidered cushions which served as pews were disarranged, as though agitated. But it was a very short distance to the altar, towards which Dr. Fell was lumbering now.

To Butler, going down the aisle with Lucia clinging to his arm, there occurred the grotesque fancy that he and Lucia were approaching for some kind of wedding ceremony. The idea amused and rather shocked him. Besides, bride and groom didn't go arm-in-arm down an aisle.

And besides that. . . .

In the faint sweet-stale haze of the room, which seemed to heighten senses rather than drug them, he detected another even more faint.

"Paraffin oil?" he muttered.

"What did you say?" Lucia asked quickly.

"I was only mumbling to myself, pet."

Probably he had imagined it. One touch of a match or a lighter in this warm, stuffy, be-curtained chapel would be more than a tribute to the lord of darkness and poison. Behind them, Bierce was also mumbling.

Dr. Fell had reached the apsidal sanctuary, or deep curved recess, within which on the footpace stood the altar like a couch covered with the softest vestment. On either side of it, a pedestal supported a candelabrum, each with seven branches, each with seven black candles. The whole back of the recess seemed to be covered by a large, shadowy tapestry.

Then Dr. Fell struck a match and slowly lighted the fourteen black candles. And real diabolism sprang out at them.

The soft, gathering light rippled through the recess and out into the black-and-red chapel. The great tapestry, seventeenth-century French or Italian, bore its lettering, *Lucifer Triumphans*. And Lucia Renshaw took one glance at its subject-matter, and hastily averted her eyes.

"Why did you have to bring us here?" cried Lucia, in almost the same tone as Miss Cannon had used. "If you wanted to search, you could have searched on your own!"

"Forgive me," said Dr. Fell gravely, "but do you notice the candelabra?"

"I don't care to look at them, thanks."

"They are imitation silver, much tarnished. I found them in a cupboard behind the hangings to the left of the apse."

"Well? What about them?"

"My dear lady," said Dr. Fell, "a gathering of worshippers, if not an actual Black Mass took place in this room not later than four nights ago. The candelabra used in that ceremony came from your house."

Lucia still stood with her back to the altar and the tapestry. But her shoulders lifted and settled with the expression of a woman almost at breaking-point. Patrick Butler touched her elbow for reassurance.

"Suppose you prove that?" he challenged Dr. Fell.

"Dash it all, look here! Today," argued Dr. Fell, "is Wednesday, the 21st. Yesterday was Tuesday, the 20th. The day before that was Monday, the 19th."

"I do not challenge the calendar, sir. I merely challenge you."

"Dick Renshaw," persisted Dr. Fell, "was poisoned on the night of

Monday, the 19th. Well, somebody and for some reason brought those candelabra back to the house. I have my own ideas regarding who that person was. But the candle-sockets weren't cleaned properly; you and I saw the traces of black wax last night, the 20th."

"But to call Lucia a murderer on the strength of—"

"Oh, a murderer!" scoffed Dr. Fell, waving a hand as though this were the merest peccadillo. "I don't think she is, if that helps you.

"*But,*" added Dr. Fell, with ferocious emphasis, "you don't see the point. Somebody, between last night and this morning, slipped downstairs and cleaned those candle-sockets. But nobody will admit doing such an ordinary household job. Inference: someone at 'Abbot's House' is closely affiliated with the witch-cult. Secondary inference: probably only one person is concerned."

Lucia, taking a deep breath, turned round to face Dr. Fell and the burning candles and the tapestry.

"There are only three of us," she pointed out. "Which one would you choose?"

"We-ell, now," intoned Dr. Fell, pulling at his underlip, "have you given any thought to your maid? Kitty Owen? Hey?"

"Kitty!" echoed Lucia, as though in dumb astonishment.

"Well, ma'am," the learned doctor said dryly. "Which one would be your own choice?"

"I don't think it's *anybody,*" replied Lucia. "I think this whole affair is silly and revolting and—and terrifying!"

"At the same time," Dr. Fell wrinkled up his face, "that damsel has a lean and hungry look. She is not, I should think, what in my generation we called green. I did not like certain little episodes I witnessed. And quite clearly she worships Somebody."

"I think it's silly and revolting and terrifying!" repeated Lucia. "Don't you agree, Pat?"

The candlelight made a golden nimbus round Lucia's hair as she turned round, appealing with her young-girl look.

But for once Butler did not notice. It was that word 'green,' used by Dr. Fell, which had opened a chink in his mind and illuminated a dark scene. Just as he had caught at inspiration earlier this evening, but now with broader and stronger effect, he saw what he ought to have seen before. He drew himself up, conscious of a pose but not caring a curse.

"Forgive me," he said, "if I seem to ignore your question. For now

I know how your husband was really murdered, and who killed him."

"Do you, by thunder!" muttered Dr. Fell, whose eyeglasses had gone lopsided again. "You see," he added apologetically, "I've been sure all along that I knew too."

Butler was at his most lordly.

"Before I state the clinching evidence," he went on, "may I refer to one point which will clear Lucia if she should ever be charged with the murder of Mrs. Taylor? I thought of it early this evening. And I mean the question of transportation."

Dr. Fell, behind the altar, blinked at him. "Transportation?"

"Yes. No taxi would have driven her from Hampstead to Balham, or back. It wouldn't have enough petrol. If she went at all, late at night, she would have had to use a drive-hire service; and there would be a record of it. You will find no record."

"O Bacchus!" intoned Dr. Fell, his mouth falling open under the bandit's moustache. "Do you suggest this evidence—harrumph—for the defence?"

"Naturally!"

"Sir," replied Dr. Fell, "I am bound to tell you something in confidence. You have used one of Chief Inspector Soames's strongest points for the prosecution."

"What's that?"

"Perhaps you noticed, when you went to Hampstead last night," said Dr. Fell anxiously, "the Hampstead Underground Station? It's opposite the traffic-light at Hampstead High School, and close to Cannon Row?"

"Yes. I certainly recall it."

"And no doubt you've seen the Balham Underground Station? Close to Mrs. Taylor's house?"

Butler opened his mouth to speak, but shut it again.

"That's the Northern Line," said a fussed Dr. Fell. "Ordinarily, with our fine Underground maze, you'd have been whackingly right. But there's no changing, backtracking, or getting lost and infuriated at Earl's Court. It's a straight run from Hampstead to Balham in forty-five minutes. And, if you poisoned Mrs. Taylor at night at any time before 11.30, you could get the last train back."

Butler, one hand in his pocket, remained bland and smiling. He did not even blink. Many times, in court, adroit counsel thought they had him in a corner. He would show them now, especially Lucia.

"It is of small importance," he conceded, knowing in his heart that it really was. "Though I could debate that point of the last train back." His voice rose sharply. "Now will you hear how Lucia's husband was really poisoned?"

Nobody spoke. Butler continued to smile.

" 'If Mrs. Renshaw didn't do it,' we hear, 'who else could have done it?' It seems an impossible problem. And yet it isn't." Jingling coins in his pocket, Butler allowed a pause. "The real murderer," he said, "is Kitty Owen. And the clue—which has been dangling in front of our eyes—is a large dull-green knitting-bag."

Lucia stared at him in bewilderment.

"You mean my knitting-bag?" she cried.

"I do. You told us, didn't you, that Kitty was always traipsing about the house with the knitting-bag?"

"Yes, of course!"

"You further said," Butler's finger went out in courtroom fashion despite himself, "that Kitty had the knitting-bag hung over her arm while she was using the carpet-sweeper to clean the room?"

"I . . . I think I said that, yes. Why?"

"Finally, both Dr. Fell and I were present when Kitty crept in after eavesdropping. She gave you a look that I didn't like. She swept up the knitting-bag and hared out?"

"I'm not quite sure what you mean by 'a look you didn't like,' dear. But it's true about the rest."

"Just take it easy, Lucia!" urged Butler, who found the scene being recreated so pictorially that he seemed to see it on the night of the murder. He saw Kitty using the carpet-sweeper, and the water-bottle under the ivory crucifix, and all of them waiting for Dick Renshaw's return.

"You told Kitty, earlier in the evening, to 'do' the room? But she didn't actually start until past eleven o'clock?"

"That's right. Because. . . ."

"Because she knew that either you, or the tireless Miss Cannon, would be there to watch every move she made?"

"Well—I suppose so. Agnes always *is* under your feet, somehow."

"Now tell me, Lucia." Butler's voice grew as stealthy as a tiger. "In any of the other bedrooms in your house, are there water-bottles and glasses just like the one in your husband's bedroom?"

(Butler had noted, out of the corner of his eye, that Dr. Fell was listening with interest and ferocious approval. Now the good doctor listened intently for Lucia's reply.)

"Yes! In all the rooms! Dick," and the hatred in Lucia's face was almost frightening. "Dick thought *his* habit was good for people."

"Now think about Kitty. In the interval before she cleaned the room, Kitty would have plenty of time to dissolve a dose of antimony into another water-bottle? And conceal this second bottle in the knitting-bag?"

Again a pause.

Lucia seemed shaken as though by physical hands. Her mouth was loose. Dim comprehension began to glimmer in the blue eyes.

"Pat, what on earth are you—?"

"Don't try to reason. Let me do that. Just shut your eyes and remember!"

"A-all right. I'll try."

"Kitty went in to clean the room. She picked up the water-bottle from the bedside table. She walked into the bathroom, emptied the bottle into the wash-basin, rinsed the bottle, and filled it again. Was she carrying the knitting-bag at this time?"

"Yes!"

"You—and Miss Cannon too, I think—were watching her from the middle of the bedroom? Good! I noticed," Butler closed his own eyes, visualising, "I noticed that the wash-basin in that bathroom is just opposite the door to the bedroom?"

"Just opposite, Pat. You can—"

"So you could see Kitty's back as she stood at the wash-basin?"

"Yes, of course!"

"Where was Kitty carrying the knitting-bag then? Was she carrying it at one side, or in front of her?"

"In—in front of her, I think. Yes! Like an apron."

"So that you couldn't actually see what she was doing?"

"Not exactly, no."

"You heard, in fact, the very obvious sound of her pouring out, rinsing, and filling the old bottle. *And that's all you can testify?*"

"Yes."

The black candles burned steadily, without a breath of air. Butler straightened up. He did not question; he stated.

"What she did, we now see, was very simple. She slipped the old bottle, full of clean water, into her knitting-bag. From this knitting-bag she took out the new bottle already hidden there: the poisoned bottle. This second bottle she carried back to the bedside table, put it down, and inverted the tumbler over it to complete the picture."

Sweat was heating at Butler's temples, but he appeared as cool as a judge as he slowly turned to Dr. Fell.

"The miracle explained," he said. "What do you think of it?"

16

D R. FELL, making no sound on that carpet despite his bulk and his stumping cane, slowly moved round the altar and came down to face Butler. While he stood in front of that vicious tapestry, his solid English presence drained effect from it like the presence of Old King Cole.

But, as he left it, there now seemed to be a poison in the air. They were again aware of the bloodshot eye in the roof, the dimness of even fourteen candles, the odour of Satanism itself.

Dr. Fell, as though a little appalled and less red in the face, looked Butler up and down.

"Sir, you amaze me," he said.

"Pleasantly, I hope."

"Yes. And with considerable admiration."

"I've got the truth, of course?"

"Well . . . not exactly. Wait!" urged Dr. Fell, before the other could snap with protest. Dr. Fell squeezed his eyes shut, and ruffled at his temples under the heavy mop of hair.

"Never have I known a man," he declared, looking at Butler, "who stood so face to face with truth. With the simple but very ugly truth you stand forehead to forehead, eye to eye, nose to nose, pressed together. Archons of Athens! You have reasoned closely and accurately. Move your head one inch from that mirror-stare against truth, and you will see it. Not otherwise."

"Kitty Owen, I tell you, is as guilty—"

"Ah, yes. Kitty. Put her under severe police-examination, as I shall tell Hadley to do, and you may well break her down. You may not learn the name of the murderer-cum-head-of-witch-cult, though you have a sixty-forty chance in your favour. But you will probably clear Mrs. Renshaw of any charge of murder."

"Pat," Lucia whispered, "I still can't understand any of this. But I do think you're rather wonderful."

Again, for once in his life, Butler did not tut-tut a compliment while quietly preening himself about it.

"Look here!" he said. "Did Kitty put poison in that bottle?"

"No."

"Then what in hell are we talking about?"

"Hell," Dr. Fell answered simply.

"If you know so much about all this," Butler shouted, "why don't you tell me?"

"I can tell you," retorted Dr. Fell, "and tomorrow morning I will. But it will lead, I fear, to one of my eternal wanderings round Robin Hood's barn. Confound it, sir, we came here to find the records of the witch-cult! We *must* find them or we can get nowhere! We...."

Here his eye fell on Dr. Arthur Bierce. All three of them had forgotten Bierce. Bierce, his cap pushed to the back of his freckled skull, his sandy eyebrows drawn down, had never left off staring at the tapestry behind the altar.

"I am sorry," he spoke in a normal voice, swallowing a large Adam's apple, "I've been so little and so dismal a help in this investigation...."

"Little help?" exclaimed Dr. Fell. "My good sir, next to Mr. Butler's reconstruction, you have made the most helpful remark that has been made tonight."

"Thank you," said the physician, who either did not believe him or did not even hear him. "But I can help with the search. Tear down the hangings and rip up the cushions! Destroy the altar! Look there!"

His bony finger quivered as he pointed.

"It's a luxurious prie-dieu," he said. "I don't like a prie-dieu; it smells of Popery—but even Popery should not be defiled. Burn it!"

"Take it easy, man!" Dr. Fell thundered in vague alarm. "This place must be kept intact for the police. And cushions are no good, or chairs; we want a *large* mass of papers. Shall we begin?"

And they plunged into the search.

It was just on midnight, by Butler's watch, when they began. The black candles, first in a veil so light that it was scarcely perceptible, had already begun to diffuse some scented mist which had an odd effect on the brain if you went close; but they needed those candles for extra light in the thick red gloom of the chapel.

The walls and floor were of heavy concrete under hangings and carpet, excluding a secret hiding-place. The pillows, after examination, they kicked to a heap which left clear a good deal of floorspace. In a cupboard set into concrete, to the left of the apse, Bierce found priestly vestments of the finest quality: several chasubles, one sewn with occult characters in silver, another embroidered with a pig and a woman in flesh-tint.

On a shelf there was one of the prized 'missals' of the Black Mass, red characters on vellum. Bierce translated one sentence from the Latin, "We shall be saved through the flesh," then he flung the missal across the room.

"Easy!" said Dr. Fell out of a thin-scented haze.

But, on another shelf where it could be moved to the altar for worship, there was a heavy statuette of Satan in the form of a black goat. Bierce tried to smash it by flinging it down on the floor. It only rebounded and rolled to lie face upwards, grinning, under the staring eye-light.

Wilder and wilder grew the scenes in the red gloom. Lucia, she said, was convinced the records must be in some pouch or bag fastened behind one of the hangings. The hangings swayed out and rippled as she hurried behind them, emerging from them with startling effect, and going back again.

"For my choice," said Butler, "it's one of these confessional boxes."

"My dear sir," protested Dr. Fell, who was examining the ebony pillars which supported the roof, "you couldn't hide—"

And evidently you couldn't. Butler stood before one of them, against the middle of the right-hand side-wall. This grotesque parody reminded him, for some reason, of two high magician's cabinets set side by side. Their two doors, in open carving twined with designs of Satanic triumph, opened outwards. On one side sat the leader of the cult, in black goat-mask to the shoulders, head inclined towards the other compartment: where a woman whispered of. . . .

But the floors were too thin, the carved roofs too narrow, for any concealment.

There were two dull crashes as Lucia deliberately knocked over metal braziers in corners, as though she hated them for some disservice. Dr. Fell, who had somehow managed to stand on a chair, was studying the heavy carved roof-beams. Dr. Bierce, with a surgical knife—no action now seemed fantastic—carefully ripped up the hard altar-couch to find concealed papers. Half-past twelve. Ten minutes to one. . . .

"No," Dr. Fell said dully. "It's no good."

At one o'clock they gathered, four begrimed searchers not quite in their right minds, near the front of the altar.

Bierce still held the surgical knife, with which he had been trying experiments on cushions and carpet. Lucia had lost her scarf; her old black gown, as well as her bare arms and shoulders, were smeared with dust. The haze from the flames of the black candles, burning down, drifted out past them through the chapel.

"The records aren't here," said Dr. Fell in the same heavy voice. "They ought to be, but they aren't. I regret to tell you that I am beaten. They may be hidden away, perhaps at some bank. . . ."

Lucia whipped round. "Whose shadow was that?" she asked.

"What shadow?" Dr. Bierce looked up from his surgical knife.

"Just now! It moved behind one of the pillars there. It—it seemed larger than life."

It would not be true to say that a wing of panic brushed that group. Yet Satan, even if we consider him as an abstraction, can become oppressive in his presence.

"There's nobody here." Bierce spoke curtly. But he replaced the surgical knife, and closed his medicine-case with a snap. "Those candles are throwing our own shadows. As for the candles, I want to have them analyzed. There's some kind of accursed magical scent that's putting images in front of my eyes, and . . . let's get out!" he cried thickly.

"I agree," grunted Dr. Fell.

"And I!" said Lucia, with her hand at her throat. "Ready to go, Pat?"

" 'Magical,' " said Butler, staring into vacancy. Then he woke up, all his theatricalism flowering.

"No, my dear," he smiled. "You people go on up and stand by the outer door of the chapel upstairs. I shall join you in exactly three minutes."

"Pat, what's wrong? Why do you want to stay down here?"

"Because," answered Butler, "I know where the records are hidden."

To use the word "sensation" would be a very mild description of the effect.

"A while ago," continued Butler, filling his lungs but speaking in the same easy tone, "I proved how your husband was really murdered. When I challenged Dr. Fell, he replied with mumbo-jumbo or plain mystification. Very well. But now, with your kind permission, I will do the mystification for a change. I promise to put those records in your hands in three minutes. Will you go upstairs and wait for me? Or shall we postpone it, like Dr. Fell's explanation, for tomorrow?"

And he leaned back against the black-and-red curtain of the wall, folding his arms.

"Look here, dash it all!" protested a genuinely puzzled Dr. Fell. "I only meant that. . . ."

"Sir, will you go?"

"We'll go," replied Dr. Bierce, taking a firm hold of Lucia's arm when Lucia began to turn back. "Three minutes, you said?"

"Three minutes."

Arms still folded, leaning against the wall beside the apse, Butler watched them move away in the red gloom. Lucia was protesting. Now they were at the little ebony-railed staircase, almost invisible. Now he was alone.

To be alone here, Butler hoped, wouldn't start his own nerves twitching like a drug addict's. All he had to fear was imagination. When he had first thought of that confessional box as a magician's cabinet on the stage, the idea should not have dropped away in his mind until it was jabbed to wakefulness by Dr. Bierce's term 'magical.'

The tops of magicians' cabinets, he had heard, were always made to *look* so shallow that nothing could be hidden in that shallow space. At a casual glance, especially at carving, the eye was deceived.

Butler, as quick on his feet as a cat, raced over to the parody confessional box he had examined before. He sat inside one compartment, which would have been occupied by the goat-deity. He closed the door of the compartment, with its black design of open scroll-work. Fishing out his pocket-lighter and snapping it into flame, he stood up to examine the roof.

The roof, on this side at least, was only plywood painted black.

Butler's heart was beating heavily. He ran the fingers of his right hand round the edges of the plywood. . . .

The whole thin underside of the roof fell down on hinges. When he saw it fall, showering him with paper-bundles, documents, notebooks, he instinctively shied back and sat down as though under attack.

"Got it!" he said aloud, hardly realizing that he actually had got it.

Papers or bundles, of all sizes, thumped or fluttered round him to fall on the floor of the box. They lay there at his feet, no small pile, while he sat in the confessor's seat and looked at them. Presently he raised his head to the door—and remained motionless.

Through the black Satanic scroll-work, very close, he was looking straight into the face of Gold-teeth.

Gold-teeth, with even his dental fittings. The upper lip, swollen badly and crossed with half-dried cracks, showed the two gleams below.

For perhaps two seconds, while both he and Butler remained motionless, every detail of appearance and every detail of thought went through Butler's mind.

Gold-teeth couldn't have got in here! Oh, yes he could. Lucia's key, to the door of the upper chapel, was in her handbag. That handbag, left behind with her coat at the Love-Mask Club, could quickly have been identified as belonging to the woman who ran away from the club with Patrick Butler. If Gold-teeth knew anything whatever about this red chapel. . . .

He did.

Butler, staring through the scroll-work, saw that Gold-teeth held his right hand a little away from his body. It gripped a small bundle of papers, some white and some grey or greenish, loosely fastened with a paper-clip.

Gold-teeth had been here before. Those papers he held were the only deadly or compromising documents in the files of the Murder Club. He had them now; but he wouldn't have them for long. These papers inside the box were rubbish.

" 'Ullo," said Gold-teeth through the black carvings.

"Hello," answered Butler—and instantly charged at the door.

He burst out of that confessional box like a mad bull, the flimsy door whacking back. Gold-teeth, still facing him, was backing away with a footwork which to anyone except Butler would have suggested the boxer.

Abruptly Butler stifled his rage, steadied his eyesight; he became bland and negligent, with a half-smile. They were both in an open space in front of the altar, with no black pillars or cushions against dark-red carpet. A little way to Butler's right, the black goat-face of Satan lay on the carpet and grinned up at the light of the eye.

"Hand 'em over," said Butler.

"Wot?"

"Those letters, or whatever they are."

Gold-teeth, still in soiled evening clothes except for collar or tie, seemed to have something else on his mind.

"You 'it me," he stated, and touched his swollen lip. His murderous eyes never moved.

"That's right. Care to be hit again?"

"You 'it me," said Gold-teeth. "You done it when I wasn't ready. But you done it like a amateur." The upper lip lifted. "You never done much fighting. Did you, mister?"

Butler smiled. Gold-teeth was half a head shorter than he; Gold-teeth was lean, stringy, bony. Nobody told his adversary that Bob Fitzsimmons, despite height, was in actual poundage something less than a middleweight.

"I said," repeated Gold-teeth, "you never done much fighting. Did you, mister?"

"I never bothered to learn."

" 'E never bothered to learn!" crowed Gold-teeth, with that mimicry which could drive a man mad. "Could you lick *me*?"

Butler merely looked at him and laughed.

For the first time Gold-teeth showed a human expression, a really human expression.

"Gawd's truth!" he said, with the veins standing out on his forehead.

He stuffed the bundle of papers swiftly into his pocket. His right hand darted to his left sleeve, and whipped out a closed razor. But he gripped the end of the razor, and flung it far away from him into the gloom; it made hardly a sound when it fell.

"I ain't got no razor," said Gold-teeth. "I ain't got no moley. I'm a-going ter give you an 'iding—fair and square."

"You think you can do it?"

Gold-teeth tapped the papers in his pocket. "Come and get 'em," he said.

Butler walked slowly towards him. And at the same moment, in the far corner of the room on the wall behind Butler's back, there was a very soft explosion with a gush of blue-yellow flame. A streak of fire rippled up the side of the curtain, it's light flashing out through the dim chapel.

"That?" jeered Gold-teeth. "That's only some little alarm-clock things, set to go off in lots of places. Lost your nerve, mister?"

That was when Butler sprang at him, leading with a right that would have been murderous if it had landed.

It did not land. Something else was happening.

For the next thirty seconds he was conscious not so much of any pain as of splintered confusion. His eyes didn't seem to work. Somewhere ahead, as he kept his head down and flailed out, there seemed to be a number of horizontal pile drivers. One was always in his face, always in his face, whichever way he twitched his head or forced Gold-teeth backwards. The other pile drivers, at all angles, smote in and struck, smote in and struck. . . .

Suddenly, to his surprise, he found himself lying on his side on the carpet. Vaguely he smelt smoke and saw yellow light, which he associated with his own head.

"No," said a hateful voice, hard-breathing, "you never done—"

Then came the shock of humiliation.

It ran through him before the voice completed that sentence. Never in his life, not even in school days, had he been brought so low as this. He had been made a fool of, shown up as clumsy and unskilled and a braggart, by someone whom he despised like dirt. In his mind he saw all his friends, and they were roaring with laughter.

"—done much fighting. Have you, mister?"

Patrick Butler bounced to his feet, and by sheer luck landed a belly-punch that nearly ended the fight. But Gold-teeth's retreating, weaving, dodging, didn't last long. The pile drivers smashed in again. They jolted Butler's head, banged his jaw, stabbed his stomach against his backbone. If he could only grip his hands round Gold-teeth—!

But he couldn't. He was on the floor again.

(*Comic-spectacle Butler. Licked by a spiv. Funniest thing in years. Remember how he lorded it?*)

Patrick Butler was on his feet again, though staggering. From those mental images he felt almost physically sick. He started to lash out at Gold-teeth; then, bleary-eyed and bewildered, he instinctively stopped.

Gold-teeth, too, had lost his head and forgotten where he was. Now he stared round stupidly.

With a *whoom* of expanding gases, the great altar-tapestry belled out like a sail as flame soared up over it. It dragged thinly, crumpled, and swept down across the altar, knocking over the candelabra and breathing fire-sparks above the carpet.

Three sides of the room were afire. On the right-hand wall, where it started, burning welts of tapestry sagged on blackened concrete; but it had gushed out across two roof-beams, preceded by a crackling of varnish. Black smoke held to the top of the room, wriggling its way; but a fine brownish haze crawled stifling into nostrils and mouth.

Butler and Gold-teeth looked at each other.

"What's the matter with you?" Butler yelled as well as he could. "Put up your hands!"

" 'R you crackers?"

Butler walloped out with a right-hander (always the right hand!) which Gold-teeth dodged because he was already running for the stairs. Butler, diving, caught him by one ankle and brought him to the floor with a crash.

Fire-puffs from the fallen candles bloomed along the carpet. A whole row of undisturbed cushions, stretching halfway across the chapel near the back, gathered into one gust of fire. Gold-teeth, kicking out maniacally, flapped like a landed fish and again screamed, "Crackers!"

Then his shoe-laces broke. Gold-teeth, freed and with one white sock of his evening clothes, raced towards the stairs. But the line of burning cushions lay across his most direct way. He was a prudent man; he darted to the right to circle them.

Butler, not a prudent man, raced straight for the cushions; staggered, and cleared them from a standing jump which landed him overbalanced to fall rolling on his side at the foot of the stairs.

Whether or not he had the strength now, he did it. He lifted the bronze statue of nymph-and-satyr, hoisting it with both hands above his head. He was three steps up, and had whirled round, when Gold-teeth reached the foot of the stairs.

Again they looked at each other. Both were coughing; words came in short spurts. Both were blinded and stung with smoke-tears. Gold-teeth lifted his lip.

"Wot's the game?"

"Don't move."

"Why not?"

"This bronze comes down on your skull. I can't miss."

"Come off it, mister! You won't stay there!"

"Why not?"

Gold-teeth grew frantic with reasonableness. " 'Cos we'd both burn to death! That's why!"

"Then we burn."

Gold-teeth's smoke-grimed face changed a little.

Behind him the crackle of the fire had thickened into a faint roar as roof-beams grew as bright as Christmas logs, and a gush of flame ran up the hangings of the fourth wall: intolerably vivid except where the fast-

blackening smoke strangled it. And the coughing, murderous dialogue
went on.

"Wotcher want?"

"Those letters."

"You ain't sane!"

"Stay there then."

Gold-teeth's streaming eyes strained upwards.

"There's a roof-beam all a-burning—" His scream became choked.
But he pointed above Butler's head, and kept on pointing until breath
returned. "She's a-shaking loose! She'll fall bang on your head!"

"I know that. Letters?"

Hitherto Butler had been scarcely conscious of the intense heat, as he
had been unconscious of injuries in the fight. Now the heat fanned him,
enveloped him, slipped a fiery mask on his face. The black smoke, now
pressing down, swirled closer. With a sudden crash the eye-light in the
roof exploded.

"Letters?" said Butler. He could scarcely see or breathe.

Gold-teeth made a dart for the stairs, but jerked back again as he saw
Butler's arms tighten to throw.

"Godamighty!" coughed Gold-teeth, shivering in an agony of reasonableness. Suddenly he pointed above. "She's a-going! She's—"

In the ceiling, with a long movement, something slithered and
ripped. And the burning roof-beam fell.

It crashed down some five inches in front of Butler's face, aureoled
with sparks. It hit the stair-banister without smashing the rail, because
its other end landed first. Then it spun over in a flaming wheel—straight
for Gold-teeth's face until its upward impetus swept it over his head to
thud in a geyser of fire beyond.

And it broke Gold-teeth's nerve as a stick is snapped. He dragged out
the paper-clipped bundle from his pocket.

"Wha' do?"

"Throw"—a gush of smoke billowed up the stairs—"on the step
where I am."

"Ain't sane! 'Ow I know you don't bash me anyway?"

Butler, despite a burning throat, would have found breath to speak
clearly if he spoke it in hell.

"The word of a gentleman."

Gold-teeth never knew, never guessed, that the look on his own face
at that word 'gentleman' brought him very close to death. Butler's arms

quivered as he held up the bronze weight; but he controlled himself.

A bundle of papers, white and grey and greenish, flew out of the murk and landed on the step by his right foot. Butler set his foot on it. Then, an intolerable weight released, he tipped the bronze statue to his left over the stair-rail.

"Get out."

Gold-teeth wavered, half paralyzed. "Wossat?"

"You fought fair. Withdraw all charges. Get out."

Gold-teeth hesitated. Then he ran stumbling up the stairs, unable even to cough, blinded and beaten, past Butler to the trap at the top of the stairs and out.

Butler, trying to shift his foot, reeled and almost pitched down the steps. Bending over, he seemed in his own mind to take minutes before he groped for and gathered up the hot bundle of papers. With fire crawling up the hangings beside him, he ascended the stairs.

In a room now impenetrable with smoke except where yellow gushes shot upwards and rolled, the black statuette of Satan grinned alone among the flames.

17

AT HALF past two on the following afternoon, Mr. Charles Denham sat in his office digesting lunch and glancing over the newspaper, which the morning's pressure of business had not enabled him to read.

It was Thursday, March 22nd, precisely one month to the day after the death of Mrs. Taylor. Though there has been much shifting-about of offices between barristers and solicitors in the Temple, after the blitzes and the V weapons, Charlie Denham steadfastly maintained his former rooms in an entry in Johnson's Court.

In his own privacy, sitting by his desk at a window opening on a narrow passage outside, Charlie Denham was as neat as a cat—the thin black line of moustache, the dark hair parted and polished, the steadfastness of purpose about him. A brisk coal fire burned in the grate.

Denham, for good moral effect, always brought the *Daily Telegraph* to the office. But invariably he read the *Daily Floodlight*, which, though of only a few pages, has managed to become more American, and infinitely worse American, than any American tabloid.

Frowning, Denham caught one headline:

PRIVATE INQUIRY AGENT
STRANGLED WITH RED BAND

And, in a hanger:

Have Clue, Police Say

The day outside the window was bitter cold, but clear and once or twice sunny. Denham ran his eye quickly down the story:

Shortly after six o'clock last night, the body of Mr. Luke Parsons, head of a Private Inquiry Agency, was found by a charwoman cleaning the offices of number 42b Shaftesbury Avenue, W.I. The victim was found sitting upright in the chair behind his desk. He was strangled with a red band or cord, looped round his neck and then slowly tightened by a pencil twisted round and round in the top. Previously he had been stunned by a blow on the head, police say.

Denham, frowning as though still more puzzled, gave an exclamation of annoyance. He read on, skipping.

Miss Margaret Villars, the dead man's secretary (picture on front page) states that Mr. Parsons appeared violently agitated since an interview with a client, who gave the name of Robert Renshaw, at 3.30 P.M. At 5 P.M. Mr. Parsons told Miss Villars that she could leave early. The time of death. . . .

On the desk at Denham's elbow, the telephone rang. He was impatient. But, when he heard from his clerk who wanted to speak to him, he became eager and almost schoolboyishly excited.

"Hello?" said the breathless voice of Joyce Ellis.

"Hello, Joyce," Denham replied, and eyed a memorandum pad. As though to hide fiercely repressed emotion, even when alone, he picked up a pencil and drew designs.

"Have you seen a newspaper?" Joyce asked.

"Yes." Denham was mildly disturbed. He sketched a couple of crosses and started on a house. "It's a bit unpleasant. I knew him slightly, Joyce."

In imagination, now, anyone could see Joyce, with her black bobbed hair and grave face and large grey eyes, sitting back to stare at the telephone.

"You knew him *slightly*? Isn't he one of your closest friends?"

"Good Lord, Joyce, I never—" Denham stopped. "Who are you talking about?"

"Pa—Mr. Butler!"

"Pat Butler?" Denham dropped the pencil. "What about him?"

"They never print the whole truth in the papers. It may be worse than they say. Not that I care, of course," Joyce said quickly, "but I do feel that. . . . Have you got the *Daily Telegraph* there?"

"Er—yes. Somewhere."

"Wait! I've got one here." There was a rustling of paper over the 'phone. "It's just a tiny item at the bottom of an inside page. It's headed, '*K.C. Injured in Fire.*'"

"Well?"

"I'll read it. It says, 'Mr. Patrick Butler, the famous K.C. sometimes called The Great Defender' "—Joyce's voice grew tense, with something like a sob in it, and then went on quietly—" 'was slightly injured in a fire which broke out early this morning in a church in Balham, S.W. Mr. Butler, whose injuries were mainly bruises, is understood to have received them in escorting others out of the church. The origin of the fire is as yet unknown.' "

Joyce broke off. "Charlie, what on earth was he doing in a church early in the morning?"

"I don't know."

"You're his friend. Couldn't you go round and make sure he's not badly hurt?"

"I'm very sorry for Pat, of course." Denham gripped the pencil hard. "But must he monopolize our conversation all the time?"

A pause. "I'm sorry."

"You could go and see him, couldn't you?" asked Denham, his face expressing a passionate hope that she would say no.

"I can't. Not yet."

"Good! I mean, that's most unfortunate. Why not?"

"Because I did go there. I wanted to give him some information." Joyce paused. "I don't mind his being inconsiderate; he can't help that. But when he started to be dramatic I rather preached him a sermon. So I said I wouldn't go back until I could prove who the real murderer is."

"Murderer? What do you know about that?"

"I think I've guessed all along," Joyce answered slowly. "But I can't prove it."

Denham hesitated, fingering the pencil and then throwing it down.

"Listen, Joyce!" (A clerk, if one had entered then, would have been astonished to see Charles Ewart Denham almost pleading.) "Let's forget Pat, can't we? Why not have dinner with me tonight? And I'll call on Pat this afternoon, if you like."

"Thanks awfully, Charlie. Dinner would be wonderful." Joyce added, "He lives in Cleveland Row. I wonder what's going on there now?"

What was going on now, at the house in Cleveland Row, could be described as a row or even a riot.

Dr. Gideon Fell, arriving on the doorstep behind a taxi-driver who lugged a box of books, was admitted by Mrs. Pasternack to a little eighteenth-century passage. The large wooden box bumped the floor.

The taxi-driver, off like a flash when Dr. Fell absent-mindedly handed him a pound note for a six-and-ninepenny drive, allowed Mrs. Pasternack to close the front door.

From beyond a closed, white-painted door on the left issued the sound of several angry voices.

"It's only the doctor, sir," Mrs. Pasternack whispered in apology.

"Now look here," said the voice of the doctor, evidently an old friend. "The swelling in your face has practically gone. You're lucky to have got off with only one black eye, and no teeth lost. Still, you've got 'em. Your body-bruises are painful, and so are your hands."

A Dublin accent answered him. "Ah, begob!" roared the voice of Patrick Butler. "And what would the likes of ye know about medicine?"

"Never mind what I know. The fact remains that Mr. . . . Mr. . . ."

"O'Brien, sorr," spoke up a hearty and confident voice, "Terence O'Brien."

"Mr. O'Brien," said the doctor, "is not going to give you a boxing-lesson today."

"'Tisn't that, Doctor!" said Mr. O'Brien with dignity. "But would ye believe it, now? The idjit expects me to tache him the noble art in one lesson!"

"And why the hell not, ye spalpeen?" yelled Patrick Butler.

"Ah, bejasus," moaned Mr. O'Brien. "I'll come again tomorrow."

"And so shall I," agreed the doctor.

Both of them, on their way out, passed Dr. Fell. Mrs. Pasternack tapped on the white door. Dr. Fell, maneuvering in, found himself in a rather small but admirable library; it's white-painted book-shelves rose to the ceiling on every side except that of the two windows facing Cleveland Row, and part of the wall opposite, where a log fire crackled under an Adam mantelpiece.

Patrick Butler, wearing a dressing-gown and not quite reasonably presentable, stood with his back to the fire. He resumed his normal speech and his easy air when Dr. Fell entered, but he was not calm. Gesturing towards the leather easy-chair at one side of the hearth, Butler sank back in the other chair beside the dictaphone.

For a time there was silence except for Dr. Fell's wheezy breathing.

"Are you—harrumph—feeling better?" asked the learned doctor.

"Frankly," replied Butler with a certain grimness, "not much. For one thing, it hurts to talk. But talking, sir, is a luxury in which I shall indulge myself even when the hearse carries me to the cemetery."

"Speaking of conversation," observed Dr. Fell, "did you 'phone Mrs. Renshaw this morning?"

Butler gritted his teeth, another painful process. But last night he had again dreamed of Joyce Ellis, and of kissing her as he had kissed Lucia. It exasperated him.

"I 'phone no woman," he said.

"My dear sir! Consider what happened last night!"

"I *am* considering it, believe me!"

"No, no! Mrs. Renshaw and Dr. Bierce and I were standing in the grounds outside both upper and lower chapel. We had no notion of a fight or a fire or anything else. All of a sudden, a smoky-faced man in something like evening dress staggered out of the door and ran for the front gate. A few moments later you appeared. Have you any idea of your appearance at that time?"

"Curiously enough, I had no time to think about it."

"You handed me the bundle of papers," persisted Dr. Fell, "made an elaborate apology for being longer than three minutes, and then collapsed in a dead faint!"

"I have never fainted in my life," Butler said coldly.

Dr. Fell made a hideous face and a bothered gesture.

"Well, say that you were momentarily indisposed. Mrs. Renshaw—don't grit your teeth!—took one look at you and your papers, and walked away. She was shocked and upset. Archons of Athens! Can't you consider women simply as women—"

"That is my invariable habit."

"—and not as feminine counterparts of yourself? How on earth she got home last night," scowled Dr. Fell, "I can't understand. She certainly didn't go with us." Dr. Fell reflected for a moment, his eye roving. "Finally," he added sharply, "I understand from Hadley that you refuse to prefer any kind of charge against this man George Grace, whom you call Gold-teeth."

Butler's mood changed. All thoughts of Lucia were swept out of his mind.

"Gold-teeth," he repeated, with soft and unholy relish.

Then he turned towards Dr. Fell an expression which gave even that seasoned person a qualm.

"I didn't know the fellow's name was George Grace," Butler said, "until I rang Hadley this morning. Do you know what was pasted on the outside of my window this morning? Two of them, one on each front window beside the door. Mrs. Pasternack found them. Look here!"

From the pocket of his dressing gown, with something very like tenderness, he took a curled and partly torn slip of paper whose printing—in block capitals—had been a little smeared by its removal from the window.

It said:

YOU AND ME HAVENT FINISHED. G.G.

An ember popped in the fireplace. It was growing colder as the afternoon drew on, with a suggestion of mist outside the windows.

"This is the showdown," said Butler, tapping the arm of his chair. "This is the third and last round."

"Yes," agreed Dr. Fell, and blinked at the floor.

Butler's voice began to rise. "Do you remember Hadley's offer last night? That they could easily arrange for me to get a firearms licence if I called at Scotland Yard?"

"Yes. I remember it."

"I've sent Johnson there. Johnson also bought a gun and ammunition. You see," Butler continued, "I've changed my mind since I talked to Hadley at Claridge's on Wednesday. These worms don't understand it if you merely outwit 'em. They don't know they're being outwitted. They understand only one thing."

From the other side of the chair, wincing as pain caught him, Butler fished up a Webley .38 revolver in an officer's leather holster.

"Let the so-and-so come," he breathed through stiff jaws. "Let him come tonight. I've stopped playing. Either I get him, or he gets me."

"If Gold-teeth visits you tonight," said Dr. Fell in a curious tone of voice, "you realize he will not be alone?"

"Good! Let him bring his pals. I don't mind."

Dr. Fell shook his head. That sense of disquiet nearing real alarm, which had been muttering inside him, grew again as palpable as the heat of a furnace.

"Gold-teeth's pals!" he said. "Very well. But I did not necessarily refer to them. Don't you see that, if anyone tries to kill you tonight, there will be two sets of enemies and two converging lines of attack?"

"How do you mean, two?"

"The leader of the witch-cult as well!" retorted Dr. Fell, beginning to fire up still further. "Dash it all, man! Gold-teeth, Em, a few unnamed others, we may class among the gangsters. I question whether any of them, with the exception of Gold-teeth, knows about the witch-cult."

"But Gold-teeth definitely does know!"

"Precisely. He knew enough to select just the right papers from all that mass in the hollow top of the confessional box, and leave the rest behind."

Butler's wits were whirling. Amid all the other excitements, he had almost forgotten those documents which nearly got him killed.

"What was in the papers?" he demanded.

"Enough," said Dr. Fell, "to smash the witch-cult and at least deeply incriminate its present leader."

"Consequently you think—?"

Dr. Fell puffed out his cheeks, with a flurry of the bandit's moustache, and rolled more uneasily in the leather chair.

"The head of the cult, and perhaps others too," he pointed out, "will be frantic. Who, presumably, got and read those papers? You did! Gold-teeth, when he rushed out of the chapel, never saw the rest of us. If he conveyed information to a higher-up, it was about you. You are the marked man."

For a moment Dr. Fell paused to draw a cigar case out of his baggy side-pocket, take out a cigar, and pierce it with a match-stick.

"Respectability!" he suddenly thundered, with distaste. "I tell you, my dear Butler, that all the gangsters in creation are no more dangerous than *that*," he snapped his fingers, "when compared with pious respectability about to be unmasked as something else. Seek first for the respectable! And you'll have the answer to the whole problem!"

Butler, tenderly weighing the Webley .38 in his hand, smiled a little.

"And yet," he said, "this goat-mask of the witch-cult seems chiefly good only at managing poison-murders in other cities."

Dr. Fell, in the act of lighting the cigar, gave him a sideways glance of consternation.

"Didn't Hadley say anything to you?" demanded Dr. Fell, blowing out smoke. "Haven't you looked at a newspaper today?"

"No."

"Your friend Luke Parsons, of 'Discretion Guaranteed,'" the doctor told him, "was strangled yesterday afternoon between five and six o'clock. It happened in his own office. He was stunned and then strangled with a long piece of elastic, privately dyed red."

Patrick Butler put down the revolver, and sprang to his feet. Through his mind for many hours—lost, but sometimes recurring—had gone those words 'band or cord or lace.' He stood with his hands dug into the pockets of his blue dressing gown, with the nightmare on him.

"Not the garter again?" he said.

"A form of it, of course. It was always used, by the witch-cult, in death by strangling, for one certain offence."

"What offence?"

"Betrayal," said Dr. Fell, and blew out a long cloud of cigar smoke.

There was a silence. Butler, with a guilty knowledge that he had paid the money for betrayal, called up in mind the sweating, terrified face with the drooping dyed moustache. He retreated from it; he wouldn't face it.

"Modern secret societies, you know," Dr. Fell mused, "are mere tyros in their quickness to flash out and kill. In Scotland, in 1618, a man named John Stewart was to go on trial for witchcraft. He was fettered in his cell when two clergymen—Scottish ministers, mind you!—visited him in his cell. The visitors had hardly left when some officers of the court entered to escort Stewart to the courtroom. They found him already dead, strangled (I quote), 'with a tait of hemp, or string made of hemp, supposed to have been his garter or string of his bonnet.' "

Dr. Fell's cheeks distended, and he blew a smoke ring.

"Then," he said, "there was that weird business of John Reid. Again in Scotland, Renfrewshire, in 1698. He was to go on trial for witchcraft; and they found him strangled with his own neckcloth. Again I quote:

" 'It was concluded that some extraordinary Agent had done it, especially considering that the Door of the Room was secured, and that there was a board set over the window which was not there the night before when they left him.'

"By thunder," exclaimed Dr. Fell, "it's among our first locked-room problems! The locked room, to ignorant persons, is supposed to exist only in the minds of fiction-writers. Even an old duffer like myself can name half a dozen real ones offhand. Er—by the way. . . ."

Butler was not listening.

"I've brought you," pursued Dr. Fell, "a box of selected books on witchcraft and its allied arts. Some of the early writers, like Scot or

Glanvil, you may find heavy going. But the later authorities, Notestein and Summers and Murray and L'Estrange Ewen and Olliver, are both sound and easier reading than most of the older ones."*

"Dr. Fell! Wait! Hold on!"

Again the wood fire crackled and popped. All day Butler had been trying to look at it casually, without having it remind him of any event last night. But the black goat-face of a statue in the fire came back to him among these logs. And there was a worse matter now.

"Luke Parsons!" he said. "What time did you tell me he died? Between five and six o'clock?"

"Yes. About that."

"I left the man at four o'clock!"

"So Hadley tells me. The description of you was good." Then Dr. Fell spoke sharply, all attention. "Parsons's secretary testified he didn't leave his office, and had no more visitors. But he did make a 'phone call just as soon as you left; the secretary doesn't remember the number. Within two hours, probably much less. . . ."

Dr. Fell's hand made a savage chopping motion in the air.

"Rather quick work. Hey?" he added.

"But how can you be absolutely certain it was a witch-cult murder?"

"The police have a clue. I mean they actually have, though it isn't mentioned in the press." Again Dr. Fell drew a deep wheezy breath, and looked up. "You observed, probably, that Parsons's office wasn't very clean or tidy? Oh, ah! In the dust on his desk, somebody drew three more reversed crosses."

"That finishes it," Butler said after a pause.

"I'm afraid so. Anybody could have entered that block of offices, after the secretary left at five o'clock, without being noticed. It's only one flight up. And no place is so anonymous as a business-place."

Butler looked at the fire, and saw Parsons's face as well as the goat-head's.

"One murderer." He kicked at the logs. "Mrs. Taylor and Dick Renshaw and Luke Parsons—one murderer!"

*Reginald Scot, The Discouerie of Witchcraft (third edition from first of 1584; London, 1665). Joseph Glanvil, Saducismus Triumphatus (London, 1681). C. W. Olliver, An Analysis of Magic and Witchcraft (Rider & Co., 1928). C. L'Estrange Ewen, Witchcraft and Demonianism (Heath Cranton, 1933). Margaret Alice Murray, The Witch-Cult in Western Europe. Montague Summers, The History of Witchcraft and Demonology (Kegan Paul, 1926). Wallace Notestein, A History of Witchcraft in England from 1558 to 1718 (Washington, 1911).

"The murder of Parsons," Dr. Fell said dryly, "would not have been trusted to anybody like Gold-teeth or Em. So you see, my dear fellow, that with two lines of attack converging against you. . . ."

Butler picked up from the chair the leather holster with the Webley. Then he shouted for his chauffeur. "Johnson!" he bellowed. "Johnson!"

When Johnson entered, stolid and bullet-headed as ever, with his chauffeur's cap in his hand, Butler was leaning against the mantelpiece with his most negligent eighteenth-century pose.

"By the way, Johnson," he said in the voice which could charm anybody. "Did you put up the practice targets in the cellar?"

"Yessir. Against piles of sandbags. No chance of trouble then."

"Now look here, old man." Butler was like an elder brother. "This is Thursday: your day off, and Mrs. Pasternack's too. Didn't I tell you both to leave three hours ago?"

Johnson concentrated hard on the cap in his hands. "Rather stay, sir, if you don't mind. I'm a handy bloke lots of ways."

"Nellie will be furious, you know."

"Nellie can wait."

"I can't do it, old man. Didn't you hear what I told Mr. Hadley over the 'phone?"

"Well, sir—"

"I told him," Butler explained agreeably, "that if he dared to give me any alleged 'police protection,' I should take great pleasure in shooting the ears off any ruddy copper who appeared. This is my show, Johnson. You're an Englishman. Can't you understand that?"

"Very good, sir."

"Then you promise that you and Mrs. Pasternack will be out of this house in ten minutes?"

Johnson nodded. He went to the door and turned. He did not speak loudly, but his voice held a violence deeper than that.

"Give 'em something-something'd blank, sir," the voice burned. "Shove it up their something-something'd this-and-that!"

"Thanks, Johnson," said the delighted Butler, "I'll try."

The door closed. Butler took the Webley from its holster, swung open the barrel so that the ends of the brass cartridge-cases gleamed, and snapped it shut with a click which sounded loudly in the quiet room.

"Gold-teeth!" he added.

"For the love of Bacchus," roared Dr. Fell, "will you tell me why you still have such an animus against Gold-teeth? From the—er—I suspect bowdlerized account you gave us last night, you broke his nerve. . . ."

"Oh, yes. That was easy."

"And got exactly what you wanted. Then what's still wrong with you?"

(He floored me twice. He could have done it till I was senseless. He made me look clumsy and idiotic and helpless. My ancestors had a good code: there are some things you don't square except with steel or a bullet.)

Aloud Butler said, "There's another matter between us, as you imagine."

"What makes you think he'll be here tonight?"

"Those papers on the window, for one thing. And of course I sent him as insulting a telegram as possible, care of the Love-Mask Club. He may not get the telegram, but he'll get the message. I warned him what to expect."

"Guns?"

"Naturally!" Butler's eyebrows went up. "I told him to bring one." Then Butler chuckled.

"It took a bit of explaining," he added, "to get all that past the post-office as a joke. But it worked."

With the colour of Dr. Fell's face, it is never possible for him to achieve any pallor. But, aside from breathing out gusts of smoke past the cigar, he spoke in a comparatively mild tone.

"And now, in addition to a possible gun-battle in Cleveland Row, you have the more subtle leader of the witch-cult approaching from another direction. Man, you don't understand!"

"No," said Butler, rounding the syllable. "No, I don't understand. But I am going to understand, according to your own promise."

"Hey?"

"Last night," Butler stated with great distinctness, "I showed you the only possible way in which Dick Renshaw could have been murdered—if we exclude Lucia, which I do. I proved that Kitty Owen was the only possible guilty one. I showed how a substitute water-bottle, in the knitting-bag, was replaced for a really poisoned bottle. All you did was gibber in meaningless phrases. But you swore you'd explain to-morrow. All right—this is tomorrow."

"Yes," sighed Dr. Fell, in a dull voice. "I think I'd better explain."

Butler sat down in his chair, his arm hanging over the chair-arm, his forefinger in the trigger-guard of the Webley.

"Let's begin with essentials," Butler suggested. "We have, as I said, three murders and one murderer."

Dr. Fell frowned. "In a sense, yes."

"In a sense?"

"Yes. One of the alleged murders—" He stopped, disturbed. "Then there is the question of servants. In this affair we have two maidservants of extraordinarily different character.

"One is Mrs. Taylor's maidservant, Alice Griffiths, the conventional middle-aged domestic. Now I know Alice Griffiths was telling the truth, just as I know Joyce Ellis is innocent. But the other one is Mrs. Renshaw's maidservant, Kitty Owen. And Kitty Owen is not a conventional domestic, and she is not telling the truth. Whereas she ought to be below suspicion."

"One of the things I like about you," commented Butler, with real interest, "is the pellucid clarity of your style. Addison is nowhere. Macaulay is left at the post. Anatole France swoons with envy. Curse it, can't you say a plain thing in a plain way?"

"Certainly."

"Then what do you mean by 'below suspicion'?"

"In a detective story"—Dr. Fell puffed at the cigar—"no person is above suspicion. But there are several types who are below it. Any person serving as a detective, for instance. Any minor character. Any servant: because a servant, who may only enter to say 'The Archbishop awaits' is a wooden mask without a character to be read. But Kitty Owen, by thunder, is in a different class. And finally . . . But I had better tell you. I may—er—have unconsciously misled you last night."

And Dr. Fell began to explain.

18

WHEN Dr. Fell began to speak, the hands of the little marble clock on the mantelpiece stood at ten minutes to four. When he finished, the clock had just pinged out half-past five.

Patrick Butler, sick at heart despite himself, sat with his head in his hands and his eyes closed.

True, it had been a lively session. Butler's quick mind, with its additional information and its sharp inferences, built up the case almost as much as Dr. Fell. It was an intellectual exercise; he had to do it.

Except for the necessary verifying of some details, the case lay complete as a jigsaw puzzle on a table. But, unlike a jigsaw, it was simple. Unlike a jigsaw, its clues were bright colours which leaped to the eye. Finally, a fact unknown to those who gabble ignorantly about jigsaws, it moved with action and was rounded out with character.

Ping! went the clock on the mantelpiece.

"You see?" inquired Dr. Fell.

The fire had dropped to red-veined white ash, with a few black stumps beyond the andirons. The room was chilly and almost dark, as Butler realized with a start. Five-thirty. He must get himself into fighting-spirit for. . . .

He got up, with difficulty from the pain of bruises. From a large wood basket he picked up several logs, and dropped them on the fire amid an uprush of sparks. Since he had landed so few good blows last night, it was odd that his hands were so numb. He switched on shaded wall candles on either side of the mantelpiece.

"Better close the curtains," he said.

Still sick at heart, he walked across to the wall opposite the fireplace, and looked out of the windows. In this part of Cleveland Row, the open and paved space of Stable Yard stretched as lifeless as a byway in ancient Rome. Over to his right, a dim street-lamp touched the blackish red-brick of the empty west wing of York House. Opposite, some little distance away, loomed the ghostly arches of what had been the Museum.

Near one arch, a shadow moved and melted. They were watching already.

Butler swept shut the curtains, and came back to the fireplace.

"It's hellish!" he burst out. "Not necessarily the murders; but when you think who is the head of the witch-cult now. It's"—he touched his chest, groping for words—"what's inside."

"Oh, ah," agreed Dr. Fell.

Wearily the doctor hoisted himself up, leaning heavily on the cane.

"Sir," he intoned, "I am no more good as a help to you than I should be at mountain-climbing. But may I remain?"

"No, sorry. You understand why."

Dr. Fell studied him uneasily. "Look here, man! There's no reason to be upset!"

"I am not upset," answered Butler, looking him in the eyes. "There is no reason why I should be."

"The documents you gave me last night definitely prove that Richard Renshaw was the former head of the cult, and Mrs. Taylor his assistant. Also a third naturally to succeed Renshaw! Therefore. . . ."

"Forgive me, Dr. Fell, but it's getting late."

Butler had in his mind, along with other things, that movement of a shadow in bleak Stable Yard.

"I'll go, then," said Dr. Fell, who seemed to sense this. "Here is my 'phone number at Hampstead, if you should want it."

"Thank you," said Butler, putting the slip of paper in his pocket.

He led the way to the door, his nerves tingling. The Webley revolver was in the deep right-hand pocket of his dressing gown, though the pocket would not conceal it and his hand on the walnut grip seemed as obvious as a waving flag. Dr. Fell, of course, stumbled straight into the box of books on the floor of the passage inside the front door.

"I am clumsy," apologized Dr. Fell, somewhat unnecessarily. "Still, you might while away your time reading some of these books. Many of them I found in Mrs. Taylor's house. I wonder if her ghost is hovering tonight."

"Somebody's hovering tonight," said Butler, with his left hand on the knob of the front door.

"Visitors already?"

"Oh, nothing much. But, when you're outside, don't loiter. Go straight left, and then left again up St. James's Street. Get a taxi if you can find one."

And he opened the door.

"Sir," replied Dr. Fell, removing his shovel hat, "I say good-night to a man who, despite certain—harrumph—eccentricities, I admire very much."

For a minute or two Patrick Butler stood in the open doorway, silhouetted against the dim light behind. Again the tingling ran through him, except to his head. Though he despised athletics, he was a good horseman and a first-class pistol-shot. How, except for a certain numbing distraction, he would have enjoyed a meeting with Gold-teeth then!

The cold air fanned up through his dressing gown. He could smell mist without seeing it, except in a thin blur round the street-lamp. Again, as Dr. Fell's elephantine tread and the tap of his cane faded away, he glanced round the bleak, lost square called Stable Yard.

The Museum, yes. One of the supports of an arch, yes! Just faintly edged out of shadow, someone was standing there and looking at him.

Far away, a taxi hooted faintly.

Butler's right hand did not move; never aim at anything you don't mean to shoot. The seconds ticked past. . . .

Very deliberately, allowing ample time for something or someone to move, Butler stepped back inside and closed the door. After consideration, he turned the key in the lock.

And why not, it occurred to him sardonically, a gun-battle in Cleveland Row? After all, and fairly recently, hadn't there been a running gun-fight in cars through the West End? Before the war, Londoners would have considered that episode so fantastic that it could have occurred only in an American film; and probably exaggerated even in America.

Moving back from the front door, Butler himself stumbled slap over that box of books. It brought him back to the distraction, the head of the witch-cult, which kept him from thinking with sensible concentration about Gold-teeth.

At the top of the open wooden box his eye caught a pamphlet, dust-grey with the age of three centuries, and a part of the title: ". . . *Lewd and Unholie Designs of.* . . ."

"This has got to stop," Butler said aloud.

In the dining-room, just across from the library, the telephone began to ring.

Since the departure of Johnson and Mrs. Pasternack long ago, the whole house had been so quiet that the *ping* of the small clock in the library could be heard anywhere. The clamour of a telephone-bell tore silence to bits.

Butler hurried into the dining-room. Mrs. Pasternack had drawn the curtains there, and set out a cold dinner under the dim-gleaming crystal chandelier. With a certain hesitation Butler picked up the 'phone.

"Pat?" asked the calm voice of Charles Denham.

Butler considered for a moment. Then his heartiest tone animated the mouthpiece.

"Hul-lo, Charlie! What's up?"

"I promised to come round and see you, Pat. But I was so swamped under with business that . . . how are you?"

"Never more fit in my life, old boy! Why not?"

Slight pause. "But there was an item in the press to say you'd been hurt in a fire! Yes, and in a church and in the middle of the night. Never knew you to be inside a church at all," commented Denham, whose orthodoxy was notorious and strict.

"It was a private chapel on an old estate," said Butler. "We were sky-larking, that's all. No harm done."

"Then I needn't worry about you?" The tone was chilly.

"Not in that way, no. Thanks for ringing up. Good-bye."

Butler replaced the 'phone, and sat for a moment deep in thought. When he roused himself, he was looking at the cold dinner on the table. That meal, which Mrs. Pasternack had queued for hours to assemble, was so meagre as to seem comic and even apologetic. Patrick Butler did not mind this. What he did mind, to put the matter as civilly as possible, was the recollection of a happy, oily voice speaking on the radio, assuring listeners that never in their lives had they been healthier than on their present diet.

Butler got up. The window-curtains were closed, but he peered out through a chink.

There were now two men in Stable Yard, watching the house.

Quickly but without hurry Butler set about his preparations. First he closed and fastened all the shutters in the downstairs rooms. After that he locked the back door.

The best household safeguards, a chatty burglar had once informed him, were ordinary old-fashioned shutters; you cannot open them without too much noise. Patrick Butler did not want to keep off attack; he wanted to know exactly where it came from.

His own footsteps, creaking on old wood, made the only noise as he went upstairs. Not even a wainscot creaked, as it usually did. Upstairs he closed and locked the shutters, ending with his own bedroom at the front.

Though he wore pyjamas under his dressing gown, he decided he would not bother to get dressed. Contempt for Gold-teeth and Company (pleasure began again) would be shown better like this. Threading a leather belt through the slits in the revolver-holster, he buckled it round his waist and fitted the Webley into the holster. And yet. . . .

"Clumsy under that dressing gown, though," he said aloud. "If I could—"

Got it! And characteristically. Whipping the cord out of the dressing gown, he fastened the dressing-gown collar round his pyjama-neck and shoulders with inside safety pins. The dressing gown hung over him like a duellist's cloak, leaving his arms free inside.

Still dissatisfied with the back door, he sauntered downstairs. Against the locked door he set the back of a chair, and on it he piled such a top-heavy edifice of pots and pans and saucepans that the slightest movement of the door would have brought down banging pandemonium. Butler took an artistic pride in this, setting a kitchen-funnel on top like a hat.

Now let 'em come!

With a grim sense of pleasure, he stalked to the front door and opened it. He stood in the doorway, like a man taking the air of an evening, and looked out towards Stable Yard. Where before there had been two watchers, now there were three.

The cold war, eh? But you needed only the superior patience of superior intelligence.

Closing the door but leaving it unlocked, Butler strolled back into the library. With the library door left open, he could watch that front door from the other end by the fire.

All evening they would gather and stare, like motionless cats, under the curious impression that his nerve would break. Was that the notion? In that case, he would show his detachment by sitting down— comfortably—and giving the dictaphone an account of the whole case against the real murderer. If only (Oh, God!) if only he didn't keep seeing a face without its mask.

Besides, he couldn't possibly use a gun against. . . .

(*Stop it!*)

Butler, with a few pain-wrenches, swung round his own easy-chair by the fire so that he could keep an eye sideways on the front door through the open library door. The fire was burning brightly again. The little clock pinged the half-hour after six.

"I haven't talked to you," he said to the dictaphone, "since I made some notes yesterday afternoon. Let's see."

He pushed the pointer a little back, to catch the thread of what he had been saying before he switched off. Then he set the machine in motion, and reversed the mechanism so that the tube should speak instead of record.

His own voice—a microcosm, from a court in Lilliput—popped out of the speaker.

"*Lucia Renshaw, from the first, showed a fondness amounting to passion for—for P. B.*" Here the speaking-tube paused, and gave a slight embarrassed throat-clearing. "*Was this,*" it went on, "*because P. B. bears a strong resemblance, in voice and general appearance, to L. R.'s late husband, Dick Renshaw? Has she unconsciously transferred her affection to a man who looks like him?*"

Abruptly Butler switched off.

With unsteady hands he took the wax cylinder from its spindle. He got up, turned round, and flung down the cylinder on the stone hearth. The smash made it sound harder than wax; its pieces flew spinning over the hearth and into the fire.

Butler sat down again, putting on another wax record. His own silliness! His own stupidity!

"I now dictate," he began in his richest voice, "a complete record of the facts in what we shall call the Witch-Cult Murders."

Never once was he unconscious of that front door, of the Webley at his hip, of the box of cartridges on the other side of his chair. At the same time, in ordered logic and with precise phrase, his voice flowed on. He finished one cylinder, put it in its container in the rack below, and replaced it.

Still the fluent voice went on. How many motionless figures now waited in Stable Yard or Cleveland Row? Would they try to rush an unlocked front door? But the voice, the brain, kept these matters in a separate compartment.

". . . thus we begin to understand," he was saying, "the workings of the murderer's mind. New paragraph.

"Let us say that I, for instance, commit a murder. It bulks large in my mind; it touches everything. Unless I am a consummate actor, I cannot help in some instance betraying—by a slip of speech, a gesture, an expression—the sense of guilt which fills me, even though this may go unnoticed.

"But let us suppose, again for instance, that someone quite sincerely thinks and believes that he or she has not committed a murder? That person will never think of the crime at all. Since there is no sense of guilt, there will be only an innocent turn of hand or eye or mouth to any questions put either by private investigators or by the police."

Abruptly Butler stopped, his finger releasing the button.

The thought which struck him, at once infuriating and ludicrous, made him plunge across the room until he remembered to hurry back and shut off the dictaphone.

Those watchers outside: what if they weren't enemies at all, but police-officers on the alert? It wasn't likely that Hadley would have sent as many as three men; on the other hand, it would explain their silence.

Butler stalked to the front door, opened it, and went out. He cared not a curse (if it even occurred to him) about going across Cleveland Row and into Stable Yard in dressing gown and pyjamas and slippers. Besides, it was a hidden nook with few or no passers-by.

The mist had thickened; the street lamp was a spark. Butler felt hard asphalt under his slippers, and a sense of loneliness among dead houses, when he emerged into Stable Yard. There were four men watching now.

Two of them were behind arches of the Museum. One stood at the far end of York House, just outlined against shadow. The fourth was half invisible against a line of iron railings whose gate led to a path down into the Mall.

"Is anybody here a police-officer?" said Butler. His voice, here, seemed to have an echo. "If anybody is, speak up!"

Nobody spoke. Nobody moved. There was the slight scrape of a foot.

The right-hand side of Butler's dressing gown had been flung back. He held the Webley ready with hammer at full cock, weight of the gun balanced on second joint of second finger.

"Last chance if this is a joke!"

It wasn't a joke.

At the same time Butler became conscious of two foolish things done in anger: they could get behind him, if there were more of them; and bad light made very poor shooting.

He heard the scrape of his own slippers as he began to back away. A small pebble rolled and bounced. Familiar London chimney pots enclosed a lost arena. Over there, in the Museum, they had once exhibited the original door of Newgate Prison and a reconstruction of the condemned cell.

(*These aren't police-officers. They're not even Gold-teeth's thugs. They're members of the witch-cult, sweating in their respectability. But they think I'm the only one who knews. And they've got to kill me.*)

Butler reached his own front door. This time he locked it quickly. He also was sweating, but not from any usual kind of fear. In his imagination, at least, they were gathering and gathering outside: directing against this house a silent pressure of evil.

"Respectability!" Dr. Fell's voice came back to him in contempt and scorn. "I tell you, my dear Butler, that all the gangsters in creation are no more dangerous than *that*," a snap of the fingers, "compared with pious respectability about to be unmasked as something else."

Butler eased forward the hammer of the Webley, replaced it in the holster, and shook his dressing gown into place.

Probably he wouldn't need it. Probably there wasn't a gun out there. But—someone must come to kill him.

Meantime. . . .

He had his dictating to complete. He was tolerant; if it had not been for the silent way of murder, he might not even have blamed the witch-cult. They sought some kind of distraction in this dismal existence. Once, when the individualist had been a national pride, England had stood alone in her glory; and her lightest breath shook the world. Now the man was subjugated by the mass, for which Butler's contempt found its outlet in (say) Agnes Cannon at its best and Gold-teeth at its worst.

Again he sat beside the dictaphone, swung round in a position so that he could still keep his eye on the front door. Seeing that the second wax cylinder was almost finished, he substituted a third and took up the speaking-tube.

"Final points for the conviction of the murderer," he said.

Then he lit a cigarette, and resumed with the same detached deadliness.

"Having considered the workings of the murderer's mind," he went on, "I now deal with the next, and perhaps the most important point in a psychological sense: Kitty Owen and the green knitting-bag.

"Richard Renshaw, as we know, had a great influence on women. It was his habit to take them up and discard them at a moment's notice, as was the case," Butler winced, "with his own wife.

"Kitty Owen is just eighteen years old, of Welsh extraction and suggestible temperament. But there is no evidence or even suggestion to connect Kitty with Renshaw. On the contrary, her remarks and attitudes suggest no more than a mild attraction, even fear. We have proof positive (see foregoing) that Kitty had a harmless schoolgirl adoration for someone else.

"Kitty, in fact, did substitute a poisoned bottle for a harmless one. My original thought was correct, but I had the whole episode the wrong way round and its meaning the wrong way round; just as so many things, in this affair, have been reversed like the cross of Satan.

"Thus the actual method—"

"*Good evening*," interposed a voice behind Butler's head.

While you might have counted ten he sat paralyzed, motionless, without turning his head. The almost noiseless whir of the wax cylinder became audible.

What held him was not fear. He could have little cause to fear the person who spoke. What struck him like a bludgeon was the knowledge of his own blunder; he seemed to have been making blunders ever since his last meeting with Gold-teeth.

For he had walked out of this house—and for several minutes left the front door wide open. Anyone at all could have strolled in and sat down in the easy-chair opposite him, while his otherwise-concentrated wits noticed nothing.

"Good evening," he said mechanically, and switched off the dicta-phone.

Joyce Ellis, in an evening gown, walked round from the hearth and stood facing him.

"I told you," she said quietly and through clenched jaws, "that I wouldn't see you again until I could prove the identity of the murderer. Well, I've brought you my proof now."

"Have you, my dear?"

Joyce's evening gown was of velvet, flame-coloured and with puffed shoulders. It did not in any way change her, except that it enhanced the beauty of the grave face, the grey eyes, the dark hair in a short bob. In front of her she gripped a bulky handbag.

"I didn't poison Mrs. Taylor!" Joyce said. "I can prove that now!"

Butler leaned back in his chair lazily.

"Sure and I know it, me dear," he said with a smile. " 'Twas an inevitable accident, acushla. And isn't it the foine chance that brings ye here?"

Again it was as though he had hit her in the face.

Subtly Joyce's face changed. Her eyes looked deeper, and there was a little twist of cunning to her mouth. Her sensual figure seemed to distend the flame-coloured evening gown.

"*I am the head of the witch-cult,*" she said. "*I killed Dick Renshaw.*"

19

IN THAT library, now, there were forces more dangerous, more subtle, more explosive, than either Joyce Ellis or Patrick Butler had ever handled. For here were two different temperaments, subtly attracted, who might have been lover and mistress, or even husband and wife.

Joyce's voice, except for perhaps a far-off amusement, became the level voice with which he was so familiar.

"Yes?" queried Joyce.

"I knew that too," answered Butler, touching the dictaphone.

"You knew it?" Faint contempt.

Butler jumped to his feet.

"By God, I did!"

"You don't alarm me, Mr. Butler. May I sit down?"

She dragged round the other leather chair, so that they both sat sideways with the chairs half turned towards each other, backs to the fire. A log crackled and popped. Joyce, her bare elbow on the arm of the chair, propped her chin on her hand. With that Mona Lisa smile under the dark hair, and the lines of the flame-coloured gown outlining her figure, Butler found his wrath returning again.

"When I first saw you at Holloway," he said, remembering vividly the little room with the red sky outside, "I summed you up in my mind as being sensually passionate as the devil. . . ."

Joyce smiled.

"Also," continued Butler, "as a ready and fluent liar, whose tears looked almost like real tears. But with such shivering a respectability, such an angelic power of acting, that you wouldn't acknowledge your guilt even to your counsel. In short, as guilty as hell.

"Didn't I tell you," he added, "that I am never wrong?

"But," he continued, looking straight into Joyce's strange grey eyes,

"I *ought* to have noticed even more than I did. Remember, acushla? We were sitting on opposite sides of a little bare table. You were absorbed, while I was talking about the death of Mrs. Taylor.

"And with your finger you drew a design on the table. You traced a vertical line, then a horizontal line across it near the lower end. The reversed cross, me dear. The foremost symbol of Satan. You did it before my own eyes. You did it again later on, when you were thinking I-don't-know-what."

"Yes. I was absorbed," agreed Joyce, her eyes half-closed and her cheeks burning.

Butler watched her. He did not mean to remind her that Dr. Fell had visited her in prison too, and noticed the same habit, and passed on the information. Indeed, he preferred Dr. Fell to be kept out of this, in his own hour of triumph.

"I was absorbed," said Joyce, breathing hard, "in worship of my deity." Her pretty face became calm again. "Do you believe in God and the power of Good?"

"Yes. I do."

"Then you must believe," Joyce said simply, "in Satan and the power of Evil. They are inseparable. Didn't I tell you I was a clergyman's daughter?"

"Yes. You also kept telling me how dull and dreary your life had been."

"To worship one," whispered Joyce, "is tedium and drabness. To worship the other," she passed her hands down over her body, "is fire and delirium and light. *He* is the deity; in my mind he was even an inferior deity to—"

"To Richard Renshaw?" Butler cut in, "the man who looked like me?"

"Yes," said Joyce. She smiled a rather cruel smile.

Butler was feeling a trifle sick.

"Anyone in his five wits," he said, quoting Dr. Fell, "should have seen—by the situation at Mrs. Taylor's house—that you were a leading member of the witch-cult. You lived there for nearly two years, as you told me. Here was Mildred Taylor, a leering old female-satyr, with few friends and a lonely existence. There were you, fretting at your own drab life. It was obvious that long ago she would have approached you with her whisperings about the delights of the 'old religion'—just as much later she approached Lucia Renshaw.

"That house, 'The Priory,' had an atmosphere of the pit; I noticed it myself on the two visits I made there. Its taint hung in corners and permeated the air. On my second visit there, when I met a policeman, I noticed on the main hall table two silver candelabra: just like those at Renshaw's house, and probably with stains of black wax too. And, when you came into my house tonight, did you notice a box of books in the passage?"

"Yes. I couldn't stop to look at them."

"They're books on witchcraft," Butler snapped. "Many of them were scattered about openly in Mrs. Taylor's house for any inmate to read. Any literate inmate, that is; we may exclude the Griffiths couple and the cook. Dr. Bierce knew what was wrong there. Yet you, as you told me—you, for two years, saw nothing and believed Mrs. Taylor was a commonplace old lady whom you liked."

Joyce's eyes had hardened, in the guileless face of the parson's daughter. Her fingernails began to scratch on the leather arms of the chair.

"Shall I tell you what happened on the night of February 22nd, when Mrs. Taylor died?" asked Butler. "It's very simple."

He turned round and threw his cigarette into the fire.

"You never dreamed of killing Mrs. Taylor," he went on. "At least, not yet. That night you went out of the house to poison Dick Renshaw."

"Why?" The bitter monosyllable came at him like acid.

"Mainly," replied Butler, "because he'd thrown you over. As he's thrown over so many other women."

He let that register, while her breast heaved and the fingers on the chair-arms became rigid.

"But, since that had happened, you knew you could get control of the witch-cult—faith, and it's profitable, me dear!—shortly after he was dead. Only Mrs. Taylor stood in the way."

Here Butler bent forward.

"You weren't at Mrs. Taylor's house at all," he said slowly, "between about half-past nine and half-past one on the night of February 22nd. You went to Dick Renshaw's house, at Hampstead, to poison his waterbottle when you knew he was away from home. That's the secret; and it nearly hanged you for the wrong death."

He sat back again. Joyce remained motionless.

"Corroboration?" said Butler. "It's everywhere. William and Alice Griffiths, maid and coachman-gardener, swore they heard the back door banging about midnight, in a high wind. Then they said its latch must have caught—which was quite true—and it stopped banging. *I* hadn't prompted them. They were truthful witnesses.

"You, of course, couldn't leave by the *front* door. It has a bolt and a chain as well as a lock, as I observed; how could you get back in again? Very well, my dearest dear!"

(Every time he used an affectionate term, whether in Dublinese or ordinary speech, it had some kind of odd effect on her.)

"At half-past nine," he went on, "you got the antimony in the Nemo's tin from the stable, took it to your own room. You removed enough antimony to poison Renshaw, and put it in a paper bag or whatever you used. You hid the tin of antimony in your room. You left the house by the back door—taking the key with you, for a very good reason —but, heart of my heart, you forgot to lock that back door."

Butler allowed the pause to register.

"And now what happens," he asked, "on that wild and windy night? Let's not look at you, for a moment. Let's look at old Mrs. Taylor, fretting and fuming in bed because she hasn't got any Nemo's salts!"

Then Butler's tone became lightly satiric.

"Let's look at Mrs. Taylor, poor old soul, who has so mysteriously left you five hundred pounds in her will! Mrs. Taylor, who in a moment of anger calls you what they delicately term 'a bad name' which means 'streetwalker.' But let us do you justice, my sweetheart. You have no need to walk streets."

Joyce was smiling, a genuine smile, with flushed cheeks and bright eyes. Round her neck she wore a very thin silver chain whose ends were lost in the bodice of her flame-coloured gown. Slowly she drew up the chain, to which a very small ebony cross had been attached upside down. Joyce pressed the reversed cross to her lips.

"I worship," she explained in ecstasy.

The fire, crackling and popping, added colour to her flushed cheeks. Over Butler's nerves stole a creepy sense that the girl was, in the old sense of the term, demoniacally possessed. But he forced his thoughts back to fat Mrs. Taylor, with her dyed hair, who had taught Joyce dark worship like a witch reading from a *grimoire*.

"We got from Dr. Bierce," he said, and Joyce's eyes flashed down, "a piece of information which Dr. Fe— which I thought was the most important we had received last night. When Mrs. Taylor thought somebody was hiding something from her, she would ransack the house to get it."

No reply.

"There she sat in her own bed," Butler resumed, "brooding and brooding about Nemo's salts. You yourself told me she was brooding on it at half-past seven, and you made no answer. It went on and on. No Nemo's! Incredible! In a house run like this one? Incredible! Somebody was hiding them! Who must be hiding the tin? Obviously, you were.

"She rang her bell—here I indulge fancy—and rang it. No answer. Presently she stormed down to your room. It didn't surprise her when you weren't there, you might well be at the black chapel near by. But she searched the room. And she found a tin labelled Nemo's salts, with the proper-looking crystalline powder inside.

"Well, we remember that your fingerprints and hers were on the tin," said Butler. "But only her fingerprints on the glass. She mixed the dose with water, in the adjoining bathroom. And in her own bed, amid whatever horrors, she died."

Butler did not look at Joyce, who had returned the reversed cross to the bosom of her gown. He sprang to his feet, with black anger and horror unconquerable.

"As for you, me dear," he said, "let's follow what you did on the same night of February 22nd, just a month ago." Then Butler paused, swallowing.

"Damn you!" he said, and Joyce looked strangely pleased. "Do you know Lucia Renshaw?"

Joyce's expression changed. "Not very well," she answered. "I thought, at the trial, she looked like a little innocent for all her size and make-up. Otherwise I didn't think much at all about her, until—" Joyce stopped.

Butler scarcely heard her.

"I never realized," he snarled, "that every bit of evidence against her, every bit I thought or spoke to this dictaphone," he pointed, "applied equally well—or far more so!—to you.

"Never mind! I repeat: we go back to you on the night of the 22nd. How did you get from Balham to Hampstead and back? By Underground, of course. You had a friend and informant at Renshaw's house, who tipped you off by 'phone to everything that happened here—"

"Who?"

"Kitty Owen. She certainly doesn't like Lucia; you should have seen the look she gave Lucia on one occasion I remember. But Kitty has a purely schoolgirl worship for you. It's abject; it likes to be abject; it'll do anything. Yet I swear Kitty knew nothing about your visit to Dick Renshaw's on the night of the 22nd. All she did was give you information.

"My evidence? You'll hear it later.

"You knew that everybody would be away from 'Abbot's House' that night except Lucia. Lucia didn't sleep in her husband's room, but in a room down the gallery. You knew that Dick Renshaw had gone away the day before on one of his trips to spot the lie of the land for witch-cult poisonings in distant cities. Above all, you believed (Lucia told several of us) that Renshaw would be back in a day or two.

"You 'believed' that, I say. Not even Miss Cannon would trouble to clean the room, to change the water in the bottle, before he returned. So you crept into the house—how? Because the lock on the back door was a Grierson, just as at Mrs. Taylor's. And you dissolved a heavy dose of antimony in Renshaw's water-bottle, almost a month before he actually drank it.

"And the picture changes. Everything becomes reversed, like that damned cross you're wearing now. In fact, you drew the reversed crosses in the window-sill dust at the same time you poisoned the bottle."

Butler paused, and sat down.

His rage was evaporating, his voice calm and sardonic. Joyce Ellis, as though not thinking of murder at all, was smiling at him in a meditative way.

"It was quite all right that night, you know," she told him. "I got home by the last Underground train. I felt nice and sleepy. I locked the back door and left the key in it. I didn't even think of the antimony tin when I went to bed. But next morning, after I'd let Alice into the house. . . ."

"You got a shock, perhaps?" he inquired politely.

"A horrible shock!" said Joyce.

She turned towards him that face of eager innocence, the lips half-parted and the grey eyes wide, which she had turned towards him at Holloway prison. It gave him a shock, because there seemed to be no parody in it.

But inwardly, always inwardly, she was rejoicing, delighting, revelling in her ability to put on these masks. He wouldn't understand; it was a part of her religion.

"You see," Joyce went on in her soft voice, "Alice Griffiths said at the trial that when she discovered Mrs. Taylor's body she'd run 'to the backstairs passage' and spoken downstairs to the cook. That's very near the door of my bedroom, of course. She shouted, 'For God's sake come up here; something awful's happened.' All of a sudden I remembered the tin of antimony I'd hidden in my room. It was gone. I knew what had happened. When the bell began to ring, I—"

"You didn't know what to do, poor innocent?"

"It was awfully clever of you," Joyce assured him, with triumph gleaming out, "to explain my saying 'What's the matter? Is she dead?' to Alice. And to twist Alice and Emma so they wouldn't swear I never touched the tin that morning. I couldn't think of a story myself. But then—as soon as I met you—I knew you were going to get me acquitted."

"And why was that, me dear?"

Joyce's eyes glittered with admiration.

"It was your confidence, your self-confidence. You treated me almost as—"

"As Dick Renshaw would have done?"

"Yes, that low swine!" Joyce touched the inverted cross to quiet herself. "But, of course," her mood changed again, "I couldn't tell you, any more than I could tell the police, where I'd really been on the night Mrs. Taylor died.

"For what's the good of me, of my Master's teaching, if any man is ever sure I'm telling the truth? So I agreed to say just what you wanted me to say. It was a dreadful moment—did you notice, in court, how upset I got?—when Alice told about that banging door? I thought I hadn't killed Dick, of course, but then they might have connected him with me and our rites in the chapel. That was sacred."

"You know," Butler said, "I should like to read your thoughts."

Joyce leaned forward with eyes which had a frank, unmistakable expression; it had nothing to do with murder.

"I should like to read yours," she said.

The attraction of the woman was like a hypnotic or a drug. We shall be saved through the flesh, said the ritual of the Black Mass. Momentarily Butler fought his way out of that allurement.

"I mean—" he stopped. "The police suspected you from the start. You were under arrest in just a week. During that time, they'd watch you if you made visits. Did you try any 'phone-calls?"

"I rang Kitty. Poor, dear Kitty! Dick himself introduced her to the worship, but she liked *me*. I asked Kitty if Mr. Renshaw had returned. Kitty said no, but he'd be back before the end of the week surely. I told her the water must not, must *not*, be changed in that water-bottle."

Butler was as tense as she.

"I thought so!" he said. "You couldn't 'phone her, and you didn't dare see her, after you were arrested. But they did allow you newspapers. And not one word did you see—as you must have, if it had happened— about Renshaw's death. You believed the water had got poured out, just as it might have been."

"Oh, yes. I was afraid he couldn't be dead. I knew it!"

"In other words," said Butler, "you regarded yourself as innocent. The consciousness of guilt never touched your mind. You could rave inwardly about irony and filthy injustice: as you did aloud to me. But, by thunder! (As a friend of mine would say) nothing else clouded you. Someone could have written down your thoughts, up to and during the trial, and it would have been quite fair in the detective-story sense. Not after the trial—any afternoon paper would have told you Renshaw was dead."

"Dead," breathed Joyce, "and *deposed*."

"And after the trial," sneered Butler, "you still tried to make me believe you were innocent. In that coffee-room across from the Old Bailey, you even had the nerve to tell me a story which gave you away: about a shutter banging instead of the back door. And I hurt you, I tore your vanity, when I told you that you were as guilty as hell."

"What a queer phrase!" smiled Joyce. "But you attracted me most horribly. I wanted to stay near you. Didn't you ever find me attractive?"

Butler, who was fighting shadows in his own mind, got up. He didn't want to say what he said; it blurted itself out.

"I dreamed about you last night."

Joyce also stood up. They were so close they could almost have touched each other. Joyce moved closer.

"Oh? What did you dream?"

"I dreamed I was kissing you, just as I kissed Lucia before that."

"Only kissing?" murmured Joyce. "How tame your dreams must be."

"And when I did have my arms round Lucia"—the impulse to reach out towards Joyce was almost irresistible—"just once, I thought of you."

The pink lips curled. "Why was that?"

"Because I knew," Butler snarled, "I knew in my heart, or whatever pretentious modern damned term you want to call it, that you were a murderer and I had to forget you. But I never knew until tonight—and I admit it was a shock—that you enjoyed wholesale poisoning for profit. Even though we got on the track of the witch-cult the very night you were acquitted."

"Oh?" Joyce said sharply.

Any mention of the witch-cult, a holy thing which she had risked her life to keep secret, turned Joyce cold and wary. She backed away.

"You said we," Joyce breathed. "Who got on the track of it?"

"Faith, me dear, I was speaking editorially! Nobody knows but me-self."

Joyce drew a quick breath. "You were saying?"

"Well! I went out to Lucia's house at Hampstead. There were such things as black candle-wax and reversed crosses and mention of red garters. . . ."

Through his mind, in the finger-snap time of pause, went everything Dr. Fell had told him late that afternoon.

Dr. Fell, arriving at Lucia's house on Tuesday evening shortly after Butler, had already seen through the real meaning of the trial. "Sir, nobody considered the evidence!" And: "Both sides were looking up into trees for the roots and digging underground for the branches." Joyce Ellis was innocent of the death of Mrs. Taylor—because Joyce wasn't in the house. Where was she? She would have explained: unless her errand had been so deadly that she dared not explain and dared not risk explaining. What errand? Well, William Griffiths had testified that two large doses of antimony were gone from the tin.

Hence that bumbling exclamation from Dr. Fell: "When I heard Mr. Renshaw had been murdered, I can't say I was surprised." And: "Surely it was at least reasonable that somebody would be murdered!"

What knocked the learned doctor into a heap, what caused him to mutter and groan and make faces, was Lucia's testimony: that the water-bottle which killed Renshaw had been rinsed and refilled before Renshaw's death. Apparently Joyce couldn't have done it.

Butler, out of his reverie in an instant, was speaking to Joyce.

"But the idea that you couldn't have done the poisoning, because you were in prison," he said, "was knocked endways as soon as an investigator looked at the water-bottle on Renshaw's bedside table."

"What about it?"

"There was still about an inch of water left. And it was stale."

"Stale?"

"Yes. Full of those tiny beads that gather in water when it's been standing for days or even weeks. Could it have got stale in twenty-four hours, since Kitty was supposed to have filled it? That didn't seem possible, with a glass inverted over the top to protect it. All the same, an experiment was tried at Mrs. Taylor's house.

"A water-bottle, with glass over it, was left to stand for twenty-four hours. At the end of that time it was crystal-clear, without a bead of any kind. It would clearly remain fresh for a long time."

In Butler's imagination, voices echoed and re-echoed out of that dark house.

(*"What do you see?" "Nothing, I am glad to say. Absolutely nothing!" And: "Poison? This experiment had nothing to do with poison!"*)

Butler lighted a cigarette. His hand was unsteady, but he forced words:

"The water in Dick Renshaw's bottle had been there for a long time. When anybody considered this with certain odd features of your case, it began to appear more than odd. But how could the water in that bottle be stale, when Kitty had refilled it?

"For meself, sweetheart, I at first slightly misinterpreted the facts. I knew Kitty had made an exchange of bottles. I knew she used the knitting-bag as a cover. But I was staring eye to eye with truth, never seeing it.

"A telegram arrived on Monday, March 19th, to say Renshaw would be home that night. The room must be cleaned, the water-bottle refilled. But Kitty, implacably true to your instructions of weeks before, would *not* let the water be changed. And what did she do?"

"She has told me," observed Joyce coolly. "Kitty is loyal, though not alone to me. To *him*."

"Him?"

Again Joyce took out the inverted cross, and kissed it.

"What Kitty did," snapped Butler, "was to take a filled water-bottle, clean water, from another bedroom. She put that in her knitting-bag. She picked up the poisoned bottle of stale water, and slipped it into her knitting-bag when she went into the bathroom. It was the *clean* water-bottle she emptied, rinsed, and refilled to put in the bag. It was the same old poisoned bottle she put back on the table.

"Didn't I tell you," Butler said sarcastically, "that we saw all evidence exactly the wrong way round?"

Joyce laughed.

"Dick Renshaw was in a temper when he got home," Butler said. "Furthermore, he was having a row with Lucia. He never noticed the staleness of the water he drank." Butler, smoking the cigarette in short fierce puffs, threw it into the fire.

"He thought Lucia had done it," Butler added. "And most people thought you were now below suspicion."

"*Below* suspicion?"

"You'd been cleared in court of Mrs. Taylor's death," Butler refrained from adding that Dr. Fell had steadfastly maintained Joyce's innocence here, which he had never called 'murder' but only 'death.' "So most people, when Renshaw was murdered, could rule you out as causing *both* deaths.

"But remember Kitty Owen! Whether Kitty guessed the water might have been poisoned before that, she was smacking well certain when Renshaw died. But she was loyal! Oh, yes! She'd already done you a service, when there was to have been a Black Mass in the Black Chapel the night before Renshaw died."

Joyce, gliding back into the chair with the bulky handbag beside her, grew rigid. "How do you know there was supposed to have been—"

Butler groaned.

"The black wax-stains were fresh. When would have been the obvious night for the Mass? You parody Christian ritual, don't you? The 18th was a Sunday!

"I don't know why Renshaw didn't get back to celebrate it; we may never know. Mrs. Taylor, his second in command, was dead. You, the third in succession, were in prison. There wasn't any priest to perform the ceremony, even though the black candles had to burn at the altar and the goat-god statuette displayed. Somebody had to go and tell the masked assembly there'd be no ceremony.

"Who would do it? Kitty, of course! She was very close to two out of three of the leaders. And those candelabra were personal treasures: Renshaw liked to have a pair at home, as Mrs. Taylor did, to gloat over them. Oh, Kitty was always ready to show her superiority over Lucia Renshaw!"

"You're wrong in saying I did it for the money," said Joyce. "I should only have used it—for *his* work."

And she touched the cross. Her unwavering, half-smiling fixity of expression began to unnerve him again. He stumbled away, past the dictaphone, and stood with his back to the dying fire.

"When you were acquitted on the 20th," he said, "what did you do after you left the coffee-room? Did you get in touch with Luke Parsons? Or with Gold-teeth? Or with both?"

"Gold-teeth? Oh, you mean poor George! I 'phoned them both, yes. But I was thinking about you."

"Possibly you were, at that time. But next morning, when you came to see me and I threw you out without ceremony—wasn't that when you began to hate me?"

"I may have been a bit annoyed. At the time."

"Wasn't that really the reason why you got Gold-teeth and Em to go for me with knuckle-dusters last night? Or try to?"

"Not . . . I'm sorry about that! You did annoy me."

"Yesterday afternoon," Butler used words like a whip, without the least apparent effect, "I visited Luke Parsons and bribed him to give me a little information (two hundred quid it cost) about where I might find Gold-teeth and Em. Didn't Parsons ring you up immediately afterwards and tell you he'd done it?"

"Yes."

Joyce was sitting back lazily, the gleam of the wall-lamps on her sleek black hair, her face one of serene gravity except for certain movements of the lips and eyes.

"Was that why he was killed?"

"The person who will betray you in the very smallest thing," said Joyce, looking full at him and pressing the reversed cross against her breast, "will betray you in anything." Then the grey eyes opened wide. "That's a law of faith."

"It was a woman's crime. Luke Parsons was old and frightened and not very strong. A man would have taken him by the neck, from the front or the back. A woman would have stunned him first, as he was stunned, and then applied the garter in the form of a tourniquet. Did you enjoy killing him?"

"Dearest darling," said Joyce, "it had to be done."

"Was he a member of your—faith?"

"Well! A private inquiry agent—don't you see?—is so useful when you want information about people."

"And Gold-teeth?"

"George? Oh, George is a very special friend of mine." Joyce's teeth gleamed; her slow smile suggested much. Then her face darkened. "But I never once thought—" She stopped. "When he slipped off those gold shell-teeth he used for a disguise, he wasn't unattractive."

"Not very fastidious, are you?"

"Don't be jealous. I'm not jealous of poor silly Lucia. The most dreadful thing I ever had to do," said Joyce, who would have raged if her self-control had not been so great, "was to give George orders to set fire to the temple under that chapel!"

"Then why did you have to do it?"

"Lucia was going there with you, wasn't she? One of George's men found her handbag, with the key and a cardboard label attached, in that club. He told George, even if he didn't understand; George 'phoned me; and—

"George," and now Joyce was fighting so hard for self-control that the flame-coloured gown writhed, "didn't know you were at Balham. But he saw the light through the shutters, and wondered. Then he went on to get very dangerous papers and do . . . the rest of it. The burning. The awful thing.

"What else could I do? I knew Lucia already suspected something. In court, when Dr. Bierce was talking about 'The Priory' being what he called an unhealthy place, I saw her get up and make shushing gestures. But I couldn't guess how much she knew."

Butler hit her, only verbally, but hard.

"Lucia knew nothing," he said. "If it hadn't been for Dr. Fe— if it hadn't been for me, we might never even have found the secret trap to go downstairs."

For several seconds Joyce was quiet, very quiet.

"You're lying," she smiled at him.

"No."

"I *should* hate you." Joyce regarded him thoughtfully, but her eyes in their steady look were as fascinating to him as fire to a child. "I can't hate you. I never could. I feel just as I said I felt at that coffee-room. Only—more so. I knew it as soon as I saw you again."

Then Joyce's smile widened, with both the cruelty and the allure.

"Did you get much pleasure from Lucia," she asked softly, "when you kept thinking of me?"

"I didn't say I 'kept' thinking of you! It only just—"

Again her expression made him pause.

"And I know you won't give me away," Joyce said. "Because I've known, all along, you were one of us."

"What the hell do you mean, *one of us*?"

"Oh, you think you're not! You like to pretend it shocks you. But look into your real character, and see if it's not true!"

Joyce rose from the chair. She walked slowly towards him as he stood with his back to the fireplace.

"You know in your heart," Joyce breathed, "that *he* really exists."

"Don't talk like an idiot! This 'Satan' of yours is an allegorical myth, intended to represent—"

"Then why do you fear him?" asked Joyce. "Why do your churches fear him? Why do they cry out with one voice, but in helplessness? Why, since the beginning of time, has he remained unconquered?"

Patrick Butler had ceased to think. The perfume of Joyce's hair and flesh, her nearness, the sense about her of diabolic possession— He felt now that all he wanted, in this world or the next, was Joyce Ellis. He hit out with one last speech.

"D'you think I'd be a rival to Gold-teeth?"

There was a faint little laugh.

"George?" she said. "Oh, George needn't trouble you. He's dead."

"Dead?"

Butler's hand fell from Joyce's shoulder, which was warmer than blood-heat.

"Dead?" he repeated. "How did he die?"

"Oh, darling, does it matter?"

"Probably not. All the same, how did he die?"

Joyce's voice, low-pitched and full of genuine contrition, was muffled as she lowered her head.

"Last night," she said, "I was annoyed with you for getting those papers. I don't feel like that now! But I—I told George to paste those bits of paper on your windows this morning. He didn't seem to like it, but he did it."

"Well?"

"Well! You sent that insulting (it was insulting, darling!) telegram, and dared him to come here with a gun. I was still annoyed, so I told him. . . . But he wouldn't do it."

"What do you mean by that? Answer me!"

"Darling, it really is frightfully funny." Faint little laughter, mingled with bewilderment, floated up past Butler's shoulder. Joyce Ellis, who could slip on any mask or assume any voice, glided into pure Commercial-Road Cockney. The voice of Gold-teeth himself might have been shrilling in the room.

"'E told me I fought fair. He said 'e wouldn't make no charges against me, and 'e kept 'is word. 'E's a real gent, Butler is, and I won't do 'im dirt if you kill me for it."

Silence.

Butler swallowed hard, and then spoke.

"What happened?" he asked.

Joyce shrugged her shoulders.

"Well, naturally—he died."

Something in the quiver of Butler's shoulders, the tensity that went through him, made Joyce look up. It stabbed through the dreamy haze of Joyce's senses. She backed very slowly away towards her chair, her eyes blank with astonishment. It was several seconds before Butler spoke.

"You swine!" he said.

His tone was not loud. Yet Joyce's bewilderment only increased.

"Darling, what's wrong?"

"I don't know where Gold-teeth is," said Butler. "But I'd like to shake hands with him. I'd like to get drunk with him. That jeering sandy-haired welterweight was a real sportsman. That means the finest breed in the world. And you had him killed!"

"Darling, I never thought—"

"No. You never thought."

Patrick Butler saw no irony in the fact that Gold-teeth, the one man he had hated most, was now the one man for whom he felt the most sympathy. Butler's voice was thick and there was a sting behind his eyes. He reached across and threw the whole dictaphone to the floor with a crash.

"And now, my handsome witch-woman," he roared, "I shall proceed to tell you something. You think I'm the only person who knows the evidence against you? Well, I'm not."

"What did you say?"

"Dr. Fell knows it. Superintendent Hadley knows it. The whole God-damned police-force know it. I haven't got your papers; the police have 'em. And do you know what will happen tomorrow morning?"

Joyce whipped out of the chair, snatching up her handbag. Her face was not now pleasant to see.

"Kitty Owen," roared Butler, "will be taken to Scotland Yard for questioning. There's nothing in those papers to convict you. But Kitty Owen can convict you with direct evidence.

"She's loyal; I grant that. She worships; I grant that too. But she's young, my handsome witch-woman; she's young. She'll break like *that*," he snapped his fingers, "under eighteen hours' questioning. And do you know what'll happen to you then? You'll hang at Holloway—where you came from."

Joyce, who was fumbling frantically at her handbag, had backed away and was facing him from about a distance of ten feet. He saw the edge of the low-calibre automatic.

"It might interest you to know," remarked Butler, throwing back the right side of his dressing gown, "that I've been covering you with this Webley for some time."

Joyce screamed at him—what words he could not afterwards remember. He looked at her for a moment. Then, drawing a deep breath of self-contempt, he tossed the Webley so that it landed in the seat of the leather chair.

"Ah, the back of me hand to ye!" snapped the Irishman. "I can't shoot a woman."

The automatic was in Joyce's hand now, ten feet away.

"So you knew I was a murderer!" she screamed at him.

Patrick Butler, his back to the mantelpiece, drew himself to his full height.

"Didn't I tell you?" he asked politely. "I am never wrong."

And he made her a bow, in the full mocking style of the eighteenth century, as she shot him twice through the chest.

20

Being a letter from *Gideon Fell, Ph.D., L.L.D., F.R.H.S.,*
to Patrick Butler, K.C.

13 Round-pond Place,
Hampstead, N.W. 3,
22nd June, 1947

MY DEAR BUTLER:

And so, it seems, you are in trouble again. Not only, as I gather from your letter, with some legal dignitary whom you appear to have accused of cheating at poker, but in a case wherein you are convinced of your client's innocence. You are never wrong; I know it; and—yes, I will help.

As for your comment about Joyce Ellis: now that the trial is over, I venture to answer it. No, the girl is not insane. She has her religion; there was recently in Germany, and now being expressed in Russia, worship just as fantastic. I think the jury knew she was not insane. But the verdict of 'guilty, but insane' strikes me as being the more merciful as well as the more sensible.

I believe I wrote to congratulate you on your engagement to Mrs. Lucia Renshaw. She is a charming lady, and I congratulate you again. I only trust that your (forgive me) somewhat unconventional temperament will get you both as far as the altar.

Never forget gallantry, my dear fellow! After all, if you had not bowed gracefully to Joyce Ellis when she fired at you, those bullets would have struck your heart instead of just below the collarbone. That you will live for a while to enliven this dull world is the hope of

Yours sincerely,
GIDEON FELL